CRIME FILE

DELL SHANNON
CRIME FILE

WILLIAM MORROW & COMPANY, INC.
NEW YORK 1974

Printed in the United States of America.

1 2 3 4 5 78 77 76 75 74

Book design by Helen Roberts

Library of Congress Cataloging in Publication Data

Linington, Elizabeth.
    Crime file.

    I. Title.
PZ4.L756Cq [PS3562.I515]   813'.5'4   74-7374
ISBN 0-688-00268-4

"What do you think of it, Moon,
As you go?
Is life much or no?"

"Oh, I think of it, often think of it,
As a show
God ought surely to shut up soon,
As I go."

—THOMAS HARDY

CRIME FILE

1

"I DIDN'T MEAN TO HURT HER NONE," SAID THE stocky bald fellow, blinking up at them. He was slumped over the little table in the interrogation room, frightened and sullen in turn, and also still surprised. "Don't seem possible I *coulda*. I didn't hit her hard, and I never hit her before, ever, she could tell you that—"

"Only she's dead, Mr. Parsons," said Hackett. He exchanged a look with Mendoza.

"I know. Don't seem possible." Parsons shook his head. "I never meant to hurt her—I wouldn't hurt Myra. It was just, I had enough o' her complainin'. Squawking about not enough money alla time. I supported myself ever since I was twelve years old. I'm a good worker, I don't sit around takin' the welfare like a bum. I haven't got much learning, so what's that say? On what a trucker earns, she's gonna starve? But she's got to have a new color TV, got to have— But I didn't go to hurt her. I'm sorry—I'm sorry." His head sank to the table.

Hackett sighed and followed Mendoza out to the anteroom of Robbery-Homicide, where Sergeant Lake sat at the switchboard reading a paperback. The office was quiet; only the subdued busy click of Policewoman Wanda Larsen's typewriter sounded as she typed up somebody's report. The men at Robbery-Homicide were still feeling appreciative about their unexpected secretary.

"And they make TV shows about the glamorous, exciting job of being a cop," said Hackett.

"Occasionally it can be exciting," said Mendoza. "Just occasionally. There's nothing to that but a report. The D.A.'ll call it manslaughter and he'll get one-to-three."

"And serve half of it," said Hackett. "The way these damn judges are letting them loose these days—"

"Don't raise my blood pressure," said Mendoza. He lit a cigarette; as usual he was dapper in silver-gray Italian silk, snowy shirt, discreet tie. "Anything new down, Jimmy?"

Lake looked up. "Dead body reported over on Stanford Avenue. George and John went out on it. Jase and Tom are out talking to witnesses on that heist, and Matt just came back. I don't know what he got—"

"*Nada absolutamente,*" said Mendoza, "probably. A very anonymous thing, a take of forty-two bucks, no M.O. to speak of. It'll go into Pending tomorrow. I do get tired, Arturo."

"You can always resign. You don't have to work for a living."

"Comes the crash, I might. Take him over to jail and give the gist to Wanda for a report."

"Oh, you've got a memo from the D.A.'s office," said Lake. "On your desk. Something about those floozies last April."

"*¿Qué?*" Mendoza went into his office, noting Wanda typing at her desk in the sergeants' office, and Matt Piggott on the phone looking earnest, and found the memo. A minute later Lake heard him swearing comprehensively in Spanish. "More equal than others, isn't it the truth. *Dios,* does he think we can make bricks without straw?" But the D.A.'s note was apologetic; the D.A. was being pressured—read hounded, thought Mendoza—by some civil-rights group: why hadn't the police found and arrested the foul racist dog who had murdered those innocent black girls two months ago?

On that one there'd simply been no leads at all, and it had been filed in Pending at the first of this month. Innocent was an ambivalent word: they hadn't deserved to be murdered maybe, but they'd all had long rap-sheets as casual prostitutes. It had been a queer one, and without much doubt the X on that was a nut, poisoning the floozies with cyanide in their liquor, but after the fourth one there hadn't been another, and all the men at Robbery-Homicide were inclined to think he'd left town. Mendoza had passed on the relevant facts to NCIC; if X showed up anywhere else murdering Negro prostitutes they could guess it was the same boy. That was about all they could do, with the dearth of physical evidence.

Resignedly Mendoza picked up his phone and told Lake to get him the D.A.'s office. If the D.A. wanted a nice apologetic letter to show the civil-righters, that was about all Mendoza could do for him. While he waited for the D.A.'s secretary to locate him, he looked out the window to the clear line of the Hollywood hills in the distance. They hadn't yet had their usual first heat wave in June; the weather was for once being reasonable in southern California—warmish, with a breeze most of the day, blue skies and sun.

And Robbery-Homicide had been busier; on the downtown Central beat, LAPD, there was always enough business, but they weren't feeling harried. They had four separate heist jobs, with no leads on any of them. There was still some paper work to clean up on a suicide, there were two unidentified bodies in the morgue, one dead of knife wounds, one of an overdose. There had been a bank heist last week, but the Feds were definitely sure who that pair was—ex-cons from the Midwest, one wanted for P.A. violation; the A.P.B.'s were out and maybe one of their pigeons would finger them.

The phone hummed emptily at him, and through the two open doors he heard Wanda's practiced typing and Piggott's voice. Piggott was saying something about dishpans and screens, and Mendoza was still wondering about the combination when the D.A. came on the line.

[3]

"Listen, damn it," he said, "look, Lieutenant, I know you worked that into the ground, there just wasn't anything to get. But these damned—"

"Racists in reverse," supplied Mendoza. "Yes, I know. Shall I write a nice letter of apology?"

"Not that it'll satisfy 'em, we both will," said the D.A.

"I'll get some screening at the hardware store on my way home," said Piggott into the phone. He sounded resigned too. It was now three months since he'd been bitten by the unlikely fascination for the pretty little tropical fish. But, he was reflecting now, it was Mammon which had prompted him to try the breeding, when that female head-and-taillight tetra proved to be full of eggs. Mr. Duff at the Scales 'n' Fins shop saying he'd pay twenty cents for every one they raised to three months. Piggott and Prudence had spent the last seven weeks frantically rescuing the smaller tetras from their bigger siblings, and at the moment had seven dishpans standing about full of baby tetras, carefully graded as to size. There had been over three hundred to start with, but the ranks had been considerably thinned.

"Well, if you would," said Prudence. She sounded distracted. "The bigger ones jump so—I've caught six of them getting clear out this afternoon. You'd better pick up another dishpan, Matt. It's funny how they grow at such different rates—and if we'd known they were cannibals—"

"Only until they grow up, Duff says. All right," said Piggott. He reflected gloomily that he should have known better than to succumb to greed: the love of money . . . By the time the baby tetras were three months old, he'd be lucky to break even on the deal. Just last Sunday the sermon had been about covetousness.

He hadn't any report for Wanda to type. All of these heists were likely going to stay anonymous. He wandered out to the anteroom and asked Lake if anything new had gone down.

"Body over on Stanford. George and John went out on it."

[4]

Wanda came out of the sergeants' office with a page in her hand and said briskly, "This just came over the telex—we'll be putting it out countywide."

Lake looked at it and buzzed the lieutenant's office. "A.P.B. from Folsom. A mean one. He went over the wall last night and they think he'll probably head here—"

Mendoza scanned the teletype rapidly. One Terry Conover, twenty-four, Caucasian, six one, a hundred and ninety, black and blue, no marks, a long pedigree of much violence, in on a five-to-ten for murder two. He had a mother and a girl and pals in L.A., and probably would be heading here: addresses were appended for the mother and girl friend. Folsom wasn't so far away; if he'd got hold of a car, he could be here by now.

"Well, we'll have to look," said Mendoza. Jason Grace and Tom Landers came in, and he added, *"Por fortuna,* just as we need you. Do any good?"

"Are you kidding?" said Landers. "Nobody could give us a description, him in that ski mask. Not even an approximate height and weight—you know people. It might have been any hood in L.A., we'll never drop on him. I guess Rich is still out asking futile questions." He and Rich Conway, inherited from the old Robbery office when the two had been merged, had taken to each other at once; and they'd both just come off night watch a month ago.

"So, we've got a new one?" asked Grace. He read the teletype interestedly, brushing his neat moustache in unconscious imitation of Mendoza, and his chocolate-brown face wore a sardonic grin. "Yeah, in case Terry has made for home and mother, we'd better go and ask—more than one of us. Consider armed and dangerous. I wonder if he had help in getting over the wall—if he did, there was probably transportation waiting, and more than likely a gun. With his pedigree of armed robbery."

"That's the general idea," agreed Mendoza. His senior sergeant, bulky and burly Art Hackett, came in from escorting Parsons over to the jail, and Grace handed on the teletype.

"Suppose you and Matt go have a look at his mother's place, and Art and Tom can look at the girl."

Hackett reached up to adjust the Police Positive in the shoulder holster and copied down addresses noncommittally. "That should take us to the end of shift just nicely. Come on, Tom. You getting anywhere with that cute blonde down in R. and I.?" They went out, with Grace and Piggott after them. It was three o'clock.

Mendoza asked Lake, "What was the body?"

"By what the uniformed men said, homicide of some kind."

"Maybe business is picking up a little." Mendoza yawned. "I do get tired, Jimmy. Ninety-eight percent of what we see is just—the damned foolishness."

"As Matt would say, the devil going about," said Lake.

At a tired-looking old eight-family apartment out on Stanford Avenue, Sergeants Higgins and Palliser were talking to a scrawny, scraggly middle-aged woman in the upper hallway. The uniformed men had gone back on tour; Scarne and Duke had arrived with a mobile lab unit and were busy in the rear apartment to the left, past the open door behind the two detectives.

"You hadn't heard anything from Mrs. Moffat's apartment before that, Mrs. Kiefer?"

"Not a thing." She kept trying to see into the apartment, what the lab men were doing, past Higgins' broad shoulders. "Not that I would. I mean I wasn't listening, why should I? I'm not anybody's keeper." She was sloppily dressed in old jeans and a white T-shirt, and her graying hair was in big fat pink curlers, with no scarf over it. "Well, I mean, I hope we're respectable—"

"And Mrs. Moffat wasn't?" asked Palliser in his pleasant voice. She looked at him with slightly more approval, at his regular lean features and neat tailoring; Higgins, of course, in his bulk and cragginess, had COP written all over him.

"Well, I—well, she wasn't a lady, is all I can say. I didn't *know* her. Just to know her name, is all. But to think of anybody getting murdered, here! It's enough to scare you to death! Like I told you, and believe me it's all I can tell you, I had a phone call from Miss Callway's sister—Miss Callway lives in Seven, right there"—the door across the hall—"and she can't afford a phone, but she's a nice woman and I don't mind taking messages for her—and I come up here to pass it on, only she's not home, and there's Mrs. Moffat's door open and her laying in there all over blood, and I screamed, but I didn't go in, no, sir, I went right down and called police—but to think of it, a murder, even Mrs. Moffat, her getting murdered right here—"

"Well, if that's all you can tell us," said Palliser, "we'll want a statement from you later on, but for now you can go back to your own apartment. Thank you, Mrs. Kiefer."

"What are they doing in there, anyways? Aren't you going to take her away?"

"After a while," said Higgins. They got rid of her finally and went back into the apartment to watch Duke and Scarne dusting for prints and taking pictures. It was a shabby place, barely filled with ancient furniture, and whatever else she had been, Mrs. Ida Moffat hadn't been a very good housekeeper; there was dust everywhere, a pile of dirty dishes in the kitchen, the windows filmed with dirt. Mrs. Moffat herself didn't look too clean, flat on her back on the living-room floor: she was wearing a faded pink kimono and it had come open to show her only underwear, panties and a bra both once white but now grime-gray. She couldn't have been less than fifty or so but she hadn't had a bad figure; the blue-mottled veins in her legs, her worn, uncared-for hands, told her age better.

"You pick up anything?" asked Higgins.

"No idea," said Duke. "Plenty of latents around, but may be mostly hers."

"Even Mrs. Moffat," said Palliser. "What do you suppose she meant by that?"

"Not a lady," grunted Higgins. "By what else she could tell us, perfectly ordinary woman."

Palliser scratched his admirably straight nose and said, "I

wonder." All Mrs. Kiefer could tell them about Ida Moffat was that she took jobs housecleaning for people; she had several regular jobs up in Hollywood, one place twice a week and helping out at parties. She didn't know if Mr. Moffat was dead or divorced, or about any family. "Well, have a look around when you boys are finished."

"Just about," said Scarne. "You can read it—probably all the action was right here." She had fallen, or been knocked down, against the fake stucco hearth, where there was blood, and more blood on top of the electric heater below; she had lived long enough to crawl a few feet toward the door. "Skull fracture for a bet. A fight with somebody."

"Over something," said Palliser.

"Her handbag's in the bedroom, on the bed. Money still in it. Place hasn't been ransacked."

"So, not a burglar. She let him in," said Higgins, looking at the apartment door. It had a lock minus a deadbolt, an easy lock for a burglar to break in, but it wasn't broken; there was a stout chain fastened to door and wall, the catch now neatly reposing in its slot. In this area, it was a good bet that a woman living alone would keep that chain fastened when she was home, even during the day. "Did you print this, Bill?" Scarne looked at him reproachfully. "All right, all right, just asking."

When the lab men had gone, they had a look through the apartment. They found a few interesting things. There were nine bottles of cheap muscatel on a kitchen shelf. "How anybody can drink that sweet stuff is beyond me," said Higgins. "Think it'd make you sick before you got tight." Her handbag, a shabby black plastic one, was open on the bed; it contained a billfold with eighteen dollars in it, some loose change, and a check for thirty-five dollars signed by Winifred Bloomfield of an address in Hollywood; two soiled handkerchieves, three used lipsticks, half a pack of Camels, a very dirty powder puff, a bunch of keys, and a little plastic book with slots for snapshots. That was full; and the twenty snapshots in it obviously dated from disparate periods, all showing Ida Moffat at various ages from the twenties on up. All the snapshots showed her with men, all different men.

"My God," said Higgins mildly. "What a gal." The men were all different shapes, sizes, and ages; one, smiling at an Ida of perhaps twenty years ago, was in Army uniform, and another—a hairy-chested fellow with a mop of dark hair—was in swimming trunks, with a plastic tag around his neck that said *Life Guard,* but aside from that there was no clue to their identities, no writing on the back of the snapshots.

"Not a lady," quoted Palliser. "I wonder if we'd get anything in the local bars. She didn't have a car, that we do know. If she—"

"By that collection, she stayed home to do her drinking," said Higgins. They began opening drawers, looking for an address book, but there didn't seem to be one. Beside the wall telephone in the kitchen was a dime-store tablet hung on a string by a nail, and on several pages were scrawled notes—*Call Al at home bef. 9—new no. Bruce CA-1498—Jean 421-4243* . . . They took that to go through at leisure. Without discussing it, they were in tacit agreement that the world was probably not going to miss Ida Moffat, and it was going to be a tedious little job, probably, to find out who had had a fight with her, knocked her down and killed her, but it was the job they were paid to do and they'd do it to the best of their ability.

The morgue attendants came for the body.

It was twenty minutes to six. They found the key to the door and locked it after themselves. They'd driven over in Higgins' Pontiac, and now went back to Parker Center where Palliser reclaimed his Rambler from the lot. By then, Wanda would be gone; dictate a first report on it to her in the morning, and go on from there. This wasn't one where they'd be asking Luis if he had a hunch, thought Higgins. A tiresome routine job.

On the way home, through end-of-workday traffic, his mind switched from the job to his family: even after this while, he wasn't taking family for granted, he'd been without one so long. His darling Mary, and Bert Dwyer's good kids, Steve and Laura, and now the baby, Margaret Emily, who unbelievably was nearly ten months old—and Mary was just kidding when she said he and Steve would spoil her rotten. . . .

And on the way home, Palliser thought fondly of Robin and their almost-brand-new David Andrew, not quite three months old; but that made him remember that very minor little thing last January, that accident on the freeway, and Miss Madge Borman of Tempe, Arizona—and her dog. He frowned. He had hoped at the time that Miss Borman might forget her promise, but he had the uneasy feeling that Miss Borman was not a woman who forgot promises. Never forget how kind you've been, she'd said, don't know what I'd have done—and when he just happened to mention Robin talking about a dog after the baby was born, Not another word, Sergeant, you shall have one of Azzie's pups . . . Damnedest name for a dog he'd ever heard, and it took Matt to unravel that: Dark Angel of Langlet, Azrael for short. And, I'm breeding Marla to him next month—and that was the biggest German shepherd he'd ever seen, he hadn't said a word about it to Robin, and she'd have a fit—nice dogs but too big for the city. And no fence around the backyard, and what it might cost to put one up. He also wondered just how long it took for dogs . . .

He'd asked the lieutenant, who would know, and Mendoza had said absently, "Sixty-three days. Don't tell me you're going in for dog breeding? Matt and his fish are bad enough—"

"No, no," said Palliser hastily. But if that creature had been bred to Marla, presumably one like him, in February, the resultant pups would be about ready to leave home and mother some time this month. And how he would ever explain it to Robin . . .

He just hoped Miss Borman had forgotten all about it.

Robin had dinner ready when he came in, and the baby—such a good baby, who seldom cried or fussed—was asleep. Palliser kissed her and she asked, "Busy day?"

"The usual," said Palliser.

Higgins pulled into the drive of the house on Silverlake Boulevard to find Steve Dwyer industriously oiling his bicycle in front of the garage, with the little black Scottie Brucie watching.

"Hi, George! Say, I just developed this last roll of negs and I've got some great shots—wait till you see! They're almost dry now . . ." Steve, going in heavily for the art-composition black-and-white photography, these days was processing it all himself, proudly, in the little darkroom Higgins had put up in the garage, with the help of Henry Glasser on the electric lines.

Higgins went obediently to look at the roll of negatives before he went into the house. Steve thought it was lucky that Higgins had been there, to take care of them all, when Bert got shot by that bank robber. Higgins reckoned he'd been pretty lucky too.

"You'd better believe I'd call you quick enough if I'd heard from Terry!" She looked from Grace to Piggott, troubled. She was a little woman, slim and good-looking, dark and vivacious. This was a modest but well-maintained single house in Hollywood, on Berendo; the name on the mailbox was Fitzpatrick. She had asked them into a neat, nicely furnished living room, and a boy about ten and a girl a little older had looked at them curiously and obediently vanished at her quick word.

"Do you think he might try to contact you, ma'am?" asked Grace.

"I don't know. I don't think so, but—" She bit her lip. "Nobody could know, with Terry." She ran a hand through her thick short hair, distractedly. "I was a fool—well, I was sixteen. I guess that says it all. He was a wild one, Jim Conover. I was crazy in love with him, and we ran away to Vegas to get married and my mother about had a fit—and of course it wasn't three months later I knew what a fool I'd been. Jim knocking me around when he felt like it—and I guess I was lucky at that, you know—him getting killed in that accident just before Terry was born. But Terry's just like him—a wild one, and nobody could do anything with him. He got into trouble—stealing—when he was only seven. I tried, but having to work—"

[11]

"Well, if he does contact you," said Piggott, "we'd like to know."

She nodded. "Before he got sent up this last time, he used to come once in a while when he was broke. Asking for money. The last time, he threatened to—to hurt the children if we didn't—but I'm really lucky now." She smiled at them. "My husband's a good man, and he—got it across to Terry all right. He knocked him down and threw him out, told him just what he'd get if he tried anything. I don't think Terry'd come here—anymore. But I've got to say I don't know. But believe me, if he does we'll call you right away."

"We have information that he has a girl here," said Grace. "A Betty Suttner—they lived together a while, a few years back."

"Oh," she said. "I wouldn't know. You mean he might try to contact her?" She laughed. "He might or he might not—when it comes to girls, it's out of sight out of mind with Terry. I suppose it's possible."

"Well, thanks very much," said Piggott.

"People, people," said Grace, sliding under the wheel of the little blue racing Elva. "It's getting on for end of shift. I'll take you back to your car."

"No snapshots today." Piggott yawned.

Grace grinned. "I guess we're getting used to having a family, after six months." And his father (who should know, chief of gynecology at the General Hospital) still saying probably now after adopting little Celia Ann, they'd be producing one of their own. . . .

Piggott stopped at a hardware store on the way home and bought four feet of screening and a dishpan. In the apartment, his russet-haired Prudence was fishing for medium-sized baby tetras to transfer to a dishpan of their own. Even as he came in, one of the larger babies neatly swallowed a smaller sibling an inch from her little net, and Prudence said crossly, "Oh, *damn!* I don't care, Matt, I know I shouldn't swear, but it's perfectly maddening!

There must have been over three hundred to start with, and I can't understand why some grow so fast and others don't—"

They got about twenty-five of the middle-sized ones into the new dishpan and covered with screening before dinner.

Landers, getting into Hackett's scarlet Barracuda, had said he hoped he was getting somewhere with that blonde. Little blond Phil O'Neill, down in R. and I.—Phillipa Rosemary, only not for a lady cop, as she said—was a very sensible sort of girl, and kept telling him they hadn't known each other long enough. She didn't, she said, believe in hasty marriages—or divorce. Well, they'd known each other over a year now, and Landers knew all he wanted to know about Phil. But women—

The address Folsom had given them for Terry Conover's girl friend Betty Suttner (and apparently he'd written her letters or Folsom wouldn't have had it) was on Barton Avenue in Hollywood. It was one of the bright-painted jerry-built new apartments, about twenty units, and at number four a thin elderly man answered the door and said he'd never heard of her. "Maybe she used to live here."

There wasn't a manager on the premises. Rent was paid to a big realty company out on Santa Monica. They went up there to ask. Betty Suttner had moved three months ago and left no forwarding address. "Are you *cops?*" asked the young woman they talked to. She looked at Landers curiously. "You don't look old enough to be a *detective—*"

That one Landers was used to hearing. It used to make him mad. Phil said that funny affair last year when he'd got suspended by Internal Affairs had aged him, apparently not all that much.

"I wonder if a moustache would make any difference, Tom," said Hackett, back in the car. "Just an idea."

"Phil doesn't like moustaches. I asked her. Funny," said Landers, "a lot of women do. The lieutenant—well—"

"Man about town. Yes," said Hackett. "Until he got caught, if belatedly. I wonder if we could trace this Suttner girl through her job. If anybody at that apartment remembers where she worked—"

"In case Conover contacts her. I have had a further thought," said Landers. "He probably hasn't much money. Even if the escape was set up by some of his pals. We may hear of him first when he pulls a heist somewhere."

"Which is also an idea," said Hackett.

It was a quarter to six. They went back to headquarters. Mendoza had already left, and Lake. Hackett left the telex message about Conover pinned down by an ashtray on Shogart's desk. This was Wednesday, Henry Glasser's day off, so the night watch would be short one man. He followed Landers' Corvair out of the lot and got on the Pasadena freeway.

At the house in Highland Park, he found all serene: his inspired cook Angel busy over the stove, her brown hair in disarray from the hot oven, nearly-five Mark absorbed in the McGuffey First Reader, two-year-old Sheila (and her hair was really going to be reddish, like his mother's) coaxing the dignified silver Persian to play—Luis, wishing that cat on them, remembered Hackett amusedly, suffering Sheila's strangling hug and patting Silver Boy.

"Busy day, darling?"

"The usual," said Hackett. And to her further automatic question, "No, I haven't weighed. The hell with it. And all the diets. After all, I am six three and a half—"

Rich Conway had been wandering around all alone since noon, questioning the various witnesses on the four heist jobs. He hadn't got a thing. He felt frustrated and lonesome. He'd rather looked forward, getting off night watch on to days, to seeing more of Lieutenant Mendoza, that rather legendary character, now Robbery and Homicide were merged; but in this last month he hadn't had occasion to, much; they'd had a lot of tiresome routine, the legwork.

He went home and put a frozen dinner in the oven, and phoned

Landers, who had just got home. "What about setting up another double date on Tuesday?" They were both off on Tuesday, and Conway was dating a policewoman too, Margot Swain, who was working out of Wilcox Street in Hollywood.

"I'll ask Phil," said Landers amiably. The girls liked each other.

Mendoza, who had walked alone so long, these days came home to a crowded house on Rayo Grande Avenue up in Hollywood. As he slid the Ferrari into the garage beside Alison's Facel-Vega, he wasn't worried or much interested in any of the various cases they had on hand. He didn't like to stash cases away in Pending but sometimes it was unavoidable. He'd hear about the body on Stanford Avenue in the morning; they'd probably pick up Terry Conover somewhere, sometime; the heist jobs were anonymous, like so many of the casual robberies, burglaries; it was to be hoped those two bodies would get identified eventually, to get buried under the right names.

He got a little tired sometimes, of the eternal damned foolishness, wanton violence, random stupidity. He had put in, for his sins, twenty-five years of watching it, on this top police force, and he got a little tired. Seeing that he didn't have to go on with it—the old man having been that rare bird, a lucky gambler—he sometimes wondered why he stayed on down at headquarters.

But at home in the big Spanish house was red-haired Alison, who had so belatedly domesticated Luis Mendoza, and Mairí MacTaggart busy over her special scones, and the livestock—the Old English sheepdog Cedric offering a solemn paw, somewhere the four cats, Bast, Nefertite, Sheba and the wicked El Señor; and, of course, the twins.

Mendoza, these days, had the vague thought that parenthood should be entered into young. The twins, such an uncanny combination of himself and his Scots-Irish girl, sometimes confounded him.

"Amador," said Alison briskly, returning his kiss. "Blue cheese

or Roquefort dressing? It's just salad, steak and Mairí 's scones. Do you want a drink before dinner? And they have really related to Lesson Twenty-four in the first reader."

"*¿Por qué?*" said Mendoza. "Why do I stay at this thankless job?"

"I often wonder," said Alison. "It's the goat. Lesson Twenty-four."

"*¡No me diga!*" said Mendoza.

"Well, go and hear."

In the nursery, a term the twins objected to, he was greeted by loud demands. The twins were not quite four; at least, mercifully, the McGuffey Readers had them talking mostly English now. "See, Daddy, a *nice* goat—named Jip—he pulls the cart— A goat, he'd be fun to have, we be all *bueno* to him—" Master Johnny was excited at the thought.

"Want a goat!" said Miss Terry simply.

"*¡Dios me libre!*" said Mendoza. He wondered how you could explain zoning laws to a nearly-four-year-old. He wondered how he'd ever got into all this.

The night watch, minus Glasser tonight, came on—Shogart the plodder, Galeano, Schenke. It was a quiet night; nothing turned up for them until nine-thirty, when they had a call from the black-and-white chased out on a call. Another heist, at—of all places—Chasen's new downtown restaurant. That was a very class place, one of the few good restaurants on Central's beat. Shogart and Galeano went out on it.

"We were just about to close," said the maître d' agitatedly. "The last customers were just out, I'd already put up the sign, most of the girls already gone—"

The manager was moaning, "Never had such a thing happen—I couldn't believe it, and for a Wednesday it'd been a good night—all the receipts—I hadn't counted it, I don't know—"

Two men, they both said: one chef had still been here, but back in the kitchen, and hadn't seen them. The restaurants which offered live entertainment, a combo, a pianist, would stay open till past midnight; but Chasen's just offered good food and a quiet atmosphere, and closed between nine and nine-thirty. Two men, and all the manager and maître d' could say was, middle-sized, stocking masks over their faces, two guns. "I don't know anything about guns," said the manager, "I don't know what kind. All the receipts—it was a busy night—and I always go straight to the night-deposit box at the bank—"

"That's kind of a smart job," said Galeano thoughtfully. "Somebody thought about this, E.M. Figured somebody'd be taking all the nice cash to a night-deposit box—get in first, just at closing time." But there wasn't much to go on. Tomorrow, the day men could ask the computers who might have records of having held up restaurants before. The only definite thing that emerged was that the heisters hadn't touched anything here, and might have been wearing gloves anyway. It'd be no use to call out the lab on it.

2

THURSDAY MORNING, AND HACKETT AND HIG-
gins off. Mendoza, coming in at eight sharp, was reading the
report Galeano had left him on the job at Chasen's when the day
men came drifting in, Piggott, Palliser, Landers, Conway, Grace.

"This Moffat thing," said Grace, following the rest of them
into Mendoza's office. Palliser, seeing Wanda come in, had cor-
nered her and was starting to dictate a report about that. Having
the gist of it from him, Grace passed on to Mendoza what they
had so far. "We're going to nose around that apartment, see what
gossip we can pick up. She doesn't seem to have been exactly the
shrinking violet. Could be somebody'll know the names of a few
current boyfriends."

"It's a place to start," agreed Mendoza absently. "Now, this
slick little heist last night—" He looked at Galeano's report
meditatively. "If we ever pick up the X's on those other jobs, it'll
be pure luck— Tom, you and Conway might as well do a little
routine on this. I've got the manager and the maître d' coming in
at ten to make statements. When you come to think of it, it's a
wonder nobody had that thought before—the genteel restaurants,
at closing times. At least I don't remember any such caper."

"There'd be quite a take, I suppose," said Conway, "if half of it
wasn't credit-card records, but they couldn't be sure—"

"Ah, but they could. Nearly," said Mendoza. "The place with
a floor show, a band, dancing, there'd be a good many people

around at closing time. The nice quiet restaurant, no. By the time the manager or whoever was ready to take off for the night-deposit box, the waitresses gone, chefs gone. An ideal setup really. I wonder what the take was."

As they went out Conway said to Landers, "That aspect of it never occurred to me. He does see things. But what do you bet that this turns out just as anonymous as the other ones?"

"No bets, with the violent-crime rate up. We can make the gestures at it." They went down to R. and I. and consulted with Phil O'Neill. She really was a very cute blonde, neat and trim in her navy uniform, with the dusting of freckles on her upturned nose, and Landers looked at her fondly. "Do we have any records of anybody heisting restaurants, lady?"

"See what the computer says," said Phil. Rather surprisingly, the computer gave them two names. One Albert Pritchard, one Sam Olinski had held up the Tail o' the Cock, three years ago. Olinski had a mild record of common theft and burglary prior to that; Pritchard only a count of drunk driving. They'd both got a one-to-three and would probably be out now. The addresses would be up-to-date if they were both on parole. Reluctantly Landers followed Conway out— Phil had agreed to the date Tuesday if it was all right with Margot—and they took the Corvair to check out the address on Olinski, which was over in Glendale.

It was an old frame house on a quiet residential street, and they found Olinski sitting in a rocker on the front porch. By his pedigree he was fifty-one, but he looked older: white-haired and rather feeble. He looked at the badges and peered at Landers. "Seems you cops look younger to me every time I see one—but so does everybody, come to that. You ain't tryin' to pin anything on me, are you?"

"Depends if there's anything to pin, Mr. Olinski," said Conway, his cynical gray eyes amused. "Can you tell us where you were last night at about nine-thirty?"

"Sure. Right here. That is, in the house. Watchin' TV. With

my daughter Eleanor and her husband Jim. Did you think I was up to something?" He laughed shortly. "I guess you picked me up the last time, boys. Can't do much of nothin' these days. I had me a big old heart attack while I was still in the joint, last year."

The daughter was there, and indignantly confirmed that. "So somebody else had the bright idea," said Landers. Olinski said he didn't know where Pritchard was; he didn't know him very well, they'd only pulled that one job together and Pritchard had got paroled before he had.

The address they had for Pritchard was in West L.A., and when they found it, he had.moved away last week. A phone call downtown confirmed that Pritchard had got off parole about the same time he moved. He still could be one of the boys they were after, so they went back to the office to sit in on the interview with the manager and maître d'.

They got there as the two men were arriving.

The manager, Dave Woodward, was still shaken. "We'd never had it happen before, Lieutenant—you don't think of a good restaurant as a place that gets held up, if you take me—and I was so surprised—I'm afraid neither of us can be of any help to you, we couldn't possibly identify anybody, they had these stocking masks on, pulled right down over their faces, and they couldn't have been there five minutes—"

"Less," said the other man, Chester Hunter. He looked very unlike a suave maître d', in a tweed suit and loud tie: he was very tall and thin, Woodward short and stocky, but they both wore mournful expressions. "Mr. Woodward had all the receipts in his briefcase, all ready to leave. They took it and went."

"¿Qué?" Mendoza sat up. "As if they knew the routine?"

"We thought about that," said Woodward, "but anybody could figure the day's receipts would be taken to a night-deposit box after we closed, and it was a good time to hit us. I scarcely think it was—er—what you'd call an inside job, Lieutenant." He smiled faintly. "Every restaurant I've ever worked in had more or less the same routine on that."

[20]

"What about the briefcase?" asked Landers, thinking about latent prints.

"Oh, they took it. Just looked to be sure what was in it, and—and went," said Woodward. "Fortunately, of course, I've got the figures. For what it's worth. Six thousand eight hundred and forty-two dollars in cash. The credit-card records—"

"They'll dump those," said Conway. "My God, would that be an average take for one day?"

"Slightly under—it was Wednesday, it's usually slower in the middle of the week," said Woodward. "But really, I was so surprised—and with the masks—I couldn't possibly describe—"

"Well, you can give us some idea about sizes—clothes," said Landers.

They consulted with each other mutely. "Both young, I'd say," said Hunter. "One about maybe five ten, other one shorter. Just dark clothes—pants and jackets. Black or dark gray." Woodward agreed. "Neither of 'em fat or thin, just ordinary."

That left Pritchard in, just about. He was thirty-three, five ten, a hundred and fifty.

Only they didn't know where to look for him. They'd get word out to the pigeons; maybe somebody knew where he was.

Grace and Palliser, at the Stanford Avenue apartment, were feeling frustrated and getting nowhere.

Miss Callway, who lived across the hall from Ida Moffat's apartment, said primly that she hadn't known her at all. "Not even to speak to. I hope I know how to mind my own business."

Mrs. Licci in the front left upstairs apartment told them she really didn't know anything about Mrs. Moffat, and hadn't wanted to know anything, but she wasn't surprised she'd got herself murdered though it was a terrible thing to have happen right here. She'd get her husband to move except that they probably couldn't find anything so cheap so close in to town. "Why weren't you surprised?" asked Grace in his soft voice. "If you didn't know her?"

Well, said Mrs. Licci darkly, she didn't *know* but there were feelings to these things. Pressed, she added that she was very busy cleaning and really couldn't spare any more time.

The three couples in the other apartments upstairs and downstairs rear all worked and weren't home. In the downstairs right front apartment Mrs. Schultz shied back from the badges and said she didn't know anything. Mrs. Kiefer was the manager, she said, if anybody knew anything about Mrs. Moffat it'd be her.

Mrs. Kiefer was just leaving for the market, and said she was in a hurry. "I told you all I know yesterday, anyway," she said to Palliser. "I mind my own business, and I don't like gossip. I told you—"

"Mrs. Kiefer," said Grace gently, "does your husband work around here?"

"Now what in time that's got to do with anything—! Yes, he's got the Shell station at Vermont and Olympic. But what you're asking for—"

"What were you asking for?" asked Palliser as they started back to the car. They'd taken his Rambler; he refused to squeeze his six feet into the little blue Elva.

"Well, I've got a simple mind, John," said Grace, "as we all know. And for all Matt's right about being back to Sodom and Gomorrah, and the devil converting all too many people, it occurs to me that there are still some—mmh—skittishly respectable females left among us. I think we've been talking to some of them. And I'd take a bet the Lieutenant'd say that when Mrs. Kiefer tells us she doesn't like gossip, that's the warning rattle."

"I believe you," said Palliser.

"I'll bet all the women in that apartment exchanged a lot of gossip about this Moffat female, but they're not about to come out plain and talk about anything with *s*-blank-*x* in it, to a couple of strange cops. Just occurred to me that one of the men living there might not be so prudish."

"You've got a simple mind," said Palliser, switching on the ignition. "Let's go and see."

[22]

At the Shell station he pulled the Rambler off to one side of the pumps; they got out and asked a dirty-looking kid with long hair and sideburns for Kiefer. "That's him there—" He pointed incuriously. Kiefer was big and blond, balding, and friendly by the grin he was giving a customer as he polished the windshield. They went up and introduced themselves as the car pulled out, and Kiefer was more than friendly; he was pleased as punch to see them.

"I wondered if any of you fellows'd want to talk to me—I'll take a break—hey, Benny, you take over, hah? Now what about that, a murder right in our building! You'd took the body away, time I got home last night, but the wife told me all about it—I can't get over her bein' the one to find the body! A body—my God. So, what you want to ask me? Anything I can tell you—"

"About Mrs. Moffat," said Grace. "We've been talking to the women at the apartment, and—"

"And they was all nervous as hell about it and too mealymouthed to tell you anything, hah?" Kiefer laughed and lit a long black cigar, after politely offering the box. "Women, my God! That old biddy was about all they talked about since she lived there. My God, it makes you wonder what gets into some women, fellows. That one, she'd been around but good. Man crazy—anything in pants, I give you my word. Made a pass at me once, shows you she'd go for anything." He chuckled comfortably. "And I don't say, if she'd been twenty years younger and sober at the time, I wouldn't 'a took her up on it, but I'm a little more particular, you might say."

Palliser grinned. "We did gather, from this and that in the apartment—"

"Man crazy," repeated Kiefer. "The wife's told me, many's the time she'd see Mrs. Moffat bring men home. Never any noisy parties, nothin' to complain about, you see, but anybody can add two and two knew what was goin' on."

"Did she have a regular boyfriend?" asked Grace.

"I wouldn't think so. The wife says she never saw the same

[23]

man with her twice. I wouldn't know where she picked 'em up. I don't think she hung around local bars, not by the hours she'd be in and out, what the wife says. She worked pretty regular every day, and then she'd go out early in the evening, see." But he couldn't offer them any descriptions, any names. "And tell you the truth, I don't think the wife or any of the other women could either. See, take this latest time it happened—last Monday night. I'm sittin' there readin' the paper, the wife says there's that woman comin' in, and opens the door a crack mighty careful to do some snoopin', see. Says she saw Mrs. Moffat in the front hall, man with her, just saw his back, but she didn't think it was the same man come home with her Saturday night anyway. It was like that. The hall's dark, and for all the women's snoopin' I don't suppose they spotted her every time she brought a man home."

"So it could just as well be she did have a regular boyfriend," said Palliser. "Or several."

Kiefer thought that over and agreed. "I guess so."

"Mr. Kiefer," said Grace, "I understand your wife manages the apartment. Collects the rents and so on. Why didn't she ask Mrs. Moffat to move, if—"

"My God, man," said Kiefer, "them women wouldn't 'a had anything nearly so damn juicy to gossip about, hadn't been for Ida Moffat! Women ain't logical, Mr. Grace. I asked her the same thing once and she just says there's no technical reason, woman don't make any disturbance."

Grace laughed. "And I ought to know human nature better by this time."

But as far as tracking down any of the men Ida Moffat had known, that was a handful of nothing. Back in the Rambler, Palliser said, "There was a check. Evidently somebody she'd worked for. I don't suppose the woman could tell us anything, but we'd better give it a try. I've got the address—Briarcliff Road in Hollywood."

*　　*　　*

Just after Woodward and Hunter left, a black-and-white called in to report two new bodies, in a car on the street. A citizen had come in ten minutes before, asking to see one of the unidentified bodies; he'd reported his son missing and Lieutenant Carey of Missing Persons had sent him up here. Piggott had taken him to the morgue. Landers and Conway had just come back from another visit to R. and I. with a list of common-garden-variety heist men to chase down, with nothing at all to say that any of them had been the X's at Chasen's last night or on the other jobs; Mendoza chased them out on the new homicides.

Fifteen minutes later he was methodically stacking the deck, practicing the crooked poker deal, when Sergeant Lake buzzed him and said business was picking up. "You've got another new body, at the Clark Hotel."

"*Caray,*" said Mendoza. "So I'll go and look at it." He reached for the perennial black Homburg.

"There's an ambulance on the way and I'll get the lab out. The black-and-white's still there."

The Clark Hotel on Hill Street, like some other hotels in downtown L.A., had once been a good hotel, a quiet middle-class place with no pretension to elegance, but eminently respectable, offering good service and comfort. It was still respectable, but with the inevitable decrease of respectable transients staying in the inner-city area, when classier hotels in cleaner areas were available, the Clark looked somewhat down-at-heel and poverty-stricken now. Its brown brick front was grimy, and inside the lobby the carpet was wearing thin. One of the uniformed men, Fred Ware, was standing by the desk; recognizing Mendoza, he came forward.

"It's the fifth floor, Lieutenant. Quigley—he's the manager—is having kittens about keeping it quiet. Seems they don't have all that many customers anymore and maybe news of a murder'd drive everybody out they've got. He's up there with my partner."

"What's it look like?" Mendoza buried his cigarette in a sand tub.

"Well, it's murder one all right." Ware was a big dark young fellow, and he'd been a cop for some time, but he looked shaken for a moment. "An old lady—Mrs. Harriet Branch. She lived here—they've got more permanent tenants than people passing through, I think. She's been beaten up—it's a mess. Place ransacked. The daughter called in when she couldn't get her on the phone, they usually talked to each other the same time every day. Quigley thought she might have had a heart attack or something, and went up and found her."

"*Así*," said Mendoza. "Funny place for a break-in. Or was it?"

"The door wasn't broken in. Looks as if she let in whoever it was herself. Which is also funny," said Ware.

"The lab team'll be along—send them up."

"It's five-fourteen, Lieutenant."

Up on the fifth floor the other uniformed man was trying to calm down Quigley—a little plump man in a tight brown suit—and an agitated Negro maid in a white uniform. He greeted Mendoza in some relief. Mendoza said, "You can get back on tour as soon as the lab shows up."

"We've preserved it tight for you, sir. Nobody in since Mr. Quigley called in."

"*Bueno.*" Mendoza introduced himself to the other two. The maid was Agnes Harvey, and even in her agitation her mind was moving faster than Quigley's.

"I just hope you won't think I had anything to do with it, Lieutenant—I can see the lock's not broken, and of course I've got a key, but you've got to believe me, she always kept the bolt up too and when I came to clean I'd have to call out who I was before she'd let me in—I wouldn't have hurt Mrs. Branch, she was a nice old lady—and to see her laying there like that—"

"I'm sure they wouldn't think that, Agnes," said Quigley, shocked all over again. "Such a terrible, terrible thing—we've never had such a thing happen—"

"We'll want a statement from you, Mr. Quigley—can you wait a little while, please? There'll be some men out from the lab, and then I'll want to talk to you." Quigley stuttered obedience. Mendoza shoved the door of five-fourteen wider with a cautious toe, and went in.

The center light was on, and showed him an old-fashioned hotel suite, what used to be called a bachelor apartment. The living room was about twelve by fifteen, furnished with shabby, nondescript, comfortable furniture, an overstuffed couch, a matching chair, a little desk with a straight chair, a thin flowered carpet; there were sheer lace curtains at the windows. A door to the left gave a glimpse of a tiny kitchenette, an apartment-sized stove, a small table. A door to the right led into a small square bedroom just big enough for a single bed, a double chest of drawers, another straight chair. There was a walk-in closet, and a postage-stamp-sized bathroom beside it.

The body of the old woman was in the middle of the living-room floor. She lay on her side, arms over her head as if she were still trying to protect herself from the blows rained on her. Mendoza bent and felt one arm; it was stiff. He thought, looking at his watch, sometime yesterday evening. There was a good deal of blood; her mouth was open in a silent scream. She'd been a thin, frail old lady; she was wearing an old-fashioned cotton nightgown with a high neck, and a fleecy pink housecoat over it, both torn and bloody. One flaccid limp breast spilled out on the carpet.

The whole place had been ruthlessly ransacked—drawers yanked out and dumped, clothes pulled off the rod in the closet, the medicine chest in the bathroom swept clean; a bottle of aspirin, toothpaste, eye lotion, and mouthwash bottles dumped to the tile floor, smashed. Near the body lay an old-fashioned black handbag, open, with a generous-sized coin purse beside it, empty. An ink bottle was overturned on the desk, and a pool of ink stained the carpet. The standard reading lamp by the upholstered chair had been knocked flat, its bulb broken.

Mendoza said to himself ruefully, *"A su tiempo maduran las uvas.* And what a harvest do we reap." The statistics every cop knew, but that was figures on a sheet of paper: Mrs. Branch, horridly and cruelly dead in this quiet room, made the figures come to life: the crimes of violence up by 622 percent in the last twelve years.

He went back to the living room for another look at the body, and this time spotted something else; he bent closer. There was a noise at the door and Duke and Scarne came in loaded down with the usual equipment. "That's pretty," commented Duke. "I wish you'd find a nice neat corpse for us some time, Lieutenant."

"Few and far between," said Mendoza. "Look, Bill—there's something under the body—I'd like a look at it."

"Wait till I get some pictures." Five minutes later Scarne put down the Speed Graphic, bent over the body and grunted, "I see it." He lifted the body slightly and with the handle of a dusting brush hooked something out to slither into full sight on the carpet. "And isn't that pretty."

"No," said Mendoza. "It's an ugly little joke, Bill." He brushed his moustache back and forth. And in one way he liked it a little, and in another he didn't. Symbols, he thought.

The object that had fallen under the body—he had a vision of the old lady trying to put up a fight, grabbing and holding—was a long string of violently colored plastic love beads, the kind worn by both sexes of the Now generation. It was broken, and several beads had slid off the thin wire that had held them. At one end of it was a crudely made bright brass circle-and-cross, the Egyptian *ankh* that was the symbol of Life.

"It's all yours," said Mendoza, and went out to talk to Quigley. The maid had disappeared; Quigley, hovering in the hall, was only slightly calmer. "Could we go to your office, Mr. Quigley? I'll want to know everything you can tell me about Mrs. Branch."

"Oh, yes, certainly, certainly." But downstairs they were intercepted by the desk clerk.

"Mrs. Whitlow's been calling every five minutes, Mr. Quigley, and I didn't know what to do—I didn't like, over the phone—but I suppose she ought to know—"

"Oh, my God," said Quigley. "I forgot all about her! I ought to have called her! Mrs. Branch's daughter! My God, how can I tell her over the phone her mother's been murdered? My God, I need a drink."

"You'd better let me do it," said Mendoza. It was another unpleasant job cops got used to. The clerk put the call through to Mr. Quigley's little cubbyhole of an office; economically Mendoza introduced himself and broke the news to Mrs. Whitlow, who sounded level-headed even in crisis. He would probably want to talk to her later, today or tomorrow; the body would have to be formally identified. She said yes, and she'd call her husband right away; she gave him the address and remembered to thank him before she began to cry and hung up.

Quigley was apologizing, recapping a bottle of Scotch. "Really, I'm not a drinking man, Lieutenant, but this has upset me so—we've never had such a thing happen—Mrs. Branch! Such a nice old lady, and a real lady too—she'd lived here for over twenty years, and the last few years with her arthritis so bad she hardly went out at all, except when her daughter came for her—she had Sunday dinner with them every week—Mrs. Whitlow's a nice woman too, and I must say I can hardly blame her for trying to get Mrs. Branch to move away, go to live with them. There's no denying that this area isn't as safe or—or pleasant as it used to be, when Mrs. Branch first lived here—it was so convenient, she used to say, just a couple of blocks up to Bullock's, The Broadway practically next door, all the shops—and we'd have missed the old lady, but I did see why Mrs. Whitlow—"

Mendoza started to get him calmed down to answer questions.

"We noticed the old heap when we came on at six," said the uniformed man to Landers and Conway. "This couple asleep or passed out. No reason to check 'em out—along here you get that sometimes." The car was an old Dodge sedan, much dented. "But when we swung round here again, half an hour ago, they were still here, so Jack said we'd better check to see if they're high on something. And they're cold. I think they were shot—there's blood. Didn't want to mess up any latents for the lab."

Landers and Conway peered into the car, which had its windows down. The bodies were a man and a woman, both young. There was blood all right. "Have to tow it in before we can get at 'em," said Conway. "There could be prints on the car." And it would be just as well anyway; this was a sleazy backwater, Naud Street down below the Southern Pacific railroad yards, and already a little crowd of noisy youngsters had collected across the street and were yelling the usual names at the uniform.

"Everybody," said Landers, straightening his slim height from the car, "has got civil rights but us. Give the garage a call." In fifteen minutes a tow truck came up; the black-and-white went back on tour and Landers and Conway followed the truck back to the garage.

When the lab men had dusted the outside of the Dodge, they got pictures of the corpses *in situ* and then opened the door and got them out. The man looked to be in his early twenties, a weedy little fellow with shoulder-length blond hair and sideburns, a straggly moustache; he was wearing old jeans and a sleeveless shirt embellished with colorful flowers. He'd been shot at least once in the body. The woman was about the same age, with long dark hair, in jeans and a dirty T-shirt; she'd been shot in the head.

The Dodge was registered to a Godfrey Booth at an address on St. Andrews Place. There was a billfold on the man, empty of money but containing an I.D. card filled out: Godfrey Booth, the same address. There was a woman's handbag, no money in it but a lot of miscellany: lipsticks, powder puffs, Kleenex, matches, a bunch of keys, an address book, a paperback book entitled *How to Become a Witch.*

"Drifters," said Conway. "The mod squad."

"And no money. Just the casual violence for what they had on them?" wondered Landers. The morgue attendants came for the bodies; maybe the autopsies would tell them something more. And there were rules and regulations; if possible they had to get the bodies identified. They drove out to St. Andrews Place to see if anybody there had known Godfrey Booth and who the girl might have been.

It was an old run-down four-family place. When they stepped into the lobby they could hear a baby crying somewhere. Landers punched the bell of the apartment on the left and presently a mountainously fat woman in a bright-red cotton pantsuit opened the door. "Excuse me," said Landers politely, "do you know a Godfrey Booth who lives here?"

She stared at them, shifting a wad of chewing gum in her mouth. "Sure, I know God and Sue. Why? They're gone some place."

"Sue?" said Conway.

"Sue's God's wife. It's kind of a joke, call him God. I dunno where they went. They got the left back upstairs." Landers opened his mouth to tell her they were dead, and she added resentfully, "Went off and left their brat on my hands. I got no time to tend to him—that's him yelling." In spite of which, when they did tell her, she went into hysterics and they had to call an ambulance.

"And I tell you something, Rich," said Landers when she'd passed out and they were waiting for the ambulance, "there's something wrong with that baby."

Neither of them, as ignorant bachelors, knew much about babies; they couldn't have a guess about this one, except that it was extremely dirty; but it was crying intermittently and jerking its arms and legs around as if it were about to have a fit. They eyed it nervously. When the ambulance came, the attendants said it might be epileptic, and took it along too.

Nobody else was at home in the apartment house. It was getting on toward twelve-thirty, so they went up to Federico's on North Broadway for lunch. Palliser and Grace were already there, and Piggott came in five minutes later.

"We've got the overdose identified," he said. "Douglas Horne. Nineteen. I heard all the usual tale from the father." He didn't have to go into detail; they'd all heard that, *ad infinitum*. "The devil

[31]

getting around." And maybe once they'd regarded Matt Piggott the earnest Christian a little amusedly, but these days they didn't. The devil was surely covering ground in this year of our Lord.

When they got back to the office, Landers asked Lake to start the machinery on a search warrant for the St. Andrews Place apartment. Palliser and Grace wanted to bring Mendoza up-to-date on Ida Moffat—he might have a hunch where to go looking. They found him sitting on the edge of his spine in his desk chair contemplating a broken string of plastic love beads. A cigarette smoldered on his lower lip; his normally sleek, thick black hair was ruffled where he'd run fingers through it.

"We've got to a dead end," said Grace. "You're thinking of joining the love generation?"

Mendoza laughed. *"Tal cosa, no.* Symbols. What's your dead end? . . . Oh. Well, all that occurs to me is that the woman must have had some friends somewhere. Female friends. The same kind as herself, she might have talked to about boyfriends."

"I suppose so. But would she have mentioned their names to people she worked for?" said Palliser doubtfully.

"And if it ends up in Pending, not much loss," said Mendoza. He sat up abruptly. "I'm feeling a little more concerned about Mrs. Harriet Branch. Although—*¡singular!*—they both opened their doors to murder. That bolt—Quigley said she asked permission to have it put on—" His voice trailed off; he got up. "Her daughter sounded like a sensible woman. I'd better go and talk to her."

They had called Mrs. Bloomfield at the Hollywood address, and got no answer. Now they'd try her again. "And you know she won't be able to tell us anything," said Palliser.

"No harm in asking," said Grace.

Landers and Conway were driven back to the list of possible heisters from Records, but just as they were leaving the office Lake hailed them. "It's Hollywood Receiving—a Dr. Schiller."

"Detective Landers, Robbery-Homicide, Doctor. What—"

"What kind of devilry you boys are sending us these days," said Dr. Schiller coldly, "really has to be seen to be believed. I understand it was your office sent over this baby—I don't know the circumstances—male, approximately ten months old, some malnutrition and a respiratory infection."

"Well, yes?" said Landers.

"What kind of *mentality*—" said Schiller. "Well, of course the normal sane individual simply cannot grasp the enormities possible to the addicts—but—! The baby, Detective Landers, has been subjected to probably repetitive doses of marijuana. He is in a dangerously comatose state at the moment, but I think we can stabilize him with care. What brain damage or chromosome damage may have been done is something else. I suppose you have to—"

"What?" said Landers incredulously. "The baby—*marijuana?*"

"Almighty God," said Conway mildly.

"—know something about the latest research on narcotic drugs," said Dr. Schiller sardonically. "So possibly you are aware that the new findings are that many of the effects, such as chromosome changes and the probability of deformed genes, as well as simpler brain damage, which we once attributed to LSD, have now been determined to be in fact a result of marijuana ingestion."

"My God," said Landers. "My God. Look, Doctor, we didn't feed the baby the marijuana. But, my God, yes, I saw that release—but who would—a *baby*—"

"I only thought you'd like to know," said Schiller.

Landers put the phone down and passed that on. All of them but Piggott swore, and Piggott simply said, "And if that isn't diabolical, I don't know what is. A baby."

And Conway said thoughtfully, "The Mary Jane. You know, Tom—that's kind of basic, isn't it?"

"What do you mean?"

"Well, who had access to the baby, to feed it the marijuana? The parents. Godfrey and Sue Booth. I think—"

Kind of a joke, call him God. Landers thought, perhaps irrelevantly, of a bumper sticker that had given him a chuckle on the way home the other day: *God is back—and is He mad!*

"I think," said Conway, "we go up to Narco and ask if anybody there knows anything about Godfrey and Sue."

"I think so too," said Landers purposefully.

3

THE ADDRESS MRS. WHITLOW HAD GIVEN MEN-
doza was on Creston Drive in the hills above Hollywood. It was a
sprawling old Spanish house; this was an old residential area
redolent of substance rather than new money. She opened the
door to him herself, acknowledged the badge and introduction
with a silent nod.

"I've been trying to reach Walter—my husband. He had to go
up to San Francisco to a sales convention. The hotel promised to
pass on a message as soon as he comes in. I've tried to keep my
head, but—Mother! To think of— Please, won't you sit down."
She was tall, fair, good-looking in a broad Scandinavian way, her
face now drawn with grief. The room was a little untidy,
pleasantly furnished for comfort rather than show. "I know there
are things you want to ask—but I don't understand how it could
have happened, some criminal getting in—"

"Well, we'd like to find out too, Mrs. Whitlow," said Mendoza. He offered her a cigarette, lit it for her, lit his own. "Mr.
Quigley told me you wanted your mother to move."

"Oh, good heavens, yes," she said. "When she first went to the
Clark, it was nice. And convenient, right downtown. But now, it
wasn't even very safe—not that Mother went out much down
there, since her arthritis had been worse. I used to change her
library books for her once a week, and bring her here to dinner on

[35]

Sunday— But she'd lived there so long, since Dad died, and she knew all the people at the hotel, it was home to her."

"Did she have any friends living there too?"

She nodded. "Especially Mrs. Davies, she was about Mother's age—she died last month. I know Mother said she was going to miss her—they used to spend afternoons together, Mother's apartment or hers. Most of the permanent tenants there are older people, but a lot of them have moved away in the last few years. But I just can't understand how a thing like this could happen, right in the hotel—Mother always kept her door bolted, Walter put that on for her—"

"Mrs. Whitlow, can you give us any idea how much money your mother might have had in the apartment?"

She nodded. "It's only the second week of the month. She'd have had her check about the third or fourth— I shopped for her, just a few groceries, last Saturday, and it came to twelve something, she'd given me a twenty. Her annuity check. Dad took it out for her when he made that killing in the market, and the agent said he was crazy—"

"How much would she have had left?"

"Well, that's it. Heavens," she said, smoking quickly, staring past his shoulder into space, "I remember Dad saying that often enough—how he knew when Roosevelt took us off the gold standard the dollar was eventually doomed—just a question of time—and when he made that killing, it was during the war, he sank a lot of it into the annuity for Mother. He thought the currency might just hold for her lifetime, more and more inflated, of course. The agent said he was crazy, the monthly payment he wanted set up, but"—she smiled wryly—"I guess Dad knew what he was doing." She stubbed out her cigarette.

"And possibly a little something about basic economics," said Mendoza dryly. "How much?"

"It was fifteen hundred a month. Usually she took just what she needed for groceries and so on—I shopped for her once a week usually, if she didn't feel like going out—but I know last week she'd said she was going to take her fur coat in for storage, and it needed some repairs—and she probably took out enough for Walter's birthday present too, she wanted to get him a nice sports jacket, I was going to take her shopping— There might have been four or five hundred dollars there."

"What bank she did use?"

"The Security Pacific just down in the next block. Oh, I should have been firmer!" she said wretchedly. "I should have made her move away from there. But it's difficult with old people, if you—if you *manage* them they think you think they're not capable anymore—and it wasn't that, but—"

"Would you say your mother was—mmh—gullible, easily taken in? Would she have, say, got talking to a stranger, someone who seemed friendly, a woman especially—asked her to her apartment?"

"Oh, I don't think so—no, Mother was pretty shrewd, she had all her faculties all right. Strangers—but where would she meet any? She didn't get out much any more. Years ago she used to go up to Echo Park, MacArthur, on the bus, on nice days. But her arthritis the last few years—she was eighty-one, you know— And she'd have told me about anybody like that—"

"Did she know any young people?" asked Mendoza.

"*Young* people?" She stared at him. "Why, what do you— down there, do you mean? Oh, I don't see how—she never said anything about— Why?"

Mendoza looked at his cigarette. "You said she kept her door bolted. But suppose someone knocked and said there was a telegram, a special delivery letter. I suppose the hotel staff changes occasionally. Would she have opened her door, you think?"

"Oh, dear," she said inadequately, "I suppose so. Do you think that was how—? Oh, she would have. If they said they were from the desk. Right there in the hotel, feeling safe—" She sobbed once, and the phone rang in the hall. "Oh, thank God, that's Walter—" She ran. He listened to her murmuring voice out there for less than five minutes; when she came back she said, "He's flying right down, as soon as he can get a plane. He said something about—probably you have to have a formal identification."

"That's right," said Mendoza. "He can come to my office, take care of that tomorrow. Thanks very much, Mrs. Whitlow—if I think of anything else, we'll be in touch." He was thinking now, with this much background, it could very easily be as simple as that: probably was. The old lady a fixture in the hotel, and all too probably chatting idly with the maids, Quigley, other people: the bit about the annuity, possibly even the amount, getting around by word of mouth. Getting to the ears eventually of some of the Now generation, too many of whom seemed determined to evade working for a living. The violence in that apartment, given one frail old lady as victim, could have been the work of one adult male. And in that big lobby, one adult male might not have been noticed, or noticed idly, passing through. But it'd do no harm to ask the night desk clerk if he remembered the love beads. As a rule, the love beads went with a few other rather bizarre items of apparel: but even that might be no help: a lot of that generation affected those.

Mendoza went back to the office and heard about the baby from Sergeant Lake, who was talking about it with a horrified Wanda. *"¡Porvida! ¿Donde irá a parar todo esto?* Where's all this going to end indeed?"

"Just what I said," said Wanda. "Sometimes I agree with Matt Piggott. A *baby—*"

"Oh, well, you just can't get decent servants nowadays," said Winifred Bloomfield to Palliser and Grace. She had looked a little undecided about letting a black man into her nice clean house, even when he wasn't very black and had on a sharp-tailored suit and white shirt; she talked mostly in Palliser's direction. She was a rawboned woman about sixty, overdressed and over-made-up, and her ultra-refined accent made both of them suspect strongly that she'd once been little Winnie Whatshername from the wrong side of the tracks.

[38]

"Had Mrs. Moffat worked for you long, Mrs. Bloomfield?" asked Palliser.

"Oh, a couple of years," she said vaguely. "Two days a week. Sometimes she helped out in the kitchen when we were entertaining. I didn't know her—I really couldn't tell you anything about her." And by her expression of delighted horror when they'd told her the woman had been murdered, thought Palliser, she'd be dying to ask questions, nobly restraining herself. "At least she didn't steal my husband's liquor the way some of the others did."

"Do you remember her ever mentioning the names of any friends?" asked Grace.

"Oh, dear me, I never exchanged any *conversation* with the woman." Of course, her tone implied, he wouldn't have understood that. "Oh, I believe she did have a friend called May or Maisie or—I'm afraid I don't recall. What? Oh, she was here last Tuesday, she left about five, I think. I'm afraid I really couldn't tell you a thing about her." She graciously identified the check as the one she'd given Ida Moffat that day, payment for two days' work.

"Doesn't mix with commoners," said Palliser in the Rambler. "You annoyed her, implying she gossiped with the hired help, Jase."

"What do I know about hired help?" said Grace. "So what do we fall back on? That dime-store tablet might need a code expert."

"There were a few phone numbers. See what they turn up." They drove back downtown and upstairs in the office heard about the baby. "My God," said Palliser.

Grace just shook his head, inevitably thinking of plump brown Celia Ann at home, as Palliser thought of David Andrew.

They sat down at their desks in the original communal sergeants' office and pored over Ida Moffat's personal memo-minder, sorting out decipherable phone numbers. They divided them up and started calling.

[39]

Palliser contacted four people who denied ever hearing of Ida Moffat; all four numbers belonged to rooming houses where the rate of transience would be high. On his fifth call he got a cautious male voice saying, "Yeah, I know Ida. Who's this?"

"I'm sorry to tell you she's dead, Mr.—"

"Molnar, Al Molnar— Ida's *dead?* For God's sake, what happened?"

"She was killed, Mr. Molnar, probably Tuesday night. This is Sergeant Palliser, LAPD. We'd like to talk to you, whatever you can tell us about Mrs. Moffat—"

"Me? *Killed?* You mean *murdered?* Ida? Well, for Christ's sake!" Naked astonishment in his voice. "I don't know nothing about it—last time I seen Ida was Saturday—"

"We aren't suspecting you," said Palliser. "We'd just like to hear what you could tell us about Mrs. Moffat's friends. If you'll give me your address—"

"Well, my God, if that's so, Ida *murdered,* my God, what a thing, you knocked me all of a heap— I'd sure be glad to help you find whoever—but my God, nobody Ida knew 'd do a thing like that— How'd you find me, anyways? Oh, the phone number. Yeah, well, look, I'm at work—this is where I work, Mac's garage down on Vermont—but it's O.K., you can come here, the boss is gone for the day. My God, Ida murdered—"

They went out to talk to him. He was a big burly fellow in his fifties, fairly stupid, probably honest. He didn't mind telling them that he knew Ida went with other guys. She was good fun to be with, you had to have people to have fun with, going out and all, and he'd never got round to getting married. "What the hell?" he said simply. "It wasn't no skin off anybody's nose. I didn't own Ida or she me." He'd known her maybe five years or so. "She'd never been hitched either, just thought it sounded better, get called missus." She'd told him once she'd had a baby when she was just a kid, but she'd given it out for adoption, didn't even know if it was girl or boy.

"Could you tell us about any of her other friends?" asked Grace.

"Well, there's May. May McGraw, she was about Ida's best pal, I guess. She works at a place out on Union, the Tuxedo Bar n' Grill. I guess she'd know most of Ida's friends. Matter o' fact that's where I met Ida first—she useta like to go there for dinner sometimes, sit and talk to people, it's a nice little place." He asked eager questions about the murder; they were vague. "My sweet Jesus, I can't get over it, Ida murdered! Don't seem possible— I sure hope you get whoever it was!"

It was four-fifteen. They looked up the address of that bar and grill and drove down there. It was May's day off; the bartender obligingly gave them her address, Pennsylvania Street in Boyle Heights, and they tried there, at an old apartment house, but she wasn't home.

"One like Ida," said Grace, "out sitting talking to people in some nice little bar. Picking up the men."

"So maybe we'll get to talk to her tomorrow," said Palliser.

Piggott, said Lake when they got back, had gone out to untangle a freeway accident with two dead. Palliser thought again about that accident last January, and that enormous dog, and felt uneasy.

"Where's everybody else?"

"I haven't seen hide nor hair of Tom or Rich since that doctor called," said Lake.

Landers and Conway had gone up to the Narco office, presided over these days not only by Captain Patrick Callaghan but Lieutenant Saul Goldberg struggling with his perennial allergies. The sergeant at the switchboard said Callaghan was out, but he thought Goldberg was available. They went into the sergeants' office and found Detective Steve Benedittino talking to one of the mod squad—a tall young fellow with all the expectable accoutrements, tight black pants, leather jacket, boots, a T-shirt bearing the so-called peace symbol; he sported a thick blond handlebar moustache, curly hair down to his shoulders, and sideburns.

"Hi, fellows, what can I do for you?" asked Benedittino.

"Goldberg in?" Landers cast a glance at the flower child, who gave him the usual belligerent glare.

"Are we overlapping with Robbery-Homicide again? It will happen. He was on the phone to Sacramento a minute ago; maybe I'll do. What's the problem?"

Conway said, "No hurry—you were prodding at the junkie." His tone was low enough not to reach that one, but he scowled at them all the more. "I see he doesn't think much of our nice expensive plant."

Benedittino burst out laughing. "He doesn't think a hell of a lot of the job he's on, that's for sure. Hey, *paisano,* come and meet some Homicide dicks. Bob Miliani—Landers and Conway. Bob graduated top of his class at the Academy back in February."

"And I thought, damn it, I'd be wearing a uniform," said the flower child angrily. "My wife just moans every time she looks at me. If I'd known the brass was going to send me un-derground—my God!" He shook his luxuriant locks, disgusted.

"Never mind, we're letting you loose as soon as we get the works on that supplier," soothed Benedittino, "and by what's opening up, that could be any day."

"And I'll put in a voucher for what the haircut costs," said Miliani. "All I can say is, I think they're all nuts—it's the biggest Goddamned nuisance, falling all over the place—and the damn moustache getting in my coffee—gah! Well, I'd better get back to it and try to think of some new cusswords about the pigs picking me up on suspicion." Hunching his shoulders, he strode out.

"He'll be a good man," said Benedittino after him. "We pick the rookies—new faces, not so apt to be spotted even in costume, so to speak. He's given us quite a lot. So, what can we do for you?"

"Does the name of Godfrey Booth ring any bells?" asked Landers.

[42]

"It does. A faint one. A small-timer—the grass only, so far as I know. Sometimes a seller. He's served little stretches—got let off oftener. Why?"

"A user you can say," said Conway. "He and his wife—"

"Susan. Common-law."

"—were feeding it to their baby."

"My God in heaven," said Benedittino. "And that latest report, I suppose you saw it—the research boys have decided it's worse than the acid— My God. How'd you turn that up?"

They told him. "Would you have a guess about who they were running with? It could have been the casual thing, for what they had on them," said Landers, "but a gun—and in Booth's own car—it could also be a personal kill."

"I'll agree with you. Lessee, I can tell you something. I picked Booth up for possession about six months ago—he's got a pedigree back to age sixteen. Right off I'll say two of his best pals are Randy Wyler and Bud Packer. They've got about the same pedigree, only not as sellers. We've probably got some addresses, not guaranteed recent."

"Anything you can give us," said Conway.

Goldberg, by the sounds from his office, was still on the phone, irately. In the end, Benedittino turned up six names for them, five men and a girl all about the Booths' age, who had been picked up with them before or were known associates. There were addresses appended, but these people tended to move around. "Good luck on finding them," said Benedittino. "Not that the Booths are any loss. The baby, my God. The things we do see."

Before they went out looking, Landers called Bainbridge's office to find out if any doctor had got to the corpses. One of Bainbridge's young surgeons told him that they wouldn't get to autopsies right away but he had probed for the slugs. Only one was intact, out of Booth, and he had sent it up to the lab, to Ballistics. Eventually they would hear what Ballistics could tell them about that.

They went out looking for the Booths' pals; they'd got sidetracked off the heisters. They drew blanks at four addresses, the pals moved on somewhere; but at four forty-five they found Randy Wyler and Bud Packer at a ramshackle rooming house on Magdalena Street the other side of the railroad yards, one step short of Skid Row.

Wyler and Packer had little records of possession, mostly suspended sentences; they took cops as a natural hazard of life and while they weren't exactly eager to answer questions, this and that emerged, back at an interrogation room at headquarters. The news that Godfrey and Sue had been shot opened them up a little farther.

"Gee, that's terrible," said Wyler. He was short and thin, pockmarked with old acne, and looked as if he hadn't been eating regularly. "That's real bad, man. They were all-right people, God and Sue. Say, what about the baby? Did you know they had a kid?"

"That's right," said Conway. "Did you know they'd been giving the baby grass?"

Packer brayed a hoarse laugh, and sobered. He was about Conway's size, not tall, a stockier fellow with stringy long hair and a silly little wispy moustache. "Yeah, God thought it was a real kick, give the kid a high with its bottle. Like a fun thing. But, geesiz, who'd want to go and kill God and Sue? They wasn't doing nobody any harm."

Landers and Conway looked at each other. It would be a complete waste of time to try to reach this pair.

"It'll get to be legal pretty soon anyways," said Wyler.

"All right," said Conway, sounding tired, "did the Booths have any to sell recently? Do you know any of the people they'd been running with the last month? When did you see them last?"

Wyler and Packer exchanged glances. "Well, uh, last Saturday night, I guess," said Wyler. "There was a kind of party at their place. I dunno everybody was there—different people dropped in, like, you know—"

"Was there any grass floating around?" asked Landers.

[44]

Again the glances. "Well—some," said Packer. "Neither of us holding now," he added hastily.

"All right. Did you buy any?"

"It was a party—we were God's pals. He wouldn't make me or Randy hand out— I guess some of the rest of 'em, though. I don't know. No, I don't know where he got it—but it was no damn good, and I told him so—told him he got cheated on—"

"Bud, shut up."

"You said so yourself, damn it—it was just cut dust, it dint have no kick at all—" Packer subsided sullenly, and Landers raised his eyebrows at Conway. That was interesting.

"So, see if you can remember who was at the party," said Conway. They went on prodding at them, and came up with half a dozen reluctantly yielded names, two girls and four men. No, they hadn't seen any money handed over. They didn't know anything about Booth's supplier. Sometimes he had the stuff to sell and sometimes he was in the market—they didn't know any more, period.

It was getting on toward six o'clock; they let Wyler and Packer go.

"Say, has anything showed on that escaped con?" Landers asked Lake. "That Conover."

"Nary a thing. A.P.B.'s out statewide, but he seems to have crawled into the woodwork."

"Nobody ever did find that Betty Suttner," remembered Conway. "Well, so we go looking for these boys and girls tomorrow."

"Unless something new turns up," said Landers. "There's that list of heisters too."

"We were shorthanded today."

Wanda Larsen came past with a brisk Good Night; Lake went out. Mendoza's office was empty: eloquently, in the middle of his desk blotter was a long string of plastic love beads with a brass *ankh* at one end. "I wonder what that's all about," said Landers, yawning.

*　　　*　　　*

Mendoza came home looking preoccupied to find his household much as usual. With daylight saving on, the twins were out in the backyard chasing Cedric in circles, Cedric barking joyously. Their mockingbird, at least, had vanished again—doubtless temporarily; having raised a family in March, he and his wife would be back later this month to start another. The twins flung themselves on Mendoza; away from the reminding pictures in the McGuffey Reader they seemed to have forgotten the goat.

He went on into the house and found Alison and Mrs. Mac-Taggart busy over dinner. "And I need a drink," he said, kissing Alison. "The dirty job gets dirtier all the time, *cara.*" He told them about the baby.

"Guidness to mercy!" said Mrs. MacTaggart. "The puir wee mite! It's enough to make a body believe Satan's got the upper hand, the way Holy Scripture says he will, whiles."

"But, Luis, that's—well, incredible is hardly the word," said Alison, horrified. "The things that go on—"

"And ninety-eight percent of it the damn random idiocy," said Mendoza rather savagely. "Doing what comes naturally—consequences five minutes ahead just not there for the idiots. I need a drink," and he reached for the bottle of rye in the cupboard.

El Señor the wicked, of the blond-in-reverse Siamese markings, heard him and came at a gallop from the front of the house. Automatically Mendoza poured him an ounce in a saucer, and Alison and Mrs. MacTaggart, still thinking about the baby, said never a word about alcoholic cats.

Hackett, as usual, had used his day off to get the lawn mowed and a little trimming and weeding done. Angel took the children to a nearby playground in the afternoon, warning him not to touch the angel food cake just out of the oven. But he was still feeling what-the-hell about the diet, and had a piece anyway.

Higgins, at loose ends, mowed the lawn front and back; Steve was good about doing it, but Higgins didn't mind. School would be out next week, and Steve would have more time.

The night watch came on—all of it but Glasser: stocky dark Nick Galeano, sandy slim Bob Schenke, the stolid plodder Shogart. "What's happened to Henry?" wondered Galeano. Anybody could get rammed by a drunk on the freeway.

Mendoza had left them a note on a homicide at the Clark Hotel: somebody to see the night desk clerk. Galeano said he'd go.

At the hotel, he talked to a friendly elderly man named Perkins, who was genuinely distressed at the old lady's death. A terrible thing, he said, didn't seem possible, right here in the hotel. She'd been such a nice old lady, it didn't bear thinking about.

There hadn't been an autopsy yet but Mendoza thought she'd been killed last night. Galeano asked questions. A young man, maybe a couple of young men dressed the way some young people did—the wild colors, the headbands and beads?

"We don't see any of them in the hotel," said Perkins. "I know the kind you mean. Why? You see them in the street, but not in here. Most of the people living here now—we've got mostly permanent tenants, not so much real hotel patrons like we used to have—are older people, Mr. Galeano. Oh, they'll have the younger people come visiting, family-like, but I can't recall I've ever seen one of the kind you're talking about, the funny clothes and all, right in here. Last night? No, sir. Yes, sir, I was here all evening, I came on at six and I was here till midnight when we lock up. We didn't used to do that, you know, a hotel is a kind of public place, open so people can come and go, but the last few years we do. In this area, the crime rate up—"

"You'd see anybody who came in the front door." The elevators were at the back of the lobby; anyone would have to pass the desk to reach elevators or the stairs beside them. "What about another way in? Is there a back door, to the kitchens or—"

"Oh, we don't have a dining room anymore," said Perkins sadly. "It got so there wasn't any call for it. The kitchens are all shut up. I can't recall when the back door, out to the alley, 's been used—it's always locked now. There's another front door, of course—it used to be the street entrance to the restaurant, but it's locked now too—"

"Are you sure it was, last night?"

"Oh, I'm positive," said Perkins. "Nobody uses it now."

"Are you sure," persisted Galeano, "that you were here at the desk from six to midnight?"

"Well," said Perkins with dignity, "I did once visit the lavatory adjoining Mr. Quigley's office. There wasn't a soul here. It was about nine o'clock, I suppose. I wasn't gone three minutes."

But maybe long enough. Galeano thanked him and went back to the office. Glasser still hadn't come in. "I tried his apartment," said Schenke. "He's not there. Should we start calling hospitals?"

Five minutes later Glasser came in. As a rule Henry Glasser was an amiable man, a middle-sized sandy fellow with an unblemished record as an LAPD officer; but now he looked mad enough to breathe fire. "What happened to you?" asked Schenke.

"That Goddamned car!" said Glasser forcefully. "I swear to God, I try to be a good citizen and a good cop—what God had against my car I'll never know!" Glasser, figuring his budget last August, like a lot of other citizens hadn't reckoned on an earthquake. The earthquake had demolished his perfectly good car, and he'd been forced to buy new transportation. Being a cautious man with an instinctive distrust of installment buying, he'd got what he could pay for without interest.

"I told you then, it's false economy to buy cheap," said Schenke. "What happened?"

"The Goddamned thing lay down and died on the Pasadena freeway," said Glasser. "I couldn't even get it over on the shoulder. Traffic piled up and the Goddamned Highway Patrol came along and—it would be the Highway Patrol—"

"Brother officers," said Shogart.

"—be damned," said Glasser. "It was forty-five minutes before the tow truck showed and I thought I'd better go along to find out if it's worth the damn repair bill to fix it up. I'm still trying to decide. There's a crack in the radiator and it needs new plugs and a lube job. They said they can fix it to run, but they didn't look enthusiastic."

"So you'd better go looking for something better," said Shogart. "City employees always reckoned a good risk—"

"I don't like being in debt, damn it," said Glasser. "So all right, I'm old-fashioned. Damn it, what I don't need is another bill to pay every month."

He was still muttering about it at ten minutes to midnight when a black-and-white on routine tour called in about a probable assault: a man down and unconscious on the sidewalk alongside Pershing Square, obviously assaulted and robbed. There was an ambulance on the way.

Glasser still grumbling, he and Galeano went out on it; by the time they got there, the ambulance had been and gone, so they went on up to Hollywood Receiving Hospital. The doctor in Emergency said it was touch and go: skull fracture, a severe beating; they were still running X rays. He handed over the personal effects found on him.

There was a wallet, found beside him: empty of money. Everything else had been in his pockets, handkerchief, cigarettes, a little loose change. The suit, even bloodied and dirty, looked like a good one; it had a tailor's label in it, *Simpson, D Street, Sacramento.* In the wallet's little plastic slots was an I.D. card, photographs of a nice-looking dark-haired woman and two children, a membership card in the California Medical Association, a gasoline credit card. The I.D. was for a Dr. Bernard Ducharme, an address in Sacramento, notify wife in case of emergency.

"Well, well, a visitor to our fair city who fell among thieves," said Galeano. "I think we pass this on to the day watch, Henry. It's a little late to disturb the doctor's wife, and maybe by morning they'll know whether he'll make it or not."

"I suppose so," said Glasser morosely. He wasn't about to let the other boys know about another difficulty his suddenly carless state posed: he had a date to take Wanda Larsen to a horse show on Sunday—it seemed she was crazy about horses—and just what he was going to do now he didn't know. Well, they could use her car, but that seemed a little cheap.

Piggott was off on Friday. Before breakfast he had a look at the baby tetras swimming around in all the dishpans, and thought there were just a few less than there had been last night. It was an unexpected complication, the baby tetras—such pretty little colorful things, only a couple of inches long as adults—turning out to be cannibals in youth. He said, "I think we'd better take some of the bigger ones out of this pan, Pru."

"Honestly!" said Prudence. "Talk about, had I but known!" She looked at the array of dishpans in despair. "Honestly, what anybody would think, to see this place—"

Mendoza came in early on Friday morning, dapper as usual in gray Dacron, black Homburg in hand. He looked at the report Galeano had left and said, "Wide open. *Pues sí.* A little rudimentary planning—wait till the clerk left for a minute, which he was bound to do in six hours, and walk in. But— And business picking up as usual. Pity about Henry's car." Beyond his open office door he heard the rest of the men coming in—only short one man today—and picked up the phone. "Jimmy, get me a Mrs. Bernard Ducharme in Sacramento, this address—person to person. Wait a minute, on second thought I'd better talk to the hospital first—"

When he got her, Mrs. Ducharme had a charming contralto voice that reminded him of Alison's. She was alarmed at a call from an LAPD officer. Her husband was in Los Angeles, yes, over the weekend, for a convention of the California Medical Association.

He was staying at the Biltmore Hotel. What concern was it of the LAPD?

Mendoza told her, gently. The hospital was now saying that Dr. Ducharme would make it, he was in much better condition.

"But, my God," she cried wildly, "what could have—how could he—oh, my God, but he only left a day early so he could work on that paper—Ruth's piano practice annoyed him so—oh, my God! Yes, I'll come—have to call Mother, look after the ch— But how could it have happened? I don't—oh, thank you for calling—I'll come as soon as—but I don't understand how—"

Mendoza went out to the hall. Hackett and Higgins were back, dwarfing everybody else: Landers talking to Conway and Grace; Palliser looking worried about something. "So, somebody chase over to the Biltmore and ask what they know about Dr. Ducharme," said Mendoza, and passed on Galeano's note.

"Did somebody say women's work is never done?" said Grace. "You can go hunting May McGraw alone, John."

"And Henry's feeling annoyed, you can see."

"I told him it was false economy," said Landers. "Now he finds out. Come on, Rich. We've got all these partygoers to find."

"And then the heisters." Who were just possibles, but you never knew where you'd hit pay dirt.

Grace went over to the Biltmore. The Biltmore had Dr. Ducharme registered. "Yesterday afternoon, one-thirty," said the desk clerk. "We're hosting this convention, of course."

Grace asked questions. Did the clerk remember when Dr. Ducharme had turned in his key? It hadn't been on him. If it had been the night clerk on duty, he'd have to chase him down. But it had been this one, on up to 6 P.M.

"But—did you say, a police officer? Has anything happened to the doctor? Yes, I can tell you that—it was just before I went off duty at six, the doctor turned in his key—of course we have a great many doctors registered here for the convention, but I happen to recall Dr. Ducharme because of the name—very peculiar, my grandmother's maiden name was Ducharme and we wondered if there was any connection—"

"Did he say anything about where he was going?" Grace had a simple mind. Sometimes people did.

"Oh, he said—yes, I remember that—he said something about deserving a little holiday—a night on the town, he said. He asked me to recommend a place around here, maybe with a good piano bar—I suggested The Wild Goose over on Spring, but I did warn him to take a cab—the way the crime rate's going—"

A night on the town. Grace thought a little sadly about the phrase Hackett had coined: the stupidity and cupidity.

4

"SO I SUPPOSE WE'D BETTER GO AND ASK IF HE ever got there," said Grace. "It won't be open yet."

"That place," said Mendoza. "It came into a case before. And if he got there after six, the same bartender and waiters won't be there till around five. He was found along Pershing Square. He could have been on his way to Spring or back to the hotel—walking like a damn fool." He had slid down in his desk chair, smoking lazily, and was fiddling with the love beads. "I'm waiting for Walter Whitlow to show up for the formal identification—he called in."

"You think those things point to one of the street kids."

"Kids and kids," said Mendoza. "Enough of them, and not kids either, in the twenties—drifters, irresponsible, on the grass or the hard stuff. I've been exercising my imagination, Jase. The old lady had lived at the Clark a long time. I've got no doubt that Quigley, Perkins, some of the maids knew about that annuity. All perfectly honest people. So, the maid Agnes, off duty, says something casual to her sister—and the sister mentions it to a boyfriend who works at a gas station on Hill—and he mentions it to a pal who knows somebody who works at The Broadway, right next to the Clark— And then again you never know, it could be even simpler than that. Violence is usually damn simple, *de veras*. Just as we've heard, there are a number of elderly people living at that ho-tel—the pensions, Social Security. And in most places like that the permanent apartments will be on the upper floors. It could be that X just meant to get into any one of those apartments, where there'd be the frail old people and hopefully some cash."

"I suppose you did have the lab print those beads?"

Mendoza cocked an eyebrow at him. "Teach your grandfather, Jase. *Nada* . . . I'm also expecting the doctor's wife later this morning. When and if he comes to, he can probably tell us what happened to him—not very likely who did it."

They were still sitting there talking about the various things on hand when Palliser and Higgins came back.

This time May McGraw had been at home. May McGraw was what some people might call the salt of the earth, if not exactly the most virtuous female walking around. She'd seen a lot of life and seen it hard, if a lot of trouble was her own making, and she'd preserved in a rough sort of way her sense of humor and courage. She'd looked suspiciously at craggy-faced Higgins, narrowly at the badges, and when they told her about Ida Moffat she burst into floods of tears, asked them in, wept for five minutes, dried her eyes, and said, "Well, I will be damned. Just about the last person in the world—getting murdered! My God. I tried to call her yesterday afternoon, but I just figured she was out. My God, a person just doesn't expect to have her friends murdered, for God's sake." She blew her nose and reached for a cigarette with a hand that shook a little. Palliser lit it for her. "You don't know who?"

"No, Mrs. McGraw—is it Mrs.?"

"He was a bum, I divorced him a long time ago, but I guess McGraw's better than Stepanowsky." She was a little plump woman in the fifties, with hennaed hair and a round face raddled with years of careless makeup. She had big dark eyes and a stubborn chin.

"We'd like you to tell us about other people Mrs. Moffat knew," said Palliser. "It looks as if she had a fight with somebody—"

"But, my God, nobody knew Ida 'd go to murder her! Sure, I

can tell you people she knew, but it wouldn't be any of them, how could it be? Look, Ida, she was—you know—good-natured. Easygoing. She didn't have fights with anybody. I guess—you're thinking about men." She stopped, looking at them warily.

"We know she knew quite a few men," said Higgins diplomatically. "We aren't here to judge anybody, Mrs. McGraw—we'd just like to find out who killed her."

"Oh, what the hell," she said drearily. "Life's a drag, here we are getting older every day and no money to count much, and nobody to care much—you got to take any little fun and good company where you find it, no? What's it to anybody if Ida slept around a little? Her own business. But none of them 'd have gone to murder her. Al Molnar—"

"We've met him," said Palliser.

"Well, he wouldn't—I don't want to get anybody in trouble, none of the guys I knew about would've—"

"Well, we don't know, do we? For instance, sometimes liquor makes a man belligerent for no reason, and if—" But there hadn't, of course, been any evidence that there'd been drinking going on.

"Oh, hell," she said miserably. "I knew she'd been with Al, and Eddy Weinbeck, he's the bartender at the Tuxedo, and lemme think, that railroad man comes in—"

"Where did she—that is," said Palliser, "did she—er—drop into bars near where she—or—"

"Say, mister, Ida wasn't a pro," she said indignantly. "She was just out for a good time when she could get it. She worked hard, you better believe, cleaning houses for people for a lousy three bucks an hour. She'd come in the Tuxedo three, four times a week, to see me, have her dinner, sit around over a few beers. Maybe she'd get talking to some guy, maybe not, whose business was it? It was just"—she groped for a word and found one sounding foreign to her vocabulary—"casual. Like that. Casual. Listen, who's going to arrange about a funeral? There's got to be a funeral. She didn't have any family. Listen, I know Al 'd want to help— I don't s'pose she had much dough—and I'll ask Eddy—"

"We can let you know when the body will be released."

"Yeah, I'd be obliged. It just—isn't anything that happens to somebody you know," said May forlornly.

"Can you give us any more names?" asked Palliser.

And now, back at the office, Higgins was saying, "But listen, Luis. A woman like that—just as Molnar said, it didn't bother him that she went with other men. No great romance with any of them. There wouldn't be that much emotion involved, for anybody to be jealous of her, or get into a fight with her—over what?"

"*¿Quién sabe?*" said Mendoza. "I'll give you that, George. But why should a stranger get into a fight with her either? We have to start with what we have. How many names did she give you?"

Palliser laughed. "A dozen. She said she couldn't be sure just who Ida might have got acquainted with, this week, last week, but these she's pretty sure of. There were some others whose names she didn't know."

"It just occurs to me," said Grace, "that with those respectable females at that apartment house watching Ida so close, didn't you ask them if a strange man was seen coming in that night? With or without Ida?"

"You've had some," said Palliser. "Go and try asking 'em, Jase."

"Well, I might," said Grace thoughtfully.

"And I tell you," said Higgins, "it'll be a waste of time to talk to any of these—these imitation playboys, Luis. What kind of boyfriends would one like that pick up? The old bachelors, the winos, the—"

"Statistics tell us that murder victims are usually murdered by people they know, if not relatives," said Mendoza. "Go and start looking." Higgins uttered a rude word, and Sergeant Lake looked in and said that Mr. Whitlow was here.

Higgins, Grace and Palliser went out. Wanda, with no reports to type, was straightening out a filing cabinet. Hackett had left with Landers and Conway, presumably to chase down the erstwhile pals of the Booths or the list of heisters.

"A damned waste of time," repeated Higgins. "But we have to go by the rules."

"You can go look for the playboys," said Grace. "I want to ask Mrs. Kiefer a couple of questions."

Walter Whitlow was a tall, dark, nice-looking fellow, right now a little haggard. He said all the expectable things; taken to the morgue, he formally identified the body of Harriet Branch, and when Mendoza explained that an autopsy was mandatory, just nodded.

"It seems—I don't know," he said, "well, strange, that she should have lived to be over eighty and then—end like that. Strange." He looked down the bare empty corridor, outside the cold room at the morgue. "Of course a thing like this is always a shock. Edna—my wife—it was just bad luck I happened to be away when— She bore up pretty well, but she's gone to pieces now. What—should we do about funeral arrangements?"

"We'll let you know when an undertaker can have the body."

"What—who do you think—could have done it? Or should I ask you that? I'm sorry, I don't know much about—how you operate, Lieutenant."

"Well, we're thinking now that someone, or a couple, of the young street thugs down here slipped into the hotel on the chance of easy pickings—con their way into an apartment, strong-arm the tenant. God knows there are enough of that kind with the habit to support."

"And—it just happened to be Mother's apartment they picked? The dope," said Whitlow. He looked suddenly more haggard and worried than when he'd come in. "Why a young one? Some reason you—"

Mendoza told him about the love beads absently, and was startled at the response that got. "Love!" said Whitlow in an almost savage tone. "Love! My God, what stupidities and madness are committed in that name! These stupid, criminal, suicidal *kids*—not dry behind the ears and they think they're so God-damned smart—! Just tell me something, Lieutenant Mendoza. Just tell me what the hell's going to happen to this world when these brainwashed kids with their stupid ideas about peace and brotherly love and their immoral relative morality and do-your-own-thing-with-the-dope bit take over?"

Mendoza laughed. "There's a saying in Spanish, Mr. Whitlow—*A su tiempo maduran las uvas*. In their own time the grapes ripen. Fortunately the youngsters do get older, and some of them a little wiser. And it's still the minority running around making all the noise and devilry."

"Sense of objectivity," said Whitlow a little wearily. "I daresay. Disraeli said it better."

"*¿Cómo?*"

Whitlow's expression turned sardonic. "That anybody who isn't a Socialist by the age of twenty lacks a heart, and anybody who isn't a Tory by the age of thirty lacks a head."

Mendoza threw back his head and laughed. " 'The Gods of the Copybook Headings.' Mr. Kipling said it even better than that."

"Oh, you're a Kipling man too? I've often wondered," said Whitlow, "whether it'd do any good to make it mandatory for all politicians to read that poem over once a month."

Mendoza was still chuckling over that when he got back to his office. But the love beads on his desk sobered his expression. That frail old body in the cold tray at the morgue—

Somebody had said that at least one slug out of the Booths had been sent to Ballistics. He got on the phone to the lab and asked if they'd looked at it yet.

"Oh, that," said Thomsen. "Yeah. It's out of a beat-up old S. and W. .22. Revolver. If you ever pick up the gun, we can make it easy enough."

"*Gracias,*" said Mendoza. It was a quarter to eleven; he wondered when the doctor's wife would show up. He also wondered if anything new would break today.

*   *   *

Of the six names Wyler and Packer had given them yesterday, Landers and Conway only found two: Ron Cook and Cheryl Perry. The other four, three men and a girl, had evidently drifted on from temporary addresses, nobody knew where or nobody was saying.

Wyler had told them Cook and the Perry girl had been living together. They found them at a trailer park out toward Monterey Park, off the Pomona freeway, where Wyler said they'd be. All the trailers were old and tired-looking, and the ground overgrown with weeds, cluttered with rubbish. The old trailers sat around at odd angles, half of them obviously empty; it was a far cry from the smart modern parks of mobile homes elsewhere. This pair looked like the counterparts of the Booths, scruffy and aimless and sloppily dressed. The girl was a natural blonde, the man dark with the usual wild long hair, moustache and sideburns. They looked at the badge in Landers' hand with automatic suspicion, and at the two LAPD men with resentment—perhaps a vague resentment at two clean-shaven, good-looking young men in suits and white shirts and ties, reminder that the majority of the world still hadn't collapsed to their own low standards.

They answered questions reluctantly until Landers told them about the Booths. "Jesus, who could've done that?" said Cook. "That's real sad, man." The girl just sighed.

"So, we understand you were at a party at their place last Saturday night," said Conway. "With some grass floating around. Did you buy any?"

"You got a search warrant?" asked Cook warily.

"Not yet," said Landers. "Look, we can take you downtown to ask questions." They hadn't been invited into the trailer; they stood around the door, in the weed-grown lot.

"We're not holding. We don't know anything about who did that. We liked God and Sue O.K., man, you can't prove any different."

"We weren't going to try," said Landers, "if you can tell us about somebody who didn't. That wasn't very good grass Booth was passing out that night, was it? Cut stuff—dust."

Cook licked his lips. "I wouldn't know."

"Was he selling, or just handing it out for the party?" Cook was silent. "Let's go downtown," said Conway.

"I wouldn't know," said Cook.

"Can you tell us who else was there?"

"I didn't know everybody else there. I'm not about to get anybody in bad with the fuzz."

"You said you liked the Booths—don't you want us to pick up whoever took them off? Come on," said Landers. Cook opened his mouth and shut it. The girl was staring away from all of them, dreamily; Landers wondered if she was riding a little high. "Who was there, Cook?"

"You better tell them, Ron," said the girl in a thin voice, without looking at any of them. "What happened to the baby? They had a baby."

"That's right," said Conway. "A baby they'd been feeding the grass. It's in the hospital. Being looked after."

"Oh, was he sick? He's a cute baby."

"Come on, Ron—what's she want you to tell?" asked Landers.

"You just shut up," he said to the girl. "You just—"

"But I bet it was them," she said. She turned suddenly and climbed into the trailer, came out a minute later with a hairbrush, and sat on the trailer step and began to brush her hair with long slow sweeps of the brush.

"Who, Miss Perry?"

She giggled. "That sounds funny. Everybody calls me Sherry. Sherry Perry. I bet it was Sid and Janie. Or Sid, anyway. Because he was awfully mad at God. About that grass. It was real nothing stuff, no kick at all—God got crossed on that, wherever he got it. Ronnie was mad too—"

"Listen, *shut up!* I'm not about to get mixed in—"

"—only he didn't pay God for it so it wasn't a big thing. We went over to Sugar's and he had some pretty good—"

[60]

"*Shut up!*" Cook slapped her across the face and Landers pulled him back from her.

"That's enough of that. Who are Sid and Janie?" It could be that the Narco office could tell them.

"I don't like Sid," she said. She retrieved the hairbrush from where it had fallen and went on brushing her hair.

"Sid who?" asked Conway gently.

"Oh, it's a funny name. I don't know. What an awful name for a person to have. I used to live in Beverly Hills, you know. My mother and father have an awful lot of money—I was brought up to be a lady. That's right. I shouldn't think any girl would ever want to marry a man with a terrible name like that." She laughed and went on laughing, and Landers felt Cook's arm muscles tense with fury, and then she gasped, "*Belcher!* Isn't that perfectly awful?"

"You bitch," said Cook, "tying us in—"

"I think as material witnesses anyway," said Landers. And neither he nor Conway mentioned it, but they both wondered whether this precious pair would be out on bail within twenty-four hours, and promptly vanish. Some of the softheaded judges—

They ferried them back downtown, to the jail on Alameda, thinking of lunch afterward. In the lobby they found Mendoza delivering a lecture to the chief jailer. He was looking annoyed.

"What's up?" asked Landers.

Mendoza had just finished talking to Mrs. Ducharme at eleven-thirty; she had phoned from the hotel, having taken over her husband's room at the Biltmore. He told her the hospital expected her husband to be conscious sometime today; he told her the name of the hospital, and she said crisply he'd find her there if he wanted to talk to her. He was thinking of going out for an early lunch when Sergeant Lake buzzed him and said they had a new homicide. At the Alameda jail.

"At the *jail?*" said Mendoza. "*¡Parece mentira!*" He took up his hat and went out. "Nobody else here?"

[61]

"Art just fetched in one of the possibles off that list of heist-ers—first interrogation room."

Mendoza said, "Women's work!" and marched out to the elevators. He was curious enough that he used the siren on the Ferrari out to Alameda Street. At the jail, he met an ambulance just arriving.

The chief jailer and three of his underlings were arguing together in the lobby. On Mendoza's arrival they suddenly banded together defensively and began to explain.

"Listen," said the chief jailer, "things materialize out of the blue! My God, Lieutenant, we could search every cell once a day and things would still turn up! Do I know how? Things turn up in books in the library, lawyers I got to let in to see clients and not all lawyers are so damn law-abiding, the short-term birds work in the shop and make things—we do our best, but—"

"So what turned up this time and what happened?"

"My God," said one of the jailers, "is it a major operation, smuggle in a pair of dice? They were shooting craps—I didn't know it till the row broke out—"

"A pair of dice. What else?"

The jailer moaned. "A straight razor. I didn't know a damn thing about it till the argument started—he claimed they were loaded dice, and—"

There hadn't been much to choose between the prisoners: Willy Brisbane and Charles Ferguson, both Negro, both with long rap-sheets, both awaiting trial—Brisbane for rape, Ferguson for grand theft. It was Ferguson who had ended up with a cut throat.

Mendoza was annoyed. This kind of careless and unnecessary thing made paper work; it was a nuisance, when they had quite enough to cope with from people still outside jail. He told them so. The ambulance attendants took away the corpse. Mendoza was still expressing himself to the jailers when Landers and Conway walked in and heard about it.

They booked Cook and the girl in, and went up to Federico's

[62]

for lunch, where Mendoza heard about Sid Belcher. "We'll ask Narco if they know him," said Landers.

"That's the first place to ask," said Mendoza. "I wonder what the other boys are getting."

"That Moffat thing is—shapeless," said Landers, when they'd been brought up-to-date on that. "But that's not what you're annoyed about—or all the paper work on Ferguson." He eyed Mendoza shrewdly.

"I am really not so much interested in how that silly female came to get a knock on the head," said Mendoza, swallowing black coffee. "What I am feeling damned annoyed about, boys, is that there isn't one single damned lead on whatever mindless street thug walked into the Clark and beat Harriet Branch to death for whatever cash she had."

"It might have been any hood on the beat," agreed Conway sadly. "There's nothing to say, unless the lab picked up some latents there. I don't suppose you've had a report. Slow but sure, the lab."

"It's possible, but I wouldn't take a bet on it," said Mendoza.

Henry Glasser, after debate, had called the garage when he got up at noon and told them to go ahead and fix up that heap. They gave him an estimate of three-fifty plus, which at that was less than he'd have to pay for anything worth buying, and also said they'd let him have a loaner meanwhile. Glasser closed with this offer, and took the bus downtown to pick up the loaner. It turned out to be an old Plymouth two-door, banged up somewhat, but in running condition—about all you could say.

Driving back to his Hollywood apartment, he stopped at the nearest supermart for a couple of frozen dinners, a loaf of bread, and had to wait at the checkstand. When the checker handed him his change, she thrust a slip of paper into his hand with it. "Be sure and fill this out, sir, and drop it in the box over there. We're having a big drawing next week, you might be one of the lucky ones!"

"You'll never know how unlucky I feel," said Glasser. But he did fill out the slip with his name and address, and dropped it into the box. Fate hadn't been kind to him lately; but she was apt to be a changeable lady and you never knew.

Palliser and Higgins had spent the entire morning, to Higgins' disgust, in a very abortive hunt for Ida Moffat's recent or not-so-recent boyfriends. Only one of them they'd heard about from May McGraw was in a regular job, and he was a railroad engineer presently riding a locomotive back in the Midwest on a regular run to Chicago. May had been able to give them only one address, a regular patron of the Tuxedo, Jim Waggoner who lived at a rooming house on Shatto Street around the corner from the bar.

Him they found home, a fat man with an artificial leg and a pension from the government. He was sorry to hear about Ida, she was a real fun gal, he said, and who would have wanted to hurt Ida anyways? All these criminals around, what the world was coming to— But he also had an alibi, it transpired. He was a widower, and last Tuesday night he'd been at his daughter's place in Montebello because it was his birthday. It didn't cross his mind that they might have suspected him of the murder; that came out in the course of the conversation, and when they left he thanked them for coming to let him know about Ida. Poor Ida.

They resorted to the telephone book for the other names, but only one was listed, Peter Conroy, and he lived over in Glendale so they doubted he was the one who'd known Ida.

The Tuxedo Bar and Grill opened at eleven, and they went up there to talk to May again and hoped maybe to find a couple of the boyfriends dropping in. Higgins was still saying it was a damfool waste of time. But they hadn't been talking with May, still subdued, five minutes before she pointed out a nondescript fellow in his fifties who'd just come in and said Ida'd known him, she'd seen her talking to him one night. She didn't know his name.

It was Jack Smith. He looked at the badges in surprise, and he was shocked to hear about Ida. He was on Welfare—he had a bad back, he said, couldn't work at all—and he just couldn't think who might have wanted to hurt Ida. Tuesday night? Say, they didn't think he'd hurt Ida, did they? He'd liked Ida—a real nice girl, and accommodating. Palliser stored the word up to pass on to Robin. Tuesday night Jack Smith had spent playing cards with some other fellows at his apartment. He gave them names. He was indignant at the implied suspicion.

"Look, didn't I say it?" said Higgins. "The casual thing—for everybody, her included. Nobody felt strongly enough about the woman to care if she lived or died, John."

"But she got killed. Somehow." They knocked off for lunch, not at the Tuxedo but a coffee shop downtown, and afterward checked back with the office to see if anything new had gone down.

It was one o'clock and nobody else was there, said Lake, sounding relieved at Palliser's voice. "I just got a call from a black-and-white—a new body. It's Park View, over by MacArthur. I don't know what it is."

"Well, we might have known," said Palliser.

"And Pasadena called just before. They had a heist pulled over there last night, and they think by what the witnesses said it might have been that Conover. They didn't have a mug shot. I sent one over."

"O.K. We'll get on the new one."

When he told Higgins about it, Higgins said, "Thank God. Bricks without straw. Ida'll go into Pending."

They were using his Pontiac. They drove over to Park View Street. The black-and-white was still there and the uniformed men greeted them with relief. "We were wondering if you'd forgotten about us," said one of them. It was an ugly little square cracker-box stucco duplex in the middle of the block, painted dirty tan, and a fat middle-aged woman in a pink dress was standing on the front steps of the right side of it, watching them.

"What's it look like?"

"Another husband losing his temper," said the uniformed man. "But she's been dead awhile. Few days, maybe. Good thing we're not in the middle of a heat wave. That's Mrs. Cohen," he added, nodding at the fat woman. "She called in. Got worried because she hadn't seen this Mrs. Upton in a few days, and then there was"—he sighed—"the smell."

"One of those," said Palliser. "We'll want the full treatment." He used the radio in the car to ask for a lab truck and the morgue wagon, and sent the squad back on tour. Higgins was already talking to Mrs. Cohen.

"She was a nice girl," she was saying, shocked and a little grieved and also excited—the inevitable human reaction—at being in the middle of a murder case, Authority consulting her. "Cicely her name was, Cicely Upton. I liked her right from the time they moved in— I own this place, you see, rent out the other side. Not him, but her I liked. She was nice, a real ladylike girl. A homebody too. She asked for my recipe for molasses cookies. Over a year they'd lived here, but it wasn't till about a month ago she broke down and told me about him—like I say she was a nice girl, loyal to her husband and all, but we'd been neighborly back and forth, and after they had that argument, poor girl, I guess she had to have somebody to talk to. She didn't believe in divorce, but there'd been trouble—"

"Yes, Mrs. Cohen, we'll want to talk to you later, but right now, if you'd let us look around—"

"Anything you say. I've got nothing else to do. I just wish I'd called the police sooner, but how was I to know— The other men had to break in the door—"

There was a rickety screen door; the front-door lock had been splintered by the uniformed men. Before they went past the open door, they received the sickish-sweet message of death inside.

It was a bare little place, sparsely furnished, but a good-sized color TV sat in a corner of the living room; the few pieces of furniture were violently modern in style, vinyl upholstered. The body was in the front bedroom, where there was just space for a double bed, a couple of chests of drawers; one wall there contained a wardrobe with sliding doors. There was no closet.

[66]

"The surgeon will say how long," said Higgins, grimacing. She lay quietly on the bed, just one leg dangling off it; she had been dead long enough for her face to be a little bloated, but she might have been a pretty girl. Not very old, maybe in her twenties. She was wearing an ankle-length blue nylon housecoat, and one worn white satin slipper had fallen from the foot dangling off the bed. Her dark-brown hair was matted with a little blood, old and dry, at the left temple, but otherwise she looked quite natural lying there on the bed, as if she'd dropped down for a nap.

Palliser spotted the framed photograph on one of the chests: a glossy five by seven in a dime-store frame. It showed a smiling couple, the girl pretty with curly dark hair shorter than she had worn it now; she was clinging to the arm of a big-chested young man with crew-cut blond hair. They were obviously dressed up, he in a dark suit, she in a light-colored summer dress. "Wedding picture?" said Palliser a little sadly.

But Higgins had spotted something else. "I've seen a few," he said laconically. "Give you odds, she was knocked down and fractured her skull on that." He pointed. The bedstead was an old white-painted one, head and footboards rather high. On the top of the footboard was a little brown smear of what would probably turn out to be blood. There wasn't any carpet in here, and the small cotton-terry scatter rug at the side of the bed was wadded up in a bunch.

"You can read it," agreed Palliser. "Another one like Ida. She was knocked down, or fell, tripped on the rug—"

"Argue ahead of evidence. But there's friend hubby. If it was accidental, why was she left? Well, we'd better hear what Mrs. Cohen has to say. Leave this to the lab boys and Bainbridge."

They went back to the front step. Mrs. Cohen was still there, waiting. A few curious neighbors were out, staring and muttering. "Can we go into your place, Mrs. Cohen? We're waiting for more men, and we'd like to hear whatever you can tell us."

"Sure," she said. She turned and led them into a duplicate of the living room next door, but vastly different, with old-fashioned velour-upholstered furniture, a Boston fern in a wrought-iron stand. "It's just an awful thing, but it was him. He's gone, you know, his car and all. So it was him. Like I started to tell you, she never said a word against him—a good wife she was—till that time, about a month ago it was, they had a terrible argument one night, I heard him swearing and all, and next day—she had to have somebody to talk to—she sort of confided in me. We'd been neighborly, back and forth, and it was always her paid the rent. I took her my cookies, and she give me her mother's recipe for apple strudel. Her mother was dead—she hadn't any family left, she said. She cried and said how they'd been making a new start, Johnny'd promised to try and be a better husband. She was a good Christian girl," said Mrs. Cohen. "Oh, I suppose you'll think that's funny for me to say, but I'm Congregationalist myself—and a better man than my Joel never lived, God rest him. They'd been married five years, she was twenty-six, and there'd been trouble—he's the kind has a temper goes off like a rocket, and she said he'd beat her up once before, but he was sorry afterward. A lot of good that was! But she said he'd promised, he'd try to do better, and they came down here—they were living in Fresno then—and he got a better job, working for the city—the gas company."

"When did you see her last?" asked Palliser.

"That was it. Monday and Wednesday she usually had a wash on the line, and there wasn't any. He didn't want her to work, you see, and she was a real homebody. She told me she'd hoped to start a baby, but no luck. And I hadn't seen him—or his car—since Monday. Monday night he came home, like always, about six-thirty. And it's not once in a blue moon I'm out at night but I was that night, I went out with my friend Mrs. Rogers from down the street, to a movie. But now I look back, I'm up early as a rule, and I didn't see him leave for work on Tuesday. Unless he left earlier than usual." Her thin lips clamped shut for a moment, worked nervously.

"His name's John Upton? He's got a car—would you be able to tell us what make?" asked Palliser.

"It's a Plymouth Valiant," she said. "White. About a sixty-four. I've got to say I didn't hear any more arguing and swearing that night, before I went out, but there might've been later. But he hasn't been back since. I knocked on her door yesterday—him not coming home like that I thought maybe they'd had a fight and he'd left her, maybe she'd want to talk—but I never thought of anything so awful as this. Until—" She was silent.

Until she noticed the smell.

A car door slammed outside; there were voices and footsteps. The lab boys had arrived.

"Well, thank you, Mrs. Cohen," said Higgins. "We'll want to get a statement from you later."

"She was a nice girl," said Mrs. Cohen.

Mendoza came back from a belated lunch; Landers and Conway had gone back to looking for the just-possibles, on their several heist jobs (a dairy store, a neighborhood market, a liquor store—and of course the job at Chasen's). Hackett came in and said he was getting nowhere.

"You know how the damn routine goes. The one I found—he's still on P.A. so we had his address—had an alibi for all four jobs. He's just, for God's sake, had a grand reconciliation with his wife and they're being all lovey-dovey. The landlord can also say, and assorted neighbors."

"¡Vaya despacio!" said Mendoza, and Jason Grace wandered in looking pleased with himself.

"Good—somebody here," he said. "To come and be a witness. When I'd got just so far, I thought I'd better take a witness along. Just in case. I don't know that it's anything important, I've just got a kind of hunch."

"I'm the only one allowed hunches around here," said Mendoza. "About what, Jase?"

"Oh, Ida," said Grace. "I went and annoyed Mrs. Kiefer, and she finally got what I was driving at and said she didn't know we were interested in honest respectable people, and why were we,

[69]

because Mr. Stanhope was a very nice man. And as it turned out, the pharmacy—Mr. Stanhope's pharmacy on Olympic—was closed because Mr. Stanhope's mother-in-law just died and the funeral was this morning. But he opened at noon—"

"Stanhope? *¿Qué es esto?*"

"Well, I think maybe," said Grace, "we ought to go and talk to this William Linblad. I was just following my nose, you know."

5

"WELL, YOU KNOW WHAT WE HAD BEFORE from the women at that apartment," said Grace to Mendoza's question. He sat down and lit a cigarette; his brown face was gravely amused. "We couldn't even get any of 'em to say whether or not they saw Ida come home that night, alone or not. But I got to thinking, after we'd talked to Kiefer, and the first thought I had was, those nosy females keeping tabs on Ida pretty close, if she had had a man with her when she came home, we'd likely have heard. One of the women would have just happened to be out in the hall or something."

"So she didn't," said Mendoza. "You think one of them saw her come in?"

"I'd have laid a bet," said Grace. "Have we had the autopsy report yet? Well, that should tell us something. And then I thought, maybe our Ida had noticed the snooping and didn't like it. Maybe she told a boyfriend to sneak in after her. Anyway, I went back to talk to Mrs. Kiefer. I figured by then her husband would have told her we'd talked to him, and maybe she'd be a little less unforthcoming. She was. I pressed her, did she or anybody else see Ida Moffat come in that night? By chance or otherwise? And she finally said, well, she just happened to remember she hadn't looked in the mailbox and she'd been in the lobby and saw her come in. It was about six o'clock. And she'd been thinking it over, and Mrs. Licci felt the same way, it all went to show that we didn't know what we're doing, saying the woman was murdered."

"*¿Qué es esto?*" said Mendoza.

"Because it wasn't a very nice thing to have to say, but Mrs. Moffat was drunk. Staggering, and jolly. Not my words—hers. I deduce that Ida 'd had a few and was just feeling happy, not falling-down-drunk. I was grateful for the news, and Mrs. Kiefer went on to say that they'd decided she must have just fallen down and hit her head and killed herself. And you know, I suppose she could have—if she'd started to hit the drink hard, but we didn't gather she had. Because, said Mrs. Kiefer, she didn't have anybody with her—she was alone. Was she sure, I asked. What with the rise in crime, and her being the manager of the apartment, I supposed she took note of the people coming into the building. She did. She said nobody had come in later. What about the people who lived there, I said, and she said oh, well, of course Mrs. Licci and her husband had come home. Nobody else, I said, and she said nobody she'd ever seen with Ida. Nobody at all, I asked, and that was when she said she didn't know I meant respectable people, but aside from the Liccis there'd only been the boy from the pharmacy she knew of."

"*¡Maravilloso!*" said Mendoza encouragingly.

Hackett got up. "If you two soul mates are making head or tail of this, I'm not. I've got more legwork to do. Have fun with your gossips," and he went out.

"*¡Siga adelante!*" said Mendoza.

"Well, that's what we'd better do," said Grace, "if you'd like to come along as a witness." Mendoza got his hat without a word and they started for the elevators. "After I'd talked to Stanhope—the pharmacist—I thought you'd better hear about it so far. It's an independent pharmacy round the corner on San Pedro. He delivers, and he hires this high-school kid, William Linblad, to do it—and clean up the place and do odd jobs. Three of the people at that apartment house have regular prescriptions lodged with him—Mrs. Licci, Miss Callway, and Ida Moffat. She was taking

[72]

pills for high blood pressure. And she'd been in that day. I deduce she got home on the bus, that is to that area, about four, and after she stopped at the pharmacy she went somewhere and had the drinks. Stanhope said she usually waited for the prescription and took it with her, but that day she asked for it to be delivered. There were seven or eight deliveries, and the boy left about six."

"And it never occurred to either of them that we'd be interested, after she was found dead?"

"Not to Stanhope," said Grace. They'd taken the Ferrari, and now Mendoza asked where they were going. "That public high school out on Ninth. Stanhope's a vague old fellow about seventy, I'd say no interests outside the store. He might not even know she's dead. But I thought this Linblad—"

"*Pues sí.* It might be interesting to hear what he has to say."

When they got to the school, there were four black-and-whites and seven men in uniform with riot guns standing around. "What the devil—" said Mendoza, and edged the Ferrari up beside the group and produced his badge. "Has war been declared?"

"We didn't ask for detectives, sir." The Traffic man was surprised. "We had a tip that there's a gang rumble called for sometime this afternoon. Just thought a little show of force might make 'em think twice."

"*Dios,*" said Mendoza as they got out of the car, "I may be sorry I didn't bring any hardware along. Schools are dangerous places these days," and he wasn't kidding.

They were let in to see the boys' vice-principal and asked for Linblad to be fetched out of class. The vice-principal didn't seem to recognize the name, had his secretary look in the files for where he'd be. Five minutes later a tall boy came shambling in, looking nervous, and stood waiting silently. "Er—" said the vice-principal, "I suppose you'd prefer—? Just so. I'll just go along to the lounge." He was a tired, worried man; he didn't want any more bad news. "Er—these are police officers. They'd like to talk to you." He went out quickly.

The boy looked up fleetingly. He was a big boy, not bad

looking, with darkish blond hair not too long and childlike blue eyes, round and sandy-lashed. He looked immature, shy and awkward. "What—do the police want with me?" he asked in a high voice, and swallowed.

"Lieutenant Mendoza—Detective Grace. You work at Mr. Stanhope's pharmacy after school, don't you?" asked Grace. "Sit down, William—we don't bite. You remember last Tuesday night?"

The boy nodded. He sat down on the edge of a straight chair suddenly, as if his knees had given way, and stared at them dumbly. "You had some deliveries to make for the store—one to a Mrs. Moffat at that apartment on Stanford?" Another nod. "Well, when you got there, could you tell us if she was alone? Did she—"

"I never meant to do it!" said Linblad in a kind of wild croak. "I never meant nothing! But it was so awful—she scared me!" He was scared now: a senior here, turned eighteen, but very immature eighteen, even with all his growth. "I never—I never—"

"Take it easy," said Mendoza, interested. "Just tell us what happened. But maybe we'd better give him his rights first, Jase."

Linblad hardly listened to that little set piece, nodded again when Grace asked if he understood it. "I—I been scared ever since, I guess— I wanted to tell somebody but I didn't—I didn't know—what you might do to me. I—I—when I heard about it, couple of women in the store saying how she's dead, I didn't believe it—I thought, maybe she just—sort of died—later. I—I—"

"What time did you get there?" asked Grace.

"It was the last delivery. I'd never been there before, I had to look at the mailboxes—it was about eight, maybe. Just getting dark." And suddenly he began to gabble it out at them fast, as if to get rid of it once and for all. "It was—just awful—when she opened the door, she—I mean, she was an old lady, all this gucky makeup all over her face, and she was sort of drunk—not awful drunk but some—and she—and she—started to call me lovey-dovey names and nice boy and she t-t-tried to kiss me, she said didn't I want her to be nice to me—and it was just awful, I tried to get loose from

[74]

her, and I just gave her a shove like and she started to cry, and I just sort of pushed her away—she hadn't paid me yet but I just wanted to get *away*—" Suddenly he began to cry just a little. "I mean—I mean," he said, ashamed, getting out a handkerchief, "I'm not a *kid*, if it had been a pretty girl—but *her!* It was—like to make me sick—"

Mendoza looked at Grace. "You wanted a witness. A real hunch."

"It just crossed my mind as a possibility," said Grace. "Given what we knew about Ida."

"What—what are you going to do?" asked the boy. "It wasn't—it couldn't've been—just that little shove I gave her—was it?"

Palliser took Higgins back to the office, to dictate the initial report on Cicely Upton and fill Mendoza in, and then drove down to the gas company offices. Personnel there told him that John Upton was working on repair crews out of a station on Santa Barbara. Out there, Palliser talked to the dispatcher, Stan Rodman, who listened to him with various expletives and before he said anything else picked up the phone and told someone to send up Dickey and Collins if they were in. He leaned back in his chair and regarded Palliser with interest, a lean rawboned man in olive-green uniform.

"Well, you never know what's going to happen, isn't it the truth," he said heavily. "You think he killed his wife? I will be damned. He seemed like a good enough young fellow—good worker, I will say. But I wasn't working that close to him, say what kind he was. He hasn't showed up since Monday, or called in sick, so that fits right in, don't it? I will be damned."

"He worked last Monday?"

"Same as usual—eight to five. Reason I called up Chet and Bill, they made up a crew with Upton, they'd know him better. If this isn't the damnedest thing—but like I say, you never do know what's going to happen the next minute. I often thought it must be an interesting job, being a cop. You like it?"

"It can be interesting—and damn boring sometimes," said Palliser.

"I suppose. Here's Chet and Bill. Say, what do you know, fellows? This is a cop, Sergeant Palliser—and he says Johnny Upton's murdered his wife and skipped town. You ever hear the like?"

The two men just entering the office were both wearing olive-green uniforms with the little insignia on the left pocket—*Southern California Gas Company*. Dickey was short and stocky and very dark, Collins taller and thinner and younger. They both said they'd be damned, and Chet Dickey said, "When did it happen? He hasn't been to work since Monday—"

"I just told him," said Rodman.

"It could have been Monday night," said Palliser. "We won't know until there's been an autopsy."

"That's a real shame," said Dickey, and he looked as if he meant it. "Cicely was an awfully nice girl."

"Did you know her?" Palliser was surprised.

"Well, see, we're all—I mean me and Bill and Johnny—we were all on the company bowling team. I live up on Bonnie Brae, not so far from Johnny, and we used to take turns to drive, on practice nights."

"That's right," confirmed Collins. "And come to think, Chet, last Monday night you said—"

Dickey nodded. He looked solemn. "I didn't think too much about it," he said. "Johnny's pretty good, he could skip practice. He called me up about seven that night, said he wasn't feeling too good, I shouldn't stop by for him. I thought it was a little funny he hadn't said something before he left work, but he said he had a headache come on sudden. I bet that was when he— My God, to think of a guy you know doing something like that—I only knew her from stopping by for him that way, but—"

"Well, it looks as if it was that night," said Palliser. "That just fills in some more, thanks."

"And I'll tell you something," said Collins suddenly. "One thing about Johnny, he's got a temper goes off real hot. Remember that time, Chet, one of us left a hammer or something alongside a trench and he tripped over it? For a minute there, way he was cussing and all, his expression, he looked ready to do murder—" He stopped, and added, "Not but what he got over it in a minute, but—you see what I mean."

And murder could be done in a minute, or less, thought Palliser, and a man sorry afterward, but it couldn't be undone. He said, "We'll probably want statements from you," nodding at Dickey and Rodman.

"Sure—whatever we can do." Dickey shook his head. "That's a real bad deal for Johnny. I'm sorry to hear about it. What'll you do to find him?"

"There are things to do on it—just hope we'll pick him up."

"Did he take his car?" asked Collins.

"It's missing."

"Well, I just might mention that he'd been having trouble with it, it needed a lot of work. Maybe he might not get far in it."

"Thanks very much," said Palliser. "That might help."

When he got back to the office, Higgins had filled Mendoza in and heard about William Linblad; Grace had taken Linblad over to jail and gone to see his parents. The D.A. would probably call it involuntary manslaughter; and of course, as Palliser conceded, the thing had its humorous aspects.

"Our Ida was feeling amorous just once too often," said Mendoza sardonically. "And that poor innocent teen-ager—"

"My, what big teeth you have, Grandmother," grinned Higgins. "In ten years he'd react different. As it is, he'll get a year or so and serve half of it."

"So you've been sitting here chatting about Ida," said Palliser. "What have you done on Upton?"

"What there was to do. Gave the gist to NCIC and put out a statewide A.P.B. on him and the car. I got the plate number from Sacramento. What'd you hear at the gas company?"

Palliser told them. "Nothing very abstruse about it—how many times has it happened, husband losing his temper, wife dead. Maybe he's sorry but he's not going to come begging to be put in jail. But if that car's in bad shape, he may drop it somewhere and pick up another—though come to think, so far as we know he hasn't got a record, he might not know how to hot-wire a car."

"We know," said Higgins. "At least as far as we're concerned, he's got no record. Mrs. Cohen said they came from Fresno, I sent a telex up there to ask."

"So we wait and hope we pick him up. What's the status quo otherwise?"

Mendoza flicked a report on his desk. "Autopsy report on Ida. She wasn't legally drunk—just happy, as Jase said. Fractured skull. The more I think of that one—" he laughed. *"Se lo digo,* no happy medium with the kids! Either the smart-aleck sophisticates who know it all, or—the ones like Linblad. Yes. The ones like—*Dios,* I hope to hell the lab picked up something useful in that Clark Hotel apartment."

"Mrs. Branch. If they didn't, we're fresh out of leads—except for your love beads, a dime a dozen at any of the freaky shops for the flower children."

"Damn it, they've had two days," said Mendoza, and reached for the phone; it buzzed at him and he picked it up. "Yes, Jimmy?"

"Your assaulted doctor is now conscious and can be talked to," said Lake.

"Oh, thanks so much." Mendoza got up, reaching for his hat. As he passed Lake's desk outside, he said, "You look happier these days, Jimmy. Forgotten the diet?"

"Like hell," said Lake gloomily. "I can hardly get into this uniform, and I'll be damned if I lay out for a new wardrobe. Caroline found one that's all low protein, I'll start on it tomorrow." He sighed.

At Hollywood Receiving Hospital Mendoza was told he could talk to Dr. Ducharme just ten minutes. His wife was with him.

When Mendoza came into the little room, with only one of the single beds occupied, Mrs. Ducharme was looking rather glamorous, her color high and eyes bright.

"And here," she said to her husband, "is a police officer, and you'd better tell him all about it. Oh, I'm sorry, Bernie, but of all the crazy stupid things to do! I really thought you had better sense than that, and you're just lucky—we're all lucky—you didn't end up getting killed!" She turned away to the window. "His name's Lieutenant Mendoza," she added a little crossly.

"Mea culpa," said the man in the hospital bed in a faint voice. "I'll admit it was stupid. We all do the stupid things sometimes." His head was bandaged, and he needed a shave, his beard as thick and black as Mendoza's. He was nearly handsome, a strong nose and chin, olive skin and dark eyes.

"And now I know you'll be all right—honestly, Bernie, I'm mad at you! Risking your life like that, with me and the children—"

"So what happened, Doctor?" asked Mendoza.

Ducharme said fretfully, "I've got a hell of a headache. Deserve it, I suppose. They wanted to give me some more Demerol, but I'm leery of that stuff. Might start up that damned allergy again. Well, I was stupid, Lieutenant. I was alone, in a strange town, and I guess for a while I was feeling like a young blade again." An intern came in and told him not to talk too much or exert himself. "You run along—I'm a doctor, too, you know. I left the hotel, and I meant to find that place the desk clerk recommended, but I didn't, I went into a bar up the street, something like Romero's—Moreno's. I had a few drinks—which I don't as a rule, I'm not used to more than a couple—and I got talking to a man there. He seemed like a nice fellow—"

"With all the drinks addling your brains," she said, but then she laughed.

"Well—and I'm afraid all I recall after that is being outside again and trying to fight them—it was two men, I'm pretty sure of that, they were hitting me with something—"

"Mmh," said Mendoza. "Don't be too hard on him, Mrs.

Ducharme. That's not too safe an area around there—reason the clerk advised you to take a cab. And we used to think of the B-girls as the ones who slipped the customer a Mickey Finn to roll him outside, but there are men who go in for it too. You were wearing good clothes, Doctor, you looked prosperous—you might offer good pickings. I'd have a bet the one in the bar slipped a small dose of chloral hydrate into your drink, eased you out to where his pal was waiting. Then you woke up when they were stripping you and began to fight them, so they had to put you out a quicker way."

"I'll be damned," said Ducharme.

"What did they get?"

"My watch—Longines wristwatch—and my diamond ring. About forty dollars in cash. I'd had the sense to put the rest in the hotel safe."

"Could you describe the man in the bar?"

Ducharme shook his head and groaned involuntarily. "Not much—young, medium coloring, middle height—pretty sharp sports clothes."

"Well, we've got some mug shots of men who've pulled that kind of caper. When you're feeling better you might like to take a look. Meanwhile, if we can have a description of the jewelry we'll get it on the pawnbrokers' hot list."

"I can give you that," she said. "Honestly, Bernie—of all things to happen."

Landers had said why bother Narco again, they had their own business, and if Sid Belcher had a pedigree R. and I. would turn it up faster. Conway's cynical gray eyes were amused, but he went along with that. Down in Records, Landers looked at his girl fondly, neat little Phil O'Neill, and said, "What about Tuesday night, The Castaway again?"

"Fine with me," said Phil. "I just hope Rich realizes what he's getting into with that Margot. Did you know she's taking night classes in karate?"

"I had heard," said Conway, his lips twitching. "That's the way to keep a man from getting fresh all right."

"So what are you after now?"

"Sid Belcher. I don't know if that's his real name—"

"It'd almost have to be," said Phil. "Nobody would deliberately adopt a name like that, Tom. I'll have a look."

She brought the package to them five minutes later. Sidney Charles Belcher was described as Caucasian, twenty-four now, six feet, one ninety, brown and blue, no marks. He had a pedigree of possession, one count of assault, one of rape. He'd been off parole for six months. The last known address was Cahuenga Boulevard in Hollywood.

"Well, we can start there," said Landers. He was disposed to linger chatting with Phil, but Conway reminded him what he was getting paid for and reluctantly Landers followed him out. They took Conway's Dodge.

That was an old section of Hollywood; these days some old buildings were getting knocked down and new ones put up, and along the block they wanted the contrast was glaring: the old apartment buildings dirty white or tan stucco, square and solid and plain, the new ones sprawling with sun decks, colored plastic patio shelters and bright colors that would fade quickly in the hot sun. The one they wanted was one of the old ones. There wasn't a parking slot for a block and a half; they walked back.

"Past time we're due for a heat wave," said Conway.

"Don't call it down—it'll be coming." It was a three-story place, with steep steps up to a square-roofed porch, where the rows of mailboxes were lined. *Belcher* was listed at apartment eight. "Still here, anyway."

They went in and climbed uncarpeted stairs. Upstairs the hall was narrow, and there was a faint smell of frying onions somewhere and another of a cloying room freshener. The place was very quiet. At the door numbered eight Landers pushed the bell, and there was a shrill high buzz beyond the door. They waited. Unconsciously Landers reached up to adjust the shoulder holster.

The door opened; their eyes, adjusted for six-feet-high Sid Belcher, met space. They looked down. "Yes?" she said brightly. "What was it?"

"We're looking for a Sidney Belcher," said Conway. "Does he still live here?"

"When he's home, boys. Which is sometimes," she said airily. "Come on in. You friends of Sid's? Haven't seen you here before. I'm Sid's mother, in case you didn't know." She blinked and simpered at them.

She was a little woman, bleached blonde and skinny as a plucked chicken. She had on a purple nylon housecoat, and her fingernails matched it. She was in her bare feet; on the coffee table in front of a sagging couch was evidence of what she'd been doing—painting her toenails to match both. There was also a cocktail shaker half full and a lone cocktail glass, empty.

"You like a drink?" she asked hospitably.

"No, thanks, Mrs. Belcher," said Landers. "Do you know when Sid might be home?"

"No idea," she said. She sat down and refilled her glass from the shaker. She was facing the light and the merciless afternoon sun showed the telltale broken red veins in her nose, the splotchy skin covered with makeup. "He comes and goes, comes and goes. Come to think, he's gone. I just remembered he took a suitcase with him. He said where he was going, but I just don't call it to mind—my memory's getting terrible." She drank.

"Where does he usually go?" asked Conway somewhat inanely.

"Now there's a good question, mister," she said. "A very good question. Where does he? He was in a hurry, that I do remember. And he asked me to do something for him while he was gone. I was sitting here just now doing my toenails, and I said to myself, Bella, I said, what was it that Sid asked you to do? He said it was important, and I'd better do it right away. He used to like Disneyland, but I don't suppose he'd be going there now."

"When did he leave?" asked Landers.

"Oh, a while ago," she said vaguely. "Probably he owed

somebody some money. That's always a good reason for leaving, isn't it? Are you sure you won't have a drink?"

"No, thanks," said Conway. "Was Janie with him?"

"Which Janie you mean? Oh, *that* Janie. I'm sure I don't know," she said, and hiccupped and added, "Parm me. Does Sid owe you any money? Because if he does, you're out of luck, I couldn't oblige him—not this month. The alimony was late again, and it's what they call—vicious circle, y' know. Got you comin' and goin'. You don't get the alimony, you can't pay a lawyer to get it for you. Lawyers are all crooks anyway. Are you lookin' for something'?" she added to Conway in mild curiosity. "The john's off the hall."

"I was just noticing this," said Conway casually. "Does it belong to Sid?" He jerked his head at Landers, who came to look. It was lying there in full view on a pile of old *True Romance* magazines, a rather rusty old Smith and Wesson .22.

"What?" She padded over to look, and sudden enlightenment came into her eyes, focused on it with some difficulty. "Oh, *now* I remember what it was Sid told me to do! I was s'posed to get rid of that some way, throw it out in the trash. 'S lucky you happened to notice it—" She swayed a little, peering up at them, and suddenly she said, "Say, just who are you guys, anyway?"

"It's the plain stupidity that gets you," said Landers disgustedly. "Him relying on that lush to get rid of the gun—"

"And shooting the Booths in the first place."

"Over the no-good pot. As Jase says, people."

They turned the gun over to the lab; they'd given her a receipt for it but she probably hadn't known what it was. Landers gave Wanda the gist of it to type into a proper report, and they put out a statewide A.P.B. for Sid Belcher and flashed the word to NCIC in case he'd gone farther. They queried the D.M.V. in Sacramento and learned that he had a car registered, a VW, and added the plate number to the A.P.B. They heard about William Linblad from

[83]

Lake, and agreed that it was a funny one. You did still, in the midst of a renewed Sodom and Gomorrah, find the innocents.

They went home. Landers was feeling rather ambivalent about the double date on Tuesday night. He and Rich had taken to each other right away, and he liked Rich's girl all right, but he'd rather have Phil to himself. They'd known each other over a year now, and if she'd ever think about marrying him—

Grace told Virginia about William Linblad as he watched her giving Celia Ann her bath. "Maybe I'm growing the faculty for hunches too. But you could sympathize with the kid at that, funny as it was."

"Not funny," said Virginia. Celia Ann splashed and gurgled and they smiled at her; even after six months they hadn't quite got used to having their own baby. "What a woman, Jase. Maybe she got what she deserved."

"Not the nicest person in the world, Ginny, but maybe she didn't want to die."

Just before Mendoza left the office, the autopsy report came up on Harriet Branch. He was annoyed all over again, reading it. She had actually died of manual strangulation, though she'd been knocked around; there were bruises. Estimated time of death, between 8 and 10 P.M. Wednesday. Otherwise she had been a fairly healthy old lady, for her age: the heart slightly enlarged, the arthritis, but she might have had some years to go, living quietly there with her little amusements, an attentive family.

The victims like Harriet Branch always annoyed Mendoza. A good many victims of murder had invited it, by being stupid, or greedy, or careless. But Mrs. Branch, the harmless nice old lady, hadn't deserved to die that kind of death: and it didn't look as if there'd be any way for them to track down who'd brought it on her. Those damned love beads—

He drove home, consciously shelving the dirt and idiocy and brutality he dealt with on the thankless job. The house on Rayo

Grande Avenue was a stark contrast, and his red-haired girl trying to cope with the twins bouncing on their beds. Mairí MacTaggart's sister was having a birthday party, and their treasure had deserted them temporarily.

Terry and Johnny abandoned persecution of their mother to fling themselves at Mendoza. "Show you how good I read!" said Johnny peremptorily. "I show you better!" said Terry instantly. "But, *Padre,* what's a pond?"

"That is a marvelous book," said Alison as they scrambled to fetch their McGuffey Readers. "They hardly ever get confused with Spanish now—but raising children in the city, there are a few things—"

"What's a pond, Papa?" Johnny pulled at him. "It says they went there. *Mamacita* says water but water's in the faucet."

"Yes, I do see what you mean," said Mendoza. Occasionally he felt his years. Automatically patting all four cats curled in a heap at the foot of Terry's bed, he added, "Parenthood is for the young."

"Speak for yourself, *amador.* Statistics say children of elderly parents are more intelligent."

"I'm not feeling quite elderly yet, my love."

"Oh, you needn't tell me *that,"* said Alison.

The night watch drifted in. Glasser told the rest of them about the car. "Lesser of two evils," he said.

"I don't see it," said Schenke. "You'd be better off to buy a good used job. I could recommend a lot—"

The first thing turned up at nine forty-five, and maybe they should have expected it. Another heist at a restaurant just closing. This time it was that place so improbably popular, Le Renard Bleu, the unpretentious French family restaurant over past New Chinatown. It offered nothing but good food and good service, and you always had to make reservations. Glasser and Shogart went out on that, and heard very much what they'd heard about the Chasen job.

The shaken proprietor, Monsieur Robineau, was comforting a

more shaken cashier, who turned out to be his niece, Mademoiselle Guillaume.

"We had only just closed—nearly everyone is gone, the chefs, the waitresses, and we are just counting up the money, it was a good night, when they came in—" Robineau gestured dramatically. "I am careless, there was a last couple lingered, and they had just left, I should have locked the door then—"

"Such big, big guns!" said the pretty, dark cashier.

It sounded like the same pair, stocking masks, the big guns, in and out fast. "I do not have to figure to tell you," said Robineau. "They stole five thousand eight hundred and thirteen dollars and thirteen cents. In the little canvas bag I use to carry money home. But I saw something. I would not know their faces, no. But one of them, he has on his right hand—I am sure!—a great long scar, like from a knife, on the back of the hand. Perhaps the police know a criminal with such a scar, eh?"

It wouldn't be much help. They'd want formal statements on it, but it looked, as Glasser said, as if that pair had realized they'd stumbled on a very nice M.O., and were bent on building up a good take. None of them had grasped before what kind of cash money the good restaurant would have on hand at closing time. "I wonder," said Glasser thoughtfully, "if one or both of them have worked in places like that?" It was an idea; it wouldn't take them any further in finding them.

At eleven forty-five they had a call from a Traffic unit. "You desk boys will be taking a lot of statements on this," said the squad-car man tersely. "And there's an assault with intent at least—it looked touch and go, may turn into homicide."

Galeano and Schenke went out on that, and heard about it at length from Patrolman Bill Moss and his partner, Frank Chedorov. "We've practically been chasing this guy all night," said Moss. "We haven't laid eyes on him, but plenty of people have. I wouldn't have a guess whether he's drunk or high on something else." They were in front of a single frame house on Diana Street. "The first call we got about two hours ago, a prowler over on Westmoreland. I've got all the names for you—you'll be taking statements like I said." He leaned against the squad car, a very tough, competent LAPD man, tall, dark, grim-faced, a good-looking young man. "Householder heard him trying to break in the back door, and scared him off with a light. Got a look at him as he ran—best he could give us, a tall thin guy, Negro, ran fast, no make on his clothes. About half an hour later we got sent over on Geneva, just around the corner. Two girls, nice girls, sharing an apartment there—man broke into the place, one of these flimsy back-door locks, and they had quite a little fight with him, he mauled them both around some—we called an ambulance, but neither of 'em's seriously hurt, just bruised. Good girls, they put up a fight, banged him over the head with a flashlight, and he got away and ran. They told us, a tall thin Negro in a tan jumpsuit." Moss lit a cigarette.

"By this time," said Chedorov, "we were cruising the neighborhood on the lookout for him. And not fifteen minutes later we got a call to Diana Street here—another prowler call—half a block up, that way. Another attempted break-in, but the householder had a gun, turned a light on and showed it, and the prowler ran through the backyard and got away. But the householder got a good look, in the floodlight at the back. Tall thin Negro in a tan jumpsuit. We were just behind him all the way."

"So then we get a call, prowler, right here," said Moss. "We came up in a hurry, it's got to be him, but we're just too late. We heard about it from the neighbors." He gestured.

This block was in a mild uproar, lights on and people out in the street with flashlights, clustering, talking excitedly. The ambulance had just taken off as Galeano and Schenke arrived.

"It's a Mrs. Elsa Short. Widow, lives alone in this place. The Leemings live next door," said Moss. "That's Mr. Leeming with the shotgun. Mrs. Short, by what we can figure, called in when she heard this guy at her back door, but we hadn't got here when Leeming heard her screaming. He got his gun and came out, saw the guy come out the back door running—across the backyard. He

[87]

said he didn't take a shot at him because the neighbors on the other side were coming out then and he didn't want to kill an innocent bystander. But it was a tall thin Negro in a tan jumpsuit."

"Thank you so much for nothing," said Galeano. "What about the widow?"

Moss stepped on his cigarette. "Not so good. He'd got in, and he had a knife. By what Leeming said he probably didn't have time to grab anything. Putting it all together, he's probably drunk or hopped up. A real stupid deal."

"Which so many of them are," said Galeano.

Sergeant Lake was off on Saturday, and Sergeant Rory Farrell sitting on the switchboard. Mendoza came in at ten past eight and looked at the reports the night watch had left, swore over the heist at the Blue Fox— "Do you remember that funny case, Art?"—and regarded the reported trail of the prowler with resignation. "Rory, check with the receiving hospital—Mrs. Elsa Short."

There was nothing in from the lab on Harriet Branch's apartment. "*¡Mil rayos!*" said Mendoza, Farrell buzzed him.

"Mrs. Short died about three A.M. Multiple knife wounds and shock."

"*Gracias* for nothing," said Mendoza. Something else to work, and no handle. The men were coming in—Landers, Conway, Piggott, Hackett and Higgins, Palliser, Grace. "We've got something new," said Mendoza.

At five minutes of nine, Farrell buzzed him again. The rest of them had drifted out on the endless routine legwork. "There's a Mr. Perkins here," said Farrell.

"Perkins? Oh. Well, shoot him in." And what he might want—Mendoza sat back and lit a cigarette, and the little desk clerk came in and sat down in front of the desk.

"We thought someone ought to tell you," he said earnestly. "Mr. Quigley and I talked it over, you see. Putting together what the other officers said, and that detective who talked to me. How you thought some—some person had got into the hotel while I was in the lavatory. Well, Lieutenant, I don't mean to tell you your business, you're an experienced officer, but it just occurred to both of us, you know—if that was so, how did he get out?"

Mendoza stared at him. *"¿Qué?"*

"I wasn't gone five minutes," said Perkins. "And after midnight the door was locked. And nobody came out past me after I'd been to the lavatory."

Mendoza sat up abruptly. *"¡Diez millones de demonios negros desde el infierno!"*

6

"OH, LUIS—" HACKETT CAME IN. "SORRY, I didn't—"

"Come in and listen to this, Art. Sergeant Hackett, Mr. Perkins. Night clerk at the Clark. Go on, Mr. Perkins."

"Well, that's just it," said Perkins, his nearsighted eyes behind rimless glasses a little anxious. "It's the kind of lock, you have to use the key on either side, to lock or unlock it. It's not a question of pushing a button or anything like that, and besides the door *was* locked that next morning. Anybody going out would have had to have a key."

"Now let me get this straight." Mendoza sat up and lit a cigarette. "You lock the front door at midnight. It's the only door used any more—others are all locked." Perkins nodded. "What about the permanent tenants? Suppose they're out after midnight?"

"Oh, they've all got keys."

"I see. And the ordinary hotel guests? You do have—"

"Oh, yes, sir. Not nearly so many as we used to have, but we get quite a lot of salesmen and business people passing through, who like to be in the downtown area, or are on tight expense accounts, don't care about the fancy places. People on vacation, just out for a good time, they want to stay somewhere fashionable, one of the Hiltons or the Century-Plaza. Mostly the people we get are quiet people on business, in before midnight, but there's a notice posted and if any of them are going to be late, they can borrow a key. But Mr. Quigley's very punctilious about keeping track of the extra keys—they're always locked in his desk. As it happens, I can tell you that nobody had an extra key that night—last Wednesday night."

"And you didn't see anybody in the freaky clothes, the love beads, come in."

"Oh, no, sir. Just as I told the other detective. All the guests were in by ten—they'd all gone out at various times for dinner. It's a shame to think how the hotel's gone down," said Perkins. "Really a skeleton staff these days. No room service, no dining room—it's just a glorified rooming house now—but our charges are according, and we do offer clean quiet rooms. I—"

"You went to the lavatory at nine o'clock."

"Somebody—of the kind you mean—could have slipped in then, yes, sir. But there was only one guest came and got his key after that, about ten o'clock. I was sitting there reading, but I'd have seen anyone go across the lobby and out. I—"

"Look here," said Hackett, "how about the fire department regulations? Aren't you supposed to have an emergency exit open at all times?"

"Certainly," said Perkins. "It's in Mr. Quigley's office off the lobby, out to Hill Street. There are three signs about it in the lobby. The door only opens out, of course." He looked uneasy. "Or it's supposed to. The fact is, it's out of order. That's actually what got Mr. Quigley and me talking about this. It's stuck. Mr. Quigley's been calling all around trying to get somebody to come and fix it, or if necessary put in a new door, but"—he sighed—"you know how it is, try to get a workman to come. Ordinarily, anybody could have come downstairs after midnight and gone out that way, and nobody the wiser. But now, no. They'd have to have a key to unlock the front door. Well, to go on. I locked up at midnight and went to bed. I have an apartment on the fifth floor. Mr. Quigley is on the sixth. He tells me when he came down to unlock the door next morning it was just as usual, locked up just as

[91]

I'd left it. So whoever it was did that terrible thing to Mrs. Branch, he must have got hold of a key somehow, and it occurred to us to wonder—"

"*¡Por Dios!*" said Mendoza. He got up. "Come on—I want you to take a look at something." Hackett trailing them, he took Perkins out to the elevator and down to the lab. "You haven't sent up a report on the Clark Hotel job," he said to Scarne, the first man they ran into, "but right now I want a look at what you brought in to process. Any keys?"

"Sure." Scarne looked a little surprised. "We didn't fetch in all the personal effects, but anything standing out that might've collected latents— And you never do know where you'll pick some up. We took her handbag, naturally, and there was a bunch of keys in that. They're clean—smudged, but nothing liftable."

"Show, show," said Mendoza impatiently. Perkins was looking around this big, bare room with its wall benches and sophisticated mysterious equipment with interest. Scarne rummaged and came up with a brown leather handbag, a little worn, still bearing a few marks from the dusting powder. "We'll clean it up before we hand it over to the relatives. Sorry, just smudges on this too. We put everything back—you can handle it."

Mendoza upended it unceremoniously on a table. A clean handkerchief, a gold-colored compact for loose powder, a pale pink lipstick, a coin purse, a new-looking blue vinyl folder for bills, empty, fell in a heap with a bunch of keys. Mendoza pushed those away from the rest with a long forefinger. There were several keys on an old-fashioned steel ring. "What about it, Mr. Perkins? Is the front-door key here? You'd know it?"

"Oh, dear, yes. I've been at the Clark for twelve years, Lieutenant. No, it's not," he said after a minute. "It's gone."

"*Un momento.* I don't suppose she used it often—the Whitlows said she didn't go out much anymore, she wouldn't be out after midnight. It could be she didn't keep that key with the rest." Mendoza was sorting them out: a Yale key, could be the key to the apartment, a long thin key that would fit a safe-deposit box,

...other Yale key—possibly the Whitlow house?—a couple of old ones he wouldn't have a guess about.

"Oh, but she did," said Perkins unexpectedly, "and I'll tell you how I happen to know. Let's see, this is June. It was back in February, there was a series of musicals at the Music Center, and Mr. and Mrs. Whitlow took her to see *The Mikado*. Gilbert and Sullivan, you know. She did look forward to it, and as luck had it that was one of her better days, when her arthritis wasn't so troublesome. They picked her up just as I was coming on duty, and I reminded her about the door, if she'd be late coming in—and she smiled at me and said she had her key, she took that ring out of her purse and showed it to me. And as a matter of fact they brought her home after midnight, and the next time she saw me she said how Mr. Whitlow had unlocked the door for her and taken her up to her apartment."

"*Así,*" said Mendoza absently. "But that's— What it comes down to is that X knew. I will be damned. I will be—he knew you'd be on the desk till midnight, and then locking up. He thought he'd get out the emergency door, but when he found it was stuck, he knew about the keys—that Mrs. Branch would have one. And, by God, he knew the right key—if he hadn't, he'd have taken the whole bunch. But instead, he simply takes that key off her ring—"

"Like a damned fool," said Hackett, hunching his bulky shoulders. Perkins was looking from one to the other. "Because you know where that takes us. Somebody from the hotel."

"Oh, no, I'm quite sure you're wrong there!" said Perkins agitatedly. "That's quite impossible. We're reduced to a much smaller staff than we used to have, but all respectable, decent people—I'm quite sure—"

"I want to get these keys sorted out!" said Mendoza forcefully. "Bill, if you don't send me a report on all this by tomorrow I'll report you to I.A. Come on, we're going over to the hotel to go into this in depth. Did you park in the lot?"

"Oh, I came on the bus—"

Mendoza led them down to the lot; they squeezed Perkins into the jump seat of the Ferrari and had a quick ride up to Hill. There are a few advantages to being a cop; Mendoza left the Ferrari in a loading zone and they went in.

Mendoza and Hackett went first to look at the emergency door. It was firmly stuck on dead center: Hackett exerted all his strength and couldn't move it. Nobody had got out that way.

Quigley was also agitated at the implication; but both he and Perkins were experienced in the ways of hotels, and a wealth of facts was disclosed in rapid order, on consultation of the register. On Wednesday night there had been forty-nine transient guests at the hotel, all but four of them men, all probably business people, sales representatives—that type, by what both men said. Quigley said at once that he had ten duplicate keys to the front door, always kept in a locked drawer in his desk, and all ten were there now; they looked. There was his key, and Perkins' key. There were thirty single apartments on the fifth and sixth floors of the building, with twenty rented: two more were occupied by Perkins and Quigley.

On Thursday, it hadn't seemed worth the while to talk to any of the other tenants on the fifth floor. Mrs. Branch's apartment was at the end of a short corridor down from the elevators; there were only two others in that little wing. The one across the hall was empty; the one on the same side, its front door twenty feet away from Mrs. Branch's, had been occupied by Mrs. Davies until her death last month. This was an old building, very solidly built, and it was not very likely that any of the tenants farther away— ten more small apartments on that floor—had heard any little struggle and outcry from Mrs. Branch's apartment.

Now, Mendoza wanted the full treatment. He called the office and asked who was there. "John and Jase went out to get statements from all that rumpus last night," said Farrell. "On the Short woman. Henry had a little idea about the restaurant heisters and it paid off, Piggott's out on that. Tom and Rich Conway were just leaving—"

"Hold it. Send them over. We've got some questions to ask here too."

"Will do," said Farrell. "I'll just catch 'em."

"Now, I want to hear all about your employees," said Mendoza to Quigley.

"I'm sure you're wrong about that, Lieutenant. Most of them have been with us a long time, all reliable people. But of course, anything I can tell you—"

There were four maids for the first four floors, where the single hotel rooms were located. Three of them had worked there for five, six, ten years: all middle-aged women, said Quigley, never any trouble, hard workers. The fourth had only been there a month, a Laura Schoonover: she seemed like a nice quiet girl, said Quigley, about thirty. Got along with the others all right. For the two top floors, where the apartments were, there were two maids: Agnes Harvey and Louise Wilding. Not all the permanent tenants wanted to pay extra for maid service: Mr. and Mrs. Bolt didn't, or Miss Trucker, or Mr. Yates; with him it wasn't the money, he was a secretive old chap who didn't like strange women fussing about his quarters. The other seventeen apartments occupied were cleaned by the maids once a week. Usually Agnes Harvey did the fifth floor and Louise Wilding the sixth, but there wasn't any rule about it.

Landers and Conway arrived. "We're going to talk to everybody who lives here," said Mendoza. "And we're going to make sure where their front door keys are, all accounted for. This might give us some very useful ideas where to look. Art, you go and talk to the maids. Especially Harvey and Wilding."

"Yes, I think this may be it," said Hackett. "See what I turn up." He might not have the built-in radar like Mendoza, but he'd been a cop a long time and any cop got feelings about people.

By one o'clock they had talked to everybody but Mr. Yates. Miss Trucker was a sales clerk at Bullock's, and Conway had gone up there to see her, had seen her key. Everybody else living at the Clark was elderly, retired, and at home. The Bolts were the only married couple; there were two spinster sisters, the Misses Catton; everyone else lived alone. They all had their front-door keys to show; few of them ever used them. When Landers tried to talk to Mr. Yates, the door was opened a cautious few inches on a chain, and Mr. Yates said, "Don't know anything about it," to Landers' questions. "A murder? Murders all over. Dangerous. I don't go out. Get the drugstore to send up my breakfast and dinner. What say? What key? Oh, that key. I never use it."

"Have you still got it? I'd like to see it, sir." And presently, grumbling, Mr. Yates held up to the crack a single bright Yale key. Landers could recognize it by then, having looked at a dozen others.

All the front-door keys were accounted for except Harriet Branch's. Nobody who lived on the fifth floor had heard any kind of disturbance on Wednesday evening, between eight and ten. All of them had been home; most of them had been watching TV.

"¿Cuánto apuestas?" said Mendoza. He stood in front of the desk in the lobby, smoking and rocking gently heel to toe. "That puts it right here. Right here at the hotel."

"And what a damn fool thing to do," said Landers. "Anybody could figure that. Who else would know that key by sight, to take just that one?"

"He hadn't any choice about the key," said Mendoza. "Not after he found that emergency door blocked. But he'd have been smarter to take the whole bunch."

"The maids don't have occasion to use the key," said Quigley behind the desk.

"No, but they've seen it—they're familiar with it. There's the one in your office. I noticed you've got it hanging there on the wall all by itself. Why?" asked Mendoza suddenly. "Why don't you keep it with your others?"

Quigley looked distressed. "I used to. It's only there during the day—I take it with me when I go off duty. The only time I use it as a rule is when I open up in the morning. But—at the time of the Watts riots, there were several incidents—looters coming in off the street—oh, nothing like what it was down there, but we did finally lock the door when a noisy gang came by, and Mr. Perkins said then perhaps we should keep a key handy for—emergencies. If I was away from the desk, or—"

"The maids go in there, they'd know the key."

Quigley admitted it. "But really, to think that one of them could—"

"They've got personal lives," said Mendoza. "Relatives, and probably troubles. What did you get from them, Art?"

"I'll tell you over food," said Hackett. "I'm starving."

Glasser's little idea last night, expressed in a note to Piggott, had rather surprisingly paid off. Landers had said it was brilliant, and chased down enthusiastically to R. and I. to see what Phil could turn up from the computer. The criminal records of the LAPD were quite extensive; fed the proper questions, the computer turned up eighteen men with records of armed robbery who had at one time or another been employed at restaurants. Landers stared at the list, aghast.

"Well, you're setting up some legwork for yourself," said Phil, surprised too.

But as soon as Landers got back, he and Conway were chased over to the hotel. Palliser and Grace, looking without enthusiasm at the list, were just as pleased there was another job than that one to work. Piggott had started out with the first few names.

At least it was Saturday, and most people would be home. They had the names and addresses from the night watch, of the trail of the prowler last night in that neighborhood.

Alberto Perez, on Westmoreland Avenue, said he'd been in bed when he heard the prowler. His wife was visiting her mother in Bakersfield; he was alone in the house. He had got up and turned on the backyard lights, two floodlights, and scared the prowler away, having called the police first; but when they came the man had run off. He gave them a fairly good description.

Palliser thanked him; he'd taken notes for Wanda to type up

into a statement, and he explained about coming in to sign it tomorrow.

"Sure," said Perez. "I heard he ended up killing a lady. My God. Sure, you got to be a good citizen."

From there they went on to the apartment on Geneva Street, which Kathy Bryan and Linda Poling shared. The girls were there, willing and anxious to talk about it, and pleased at the attention. They were both young and good-looking, Linda a diminutive blonde and Kathy a statuesque brunette. The apartment was on the ground floor; this had been a big single house, now cut up into four apartments, and someone had done some remodeling: in this ground-floor unit, a former side door had been replaced with a sliding glass panel.

"I tell you, I've always been a little nervous about it," said Kathy. "We got that special lock for sliding doors, and I know it's awfully thick glass, but still it is glass—and of course that was where he tried first. We were both in bed, and we heard him at the same time, and I peeked around a corner of the bedroom and saw him—it was moonlight, you know." The glass door was in their living room. "It's lucky the phone's in the bedroom. I called the police as quietly as I could, and then I grabbed up this flashlight—" It was a good hefty one, metal and at least a foot long.

Linda chuckled. "I sneaked out to the kitchen and got that big cast-iron skillet. I always said it'd make a good weapon."

"And he didn't get in the glass door, so he came round and tried the kitchen door, and I think he kicked it in," said Kathy. "It made an awful noise. The lock's broken, and Mr. Winter said he'd see it was fixed today—I hope! Anyway, there he was—the man, and I was terrified but I banged him on the head with the flashlight as soon as he got in—"

"Do you think he was drunk?" asked Grace.

"There wasn't any liquor smell, but I think he might have been doped up on something, he acted so sort of wild—and he was awfully strong, I can testify to that! He grabbed the flashlight away from me—"

[98]

"This flashlight?"

"Yes, he just threw it across the room, I found it later—"

"Don't touch it!" said Palliser sharply as she reached for it again. "Just hope, if he left any prints on it—"

"I haven't messed them up already—oh, dear," she said, "I *am* sorry, I just never thought. Yes, you can have it—as long as I get it back. Anyway, he grabbed me and knocked me right down across the kitchen table—you should see my bruises—"

"And about then I tried to hit him with the skillet," said Linda, "but the darned thing's so heavy, I couldn't aim it very well—and he came at me and knocked me down, right on the floor, and I'll never forget it—there was the moonlight coming in, and he had a knife in his hand, the light hit the blade and it looked three feet long, I could feel it coming right for my middle—" She shuddered.

"And then—I guess we'd both been screaming blue murder," said Kathy, "Mr. Winter got there, yelling what was the matter—he's the landlord, he lives in front—and the man just turned and ran out. Boo! That was a real experience! It's convenient, living pretty close to work here"—they both worked at a big travel agency downtown—"but I don't know, maybe safer away from what they call the inner city." They both said they'd be glad to sign statements.

Palliser and Grace went on to the first householder on Diana Street, Rupert Lutz. He said he had his house up for sale. On account of the crime rate. "I got four years to retirement, boys," he said, "but I'm not takin' the gamble. Not here. Me and my wife are getting out, goin' up to Montgomery Creek way up north. Wide place in the road. We got a trailer house there, and an acre and a half. Grow some food, maybe have a cow." He'd gone for his gun right off, hearing the prowler, saw him at the back door; his wife had called the police, but as soon as he'd turned on the outside lights and yelled out a window that he'd shoot, the prowler had taken off. "I heard that woman down the street died—is that right? He cut her up?" Lutz shook his head. "That's awful. I sure hope we sell this place soon."

They went on to Mr. Leeming, next door to Mrs. Short's house. Mendoza had routed out the lab, and the truck was still in the drive, Marx and Horder busy packing away cameras and equipment. Palliser handed over the flashlight in its plastic evidence bag. "Think you picked up anything?"

"Anybody's guess," said Marx. "There was quite a lot of blood—looks as if all the action was in the kitchen. You'll like one thing we got—but no telling whether it'll be any use. He stepped in some of the blood. He was in his bare feet."

"What?" said Grace. "I'll be damned. Good print?"

"Fair. I'd make it about a size eleven, a wide splayed foot—he's used to going barefoot."

"Which might say this and that," said Palliser. "You'll send us a report."

"When we've looked at everything." Marx climbed behind the wheel and Horder got in beside him.

They had put a police department seal on the doors. Palliser and Grace walked around the little frame house and looked at the back door. A rather flimsy screen door had been wrenched off its hinges entirely, lay on the dry grass below the back step. But the inner door was a stout one, now crudely jimmied around the lock, splinters broken off. Grace said thoughtfully, "The girls said he was pretty strong. I'd say he had to be, to pry that open." Palliser agreed.

They went next door to talk to Leeming. He gave them the best description; he'd had a clear look at the prowler in moonlight as he ran out of the kitchen. "We heard about Mrs. Short," he said soberly. "We'd been neighbors a long time, I went out and asked the hospital to let us know. This is a hell of a thing—just a hell of a thing. He must've been drunk or doped—he didn't steal a thing, didn't have time—and there wasn't anything there to steal anyway. Mrs. Short just had the pension from her husband, he was a railroad man. There wouldn't be ten bucks in the house likely, she was careful about keeping cash around. Poor woman, not a soul of her own, they never had any kids. I don't believe there's anybody to see about a funeral, even cousins or anything. I guess she probably had enough in the bank to bury her, and she owned the house—my wife and I could do that much anyway, see to the funeral." They told him about the mandatory autopsy, the statement, and he nodded. "That's O.K., I'll be glad to."

It was getting on toward one o'clock then, so they handed all the notes to Wanda, and both of them starved, didn't waste time going out but went up to the canteen on the top floor for sandwiches.

Higgins and Piggott had been left with the new list of heisters with restaurant experience. They didn't feel enthusiastic about it, but the legwork was always there to be done. They went out looking, and found a few of them at the addresses from Records, brought them in to lean on. It was all up in the air; one had a solid alibi, the others were possible, with nothing to say yes or no.

They had just, after a lunch break, found another and were about to start talking to him when a cheerful-looking young man came in and said to Farrell, "Just checking into your nice inner-city beat. I'm from Wilcox Street—Bob Laird. Somebody like to help me make an arrest?"

"Sure," said Higgins. "Who're you after?"

"A fag by the name of Melvin Wenfer. I've got a warrant—assault with intent. He's supposed to be at a rooming house down on Temple—no guarantee he's still there. He's been living the high life up in Hollywood, little affair with one of the teachers at a public high school—"

"My God," said Higgins. "The innocent parents sending kids to those places. The teacher a fag—"

"As I'm always saying," said Piggott sadly, "right back to Sodom and Gomorrah. The love affair broke up?"

"Yep. Teacher decided Melvin was too expensive—caught him rifling his pockets and threw him out," said Laird. "Melvin missed the goodies, kept at him to start over, but finally a couple of days ago he got in a snit and attacked teacher with a knife. Teacher ran to us—he had this address from when Melvin was still begging him to forgive and forget."

"They will do it," said Higgins. "You can talk to this bird, Matt. I don't suppose anything'll come of it." The heister was a morose-looking man still on parole.

Higgins and Laird went down to the lot, to Laird's car. "And in a way," said Laird as they climbed in, "it might have been better the other way round, Sergeant."

"How do you mean?"

"Well, that Piggott's a nice mild-looking fellow, you know. I just hope you won't scare little Melvin half to death."

Higgins grinned. "Never believe I've got a beautiful wife, would you? I hope the baby takes after her."

"Boy or girl?"

"Oh, a girl—Margaret Emily, nine months," said Higgins proudly.

Laird cast a thoughtful glance at him as he started the engine. "Let's hope the baby takes after your wife, Sergeant."

At the address on Temple, they surprised Melvin Wenfer considerably. "I didn't think Eugene 'd do a thing like that—swear out a warrant for me! He's just being mean! A lousy five bucks I borrow from him—he'd have given it to me if I asked!—" He was petulant. "You damn fuzz always down on us—just because we're different—" But Higgins, with COP emblazoned on his forehead, he didn't like; he didn't give them any trouble. They put him in cuffs just to make sure and Laird dropped Higgins off at headquarters.

The possible heister had come up with an alibi for last night, checked out. "I can't understand it," said Piggott. "How there could be so many."

"Well, you think about it," said Higgins, "it's natural maybe. The thugs getting out on P.A., they'll hold a job as long as they have to, and that's the kind of job that kind can get—dishwashers, bus boys."

"That's so. But it makes the legwork." However, about then they got Landers and Conway back, from their morning at the hotel and a belated lunch.

Landers looked at the list, somewhat shortened, and said, "I suppose the quicker we get to it, the quicker we'll clean it up."

But as they came past the switchboard, an excited-looking woman came in and said, "Is this where I'm supposed to be? The man downstairs said I should come and ask to see the body—Holy Mother, a body he says—but it could be Carlos and no telling how long he'd been gone because I've been away since last Saturday, I've been on a trip with my sister—and I come home at noon today off the bus and Carlos isn't there! We live together, I'm a widow, and Carlos, he never got married after that girl jilted him—he's my brother—"

They got her calmed down a little. Her name was Vera Montoya, and she lived in a house on Miramar Street. She worked at a Manning's coffee shop, and Carlos was a checker at a Thriftimart market on Western, she said. He was off Saturdays, he always puttered around his garden, a fine garden he had in the backyard, but he hadn't been there and the neighbors hadn't seen him since last Saturday, thought maybe he'd gone off on the trip with Vera. Carlos, you could set your clock by him, a great one for routine and he'd never done such a thing— So she'd come to tell the police he was missing—

Apprehensively Higgins took her down to the morgue to look at the unidentified body dead of knife wounds. She gave one look and screamed, called on the Virgin and all the archangels, and said it was Carlos.

"That never harmed anybody his whole life, innocent as the babe unborn, how could such a thing happen to Carlos? When did you find him, how long is it? But how could such a thing—Carlos, he's the best man walking around, good, kind, everybody likes Carlos—"

Higgins took her back to the office and started to ask questions. The body had been found by Traffic just a week ago tonight, lying in the street along Loma Drive. He'd been stripped, nothing on him but cigarettes. She filled in a little, between exclamations and eulogy of Carlos. He'd been fifty-two, an old bachelor, a quiet man, Carlos Masada. He worked at his job, came home to work in his garden. No enemies. A man didn't need enemies, thought Higgins, when there were so many wild ones roaming around, to attack and maybe kill for what cash was in a pocket. Those were dark streets down there.

"Did he go out much at night, Mrs. Montoya? To a local bar maybe, or—"

"Never, never! He'd have a glass of wine before dinner, in the evening, but he never went out to sit in bars like some men, no. Go out, he would—he was crazy about the old movies, always when he saw there's an old movie playing some place, he'd go—the ones twenty, thirty years old, he remembers from when he was a young man—"

He'd probably been out to a movie, maybe up on Beverly Boulevard, close enough that he could walk there and back. And been jumped by one of the wild ones. It made more paper work; it was unlikely that they'd ever find out who it had been.

Mendoza sat at his desk chain-smoking and looking at the notes Hackett had taken on the employees at the Clark Hotel.

Those damned keys put it right back there—not, probably, to the actual maids themselves, though even that might be. But— connections. And a rudimentary plan—very rudimentary. He had a vague idea that possibly X had intended to get into more than one apartment there, quickly silencing the old people, ransacking; and then more loot than he'd expected showed up at Mrs. Branch's, and he'd stopped with that one. Or got scared when he saw he'd killed her. Because that at least they knew: he hadn't got out till after midnight, when Perkins locked up.

The two top-floor maids. Indignant and frightened, said Hackett, at being questioned—suspected. Conceivably the maids all quite innocent, just somebody taking in the casual talk?

No. The casual talk, damn it, wouldn't have told anybody what that key looked like.

Agnes Harvey was forty-two, had worked there for ten years. She was married; her husband drove a truck for Sears, Roebuck. Two children, a boy sixteen, a girl fourteen. They were buying a house on Fifty-second Street. They went to the Baptist Church regularly. Which said damn all, reflected Mendoza sardonically.

Louise Wilding was thirty, had worked there four years. She was divorced, lived with her widowed mother in the house her mother owned on Woodlawn Avenue. She had two children, a girl nine, a girl six. She went out with a man sometimes but she said she wasn't interested in marrying again. She had refused to give any names of the men to Hackett, said it was private business.

The other maids were all married: a couple of them had teen-age children. The first thing Mendoza had done on getting back to the office was to send Wanda down to R. and I. to check all of those kids. None had showed up in the j.d. records. Which again said nothing. There was always a first time.

Once a month an outside cleaning service came in to vacuum the lobby, Quigley's office, the elevators, the stairs, wash the front windows. Mendoza had just had a talk with the manager there, on the phone, and he was thinking about the cleaners as a distinct possibility, now. It was one of the big companies that took contracts for the routine cleaning of office buildings, hotels, public buildings. The manager, somewhat puzzled to be consulted by the police, had been anxious to be helpful.

"Well, if you get me—did you say Lieutenant?—it's not so easy to get good workers, in this business. We pay a good rate, but it's hard work—no denying that, and we got a reputation to keep, got to do the work right. When it's so easy to go on the welfare, and you know with all the bureaucratic red tape a lot of cheats are really taking it on seven kinds of welfare, it's not just so easy to find men willing to put in a good day's work. But I don't get why you're asking, you don't think one of our men pulled something? A—a crime? Look, I don't think any of 'em 'd do that—we got a pretty good bunch of men here now—"

And, to another question, he was uneasy and apologetic. "Well, if you get me, we're taking who we can get, Lieutenant. I got to say—we used to ask men for references, we used to check, just like we used to say no long hair and like that—and see if they got a police record, or were drunks or whatever. But we got commitments, we got the jobs to do, and these days we take about anybody shows up to apply."

The cleaners? There half a day, most of a day, cleaning? Hearing the talk from the maids, from Quigley? In Quigley's office, seeing that key hanging there.

Those damned keys. It was a tricky little point, but it did say something. And rather often, these days, Luis Rodolfo Vicente Mendoza was wondering why he stayed on at the thankless job, but admit it: Mendoza the egotist always enjoyed getting his teeth into the little puzzle like this one, ferreting out the truth.

He got up. It was four o'clock. He reached for his hat and said to Farrell absently, "I may not be back."

"Tom and Matt just brought in another one off that list. It's all up in the air—nothing to say yes or no."

"Sometimes it goes like that, Rory." Downstairs, he headed the Ferrari for the Hollywood freeway. It could be that the Whitlows—more likely Mrs. Whitlow—could tell him this and that about how Mrs. Branch had felt about the staff at the Clark Hotel, where she'd lived so long.

The maids. The cleaners. But, those damned love beads? "*¿Qué sé yo?*" he said to himself, annoyed. "*¿Qué significa eso?*"

Higgins had just brought in another man to question, at a quarter to five, and Conway had resignedly joined him in the second interrogation room, when the outside line flashed and Farrell plugged in. "Robbery-Homicide, Sergeant Farrell."

"We just got a call to a place on Ocean View. Szorbic, Traffic," said a hard young voice. "There's a body here, sir. At a house for sale—it was the realtor called us, he just found it."

"O.K.," said Farrell. "We'll be on it. Let me have the address."
The only men in were Higgins and Conway; he went down to
that interrogation room and passed on the news.

"Business picking up," said Higgins. "I suppose we'd better go
look at it."

7

AT THE SPRAWLING OLD HOUSE ON CRESTON
Drive in Hollywood, Walter Whitlow opened the door to Mendoza. "Oh— Come in. Have you—found out anything yet?"

"I've got a few more questions, Mr. Whitlow, if your wife
doesn't mind."

"Well, come in. Edna hasn't been so well—she's lying down. I
wanted to thank you—your office called to tell us we could have
the body, and the funeral's arranged for Tuesday. I don't know,
maybe I could help you?"

"I think your wife would be more apt to know about this.
Something's showed that seems to put it right there at the hotel—the staff at the Clark—and I'd like to know anything she can
tell me about Mrs. Branch's relationships with them. The
maids—"

"Oh. The staff?" Whitlow looked surprised. "That seems impossible. Why should you think that?"

Mendoza sat down opposite him in the pleasant living room, lit
a cigarette, and explained about the front-door key. Whitlow
listened in silence, grasping the implications quickly, nodding.
"Yes, I see. It still seems incredible. I don't know, Mother always
seemed to feel the people there were—nice and obliging. I don't
know about disturbing Edna, but she probably would— But,
Lieutenant, you said before—how those damned love beads—a
young person, a—one of these hippie kids?"

"We work with what we've got," said Mendoza. "This is a more important lead. It could be both—the kid connected with one of the maids some way—or somebody working for that cleaning service. We just go looking where it's indicated."

"Yes, I see that. I see that this key business does take you right back to the hotel. I'll see if Edna feels up to—" He got up.

"It's all right, Walter," she said from the door, "I've been listening. Of course I want to help any way I can. The people at the hotel—" She came in, sat down beside her husband on the couch. She looked tired and worried, her very fair skin a little blotchy, and her hands trembled slightly. She was wearing a plain black dress. "I don't see how that could be, Lieutenant. Mother liked everybody there—they were good to her. She liked Agnes, the maid who usually did her apartment, she used to look forward to those days, somebody to talk to. Agnes used to tell her all about her children and so on, it gave Mother an interest. She always gave Agnes some money on her birthday. She didn't know the other maid as well, it was just once in a while she and Agnes changed, but Mother said she was quite nice too. I just don't see how it could be—anything to do with anyone at the hotel."

"There'd never been any trouble about any of the maids, suspicion of theft or—"

"Never," she said firmly. "When Mother first went to live there, there were different maids nearly every week—well, I suppose the hotel was busier and had more employees—and some she liked better than others, but there was never anything like that. I think she was—quite attached to Agnes."

"Yes," said Whitlow restlessly. "By the way, I checked with the bank yesterday—we're both authorized to sign on Mother's account—and she'd taken out five hundred in cash when she paid in the annuity check. The rent would have been due on the fifteenth but she'd have paid that by check."

"Thanks very much," said Mendoza. "The lab's finished with the apartment now, you can go in whenever you like, by the way. I should have asked you, Mrs. Whitlow—we didn't see a jewelry case, any jewelry boxes, around—would there have been anything of value, outside the cash?"

Edna Whitlow shook her head slowly. "Mother wasn't a great one for jewelry. She didn't have anything but costume stuff—besides her wedding ring, and she couldn't get that off anymore." The corpse was still wearing it: a plain thin gold band.

Mendoza got up, feeling dissatisfied. "Well, thanks very much, but I'd hoped you could recall something more about—"

"Any trouble, but there never was any. As far as that goes," she said, a tinge of color in her cheeks, "when I say Mother was attached to Agnes, I think it worked the other way too. Really. I know about Agnes too, you know—she's worked there a long time—and I think she's a fine honest woman. A nice woman."

The trouble was, in the one brief encounter he'd had with Agnes, Mendoza was inclined to think so too.

"I don't understand all you said about that key," she told him. She looked troubled.

"Nothing much," said Whitlow soothingly. "It's just missing—but we won't be needing it, so it doesn't matter."

Mendoza got back into the Ferrari feeling as if he'd overlooked something: something had slipped past him somehow, that he should have grasped. He switched on the ignition. There was no sense going back to the office; he headed for home.

Higgins and Conway, at that end of the day, went out to look at the new corpse. At least the caustic comments of all the other men had weaned Conway from his little black cigars and he was back to cigarettes; he lit the last one in the pack as he got in the car beside Higgins.

Ocean View Avenue, so optimistically named, along here was a block of tired old frame and stucco houses dating from the twenties. There was a black-and-white and a bright new green Ford outside one about the middle of the block. Higgins parked behind the Ford and they got out; the two uniformed men were talking with a civilian on the front porch.

[110]

As they went up the front walk, the strip of uncared-for lawn on either side, they noticed the sign posted on the right side: FOR SALE, HUNTINGDON REALTY COMPANY, and across it slapped diagonally a SOLD poster.

Fred Ware was one of the Traffic men. "This is Mr. Odum," he said. "Sergeant Higgins, Detective Conway. Mr. Odum just found the body."

"Damnedest thing," said Odum, who was big and bald, with a paunch. "He was supposed to be out tomorrow, I just stopped by to confirm that. I suppose the poor old guy had a stroke or something—there's blood—damned shame."

"What's his name, Mr. Odum?"

"James Blackwood. He's a widower, about seventy-five, and it was getting to be too much for him to live here alone, he put the place up for sale and he was going into some rest home run by the church he went to. I was sorry for the old guy, he kind of resented it that his daughter didn't ask him to come live with her. Families ought to stay together."

"Yes, well, if you'd wait a few minutes," said Higgins. They went in; the front door was open.

Odum called after them, "The place was sold furnished—he'd been getting his own things packed up ready to go, poor old bastard—in the back porch."

It was a shabby little house, not very well taken care of: the furniture dusty, the couple of pictures crooked. But there was no evidence of violence until they looked into the first bedroom. There, all the empty drawers in bureau and chest had been pulled out. The second bedroom contained only a single chest, its empty drawers on the floor. The bathroom medicine chest was open on emptiness.

The body was in the kitchen. Blackwood had been a fat old man, bald and jowly. He was wearing black pants and an old-fashioned silk undershirt, black slippers on bare feet. There was blood in a pool under his head. Higgins bent and felt one wrist. "Last night," he said.

"They had a look here too," said Conway. "And in his suit-cases." Cupboard drawers were open here on emptiness. The suitcases were in the service porch, two of them, lying open and ransacked; they might have been packed up, standing ready by the back door, and rifled hastily right there. There were piles of shabby clothing, one good dark suit, shirts, two pairs of shoes, handkerchieves, an old worn leather Bible, and that was all.

"As Luis says," said Higgins, "the jungle getting junglier, Rich. A poor old fellow like this, anybody could see there'd be nothing here to steal. But—"

Conway had discovered that the back door was unlocked. He poked it open with his pen and stepped out onto the back porch. "Oh, very nice," he said. Higgins came to look.

Just at the foot of the rickety back steps was a length of wood about two feet long, part of a two-by-four. One end of it bore a few dark stains. "And as Luis also says, I do get tired," said Higgins. He went back to the front porch. "Somebody got in and beat him over the head," he told the Traffic men. "We'll want the lab."

"What?" said Odum. "You mean he was *killed?* Well, for God's sake—"

Higgins used the radio in the Traffic unit to call the lab. They wouldn't do much here tonight but take photographs of the body and weapon so both could be moved. He took Odum's address, told him they'd want a statement, asked if he knew the daughter's address. "I don't," said Odum, "but I know her name's Mackey, Mrs. Clifford, and it's on Baxter Avenue. My God, what a damned senseless thing! What a—when all the arrangements were made and all—"

"About a rest home?"

"Yeah, yeah. He just had some equity in this place, didn't own it clear, and all he got out of the sale was turned right over to the church home to pay his way there from now on. Poor old bastard," said Odum.

Higgins and Conway waited for the lab team, who said they'd

take the pictures, seal the place and come back in the morning. They went back downtown and Higgins dropped Conway in the lot; it was after six. "I'll look up the daughter," he said. "It's on my way home." Baxter Avenue was in the general direction of Silver Lake; he looked up the daughter in the phone book, after calling Mary to say he'd be late.

When he found the place, it was a neat colonial house, newly painted and smart-looking. The woman who answered the door didn't match it; she was fat, red-faced, with gray hair pulled back to a tight knob, suspicious eyes, and a sharp voice. "Yes?" she said impatiently. Higgins showed her the badge and said apologetically that he had some bad news for her, about her father. "Don't tell me he's in trouble with the police now?" she said.

Higgins told her what they had found. "It looked as if he was killed instantly, Mrs. Mackey. The place was ransacked, but Mr. Odum didn't think there'd have been anything of value to—"

"Oh," she said. "Oh. Well, poor old Dad." It was entirely perfunctory. "Shame it had to happen that way, but I guess he's better off at that. He was pretty old, you know, and getting forgetful and all—real nuisance to take care of. But thanks for letting me know."

"There'll have to be an autopsy," said Higgins, "but we'll let you know when you can claim the body."

"Oh, sure," she said. Suddenly she thought of something and her face got redder. "And my God, I bet we have to get a lawyer to get back all the money he paid that church home! I just bet."

"I wouldn't know about that," said Higgins.

"Well, thanks anyway," she said, and shut the front door.

When Higgins got home he felt grateful for the warm smell of cooking in the kitchen, and the sound of Laura practicing at the piano, and his lovely Mary a little flushed over the stove. He kissed her soundly. "It's always nice to come home, but especially tonight. I just ran into a hell of a female," and he told her about Mrs. Mackey. Mary laughed.

"People—they do come all sorts. But did it occur to you,

George, that maybe Mr. Blackwood hadn't been the best father in the world, so she isn't the best daughter?"

"It hadn't, till you said so. Could be. Where's Steve?"

"Studying for exams. And the baby's asleep."

Hackett had had a small idea, which he'd mention to Luis tomorrow, and he thought about it on the way home. Now that this business about the key had turned up, on the Clark Hotel case, could it just be that those love beads were a fake clue? Dropped deliberately to point to the hippie type, the younger generation—and away from, say, some boyfriend of one of the maids? It was just an idea.

When he got home, Angel had dinner nearly ready, and the kids were busy over coloring books, the big silver Persian asleep in his basket. "And before you sit down," said Angel severely, "you're going to get weighed. You know what the doctor said when you had your last physical, and I know you've gained."

"Oh, hell," said Hackett. "I know it too. I can hardly get into these pants."

He was up to two twenty-nine. "So back on the diet you go," said Angel. "And don't swear, Art. After all, you don't want to develop high blood pressure at your age." The trouble was, of course, that she didn't have to worry about gaining, she was a good cook, and while he gloomily ate lean hamburger and drank black coffee, she had the Roquefort dressing, the baked potato, the angel food cake. It wasn't fair, thought Hackett.

When Palliser got home that night, he was thinking about the prowler and Mrs. Short. Of course Hillside Avenue in Hollywood was a different place than that area downtown, but crime was up—violent crime—anywhere these days. He'd had good new locks installed on the doors, and iron grilles across the back windows. But, driving up to the open garage at the rear and finding Roberta placidly weeding a bed while David Andrew kicked and gurgled on a blanket nearby, Palliser suddenly felt that it wouldn't be a bad idea at all to have a big alert dog right beside those two. Behind a fence and a gate. A gate with a lock.

He locked the garage and came to lift her to her feet and kiss her. "Listen, Robin, I think we'd better figure on getting a fence around the yard."

"I know we should—on account of the baby, later on when he's walking. With everything going up, maybe we had better do it now. Of course it wouldn't need to be much of a fence—wooden pickets or something, about three feet high."

Thinking about that great big German shepherd, Palliser said, "Higher. Say six."

Roberta laughed. "You cops—you get nervous on account of all the violence you see. We can get some estimates."

Saturday night was sometimes eventful for the night watch, but this one wasn't. There was only one accident with one killed, and the only other thing turned up at midnight when they had a call from a bar on Second. Galeano and Schenke went out to see what it was.

"I wasn't never so surprised in all my life," the bartender told them. He was a little fellow with a great black handlebar moustache. "I thought he was just passed out, like always. He comes in here four–five times a week, usually he's only got money for the wine, see. He's on a pension some kind, I think. I know him—he lives around the corner on Columbia, his name's Howard. He's got a wife won't let him drink at home. I don't mind him—he never makes no trouble, sits there quiet in the corner and usually just falls asleep across the table. Most of the guys come in here don't mind him. Only, time I come to close up just now, I try to wake him up and, my God, he's deader than a mackerel!"

They looked at the corpse. He looked to be in his seventies; it was probably a natural death. They called the morgue, and went around to the address the bartender supplied and told his wife, who was annoyed at being woken up and didn't go into any hysterics.

It was, for Saturday night in Los Angeles, quiet.

Sunday morning, and Wanda Larsen off. They wouldn't see Piggott until after church. Mendoza wandered in at eight-thirty, and listened to Higgins and Conway tell him about the prowler and Blackwood while he glanced at the brief report the night watch had left.

"There weren't any neighbors home yesterday—in a neighborhood like that, they probably all work," said Higgins. "It's a funny one, Luis—one look at the place would tell anybody there wasn't any loot there. Let's hope the lab gets something."

There were still some names left on that list of heisters to find; let the rest of the men go out on that legwork. When it got to be nine o'clock and a reasonable time to expect people to be up on Sunday morning, Higgins and Conway went back to Ocean View Avenue.

At the house on the left of the late Mr. Blackwood's, the door was opened by a middle-aged man in a violently striped bathrobe. He looked at the badges, looked excited, and said, "So something did happen next door! When we got home last night, Mrs. Wells across the street came and said about a police car, and then an ambulance— What happened? Is Mr. Blackwood all right?" They told him what had happened; his wife, hair in curlers and wearing a housecoat, came to listen with exclamations.

"That poor old man! He was kind of grouchy, didn't like the kids coming in his yard, but I guess he didn't deserve anything like that! Say, Joe, I wonder—"

He nodded vigorously. "So do I, Martha. Those people."

"Well, what we wanted to ask you, Mr.—"

"Pugh."

"What?" said Conway.

"Pugh, Pugh. My name's Pugh."

"Oh, yes, sir. It seems to have happened sometime on Friday evening. The autopsy will tell us more but right now that's what we're assuming. Did you happen to see anyone around the house next door about then?"

"We sure did," said Pugh. "See, these are kind of narrow lots, houses close together, and us and the people on the other side of Mr. Blackwood's, we been interested to see what kind of people bought the house. Find out what they're like, you know, are they going to leave the radio on all day, or keep the yard up, and like that. And when we saw those freaks, my God, I was out workin' in the yard, it was about eight o'clock Friday night, still light, you know, and I come in and said to Martha, my God, I said, I sure hope I haven't just seen our new neighbors—"

"And of course I went to look, and in a while I saw them all come out in the backyard and then go right in again, and it wasn't till after dark—I was watching—they left. We sure wondered if they was the ones bought the house, but now you tell us about this, I just bet it was *them*. Did it. They was sure freaks."

"Can you describe them? How many were there?"

"Two men and two women," said Pugh. "More or less, you might say. You know how these freaks look! One of the men was black, rest of 'em white. They all looked, oh, early twenties maybe. The black one had a real bushy Afro hairdo—other man had the hair down to here, dark-brown like, and a beard and sideburns. Like they do, you know. The two girls, just long hair—both kind of dark colored. And they all looked dirty, sloppy, well, like hippies. The jeans and T-shirts."

"Did they come in a car?"

"Sure did. Drove right up in front. I got a look at that out the front window. It was a beat-up old Chevy, brown."

"Well, that's a funny one," said Higgins. "I suppose we'd better check that they aren't the new owners. Thanks very much, Mr. Pugh. We may want you to make a statement about this."

"Sure, have to help out the law. We didn't know him very good, but I sure hope you catch whoever did that. An awful thing," said Pugh.

The people on the other side were named Bowerbank, a younger couple, but they said much the same things. Noticing the freaks, they had devoutly hoped they weren't the new neighbors. They added to the description that the black one had been wearing a yellow shirt with so-called peace symbols all over it. Mr. Bowerbank said regretfully, "If it was them did that to Mr. Blackwood, my God, I coulda got their license plate for you easy, I was out in the parking trimming the edge, but I never thought. If I'd just known—well, hindsight like they say—"

Higgins and Conway went back to the office and tried to reach Odum on the phone. Sunday would be a busy day for real-estate salesmen; but after a few tries, they finally found him in the office and asked about who had bought the house, described the freaks.

"Listen, are you nuts?" said Odum. "The ones like that go around buying houses? A Mrs. Widdemer bought the house. She's a nice quiet lady, divorcée I think, and she's got a little girl about ten and a poodle."

So that drew a picture for them. And a funny sort of picture it was.

Mendoza was brooding over the cards on his desk. He still thought better with the cards in his hands. Methodically he stacked the deck for a crooked deal, and found he was still in practice.

Those love beads. He felt ambivalent about Hackett's little idea; it could be, it mightn't be. But he couldn't read anything else into the key business but that it linked X to the hotel.

There'd be people coming in today to sign statements. Mrs. Cohen, on Cicely Upton. The A.P.B. hadn't turned up John Upton or his car. The other one hadn't turned up Sid Belcher. People to sign statements about the prowler who'd killed Elsa Short—and it was to be hoped the lab would give them some lead on him. Robineau and his niece, on the second restaurant heist . . . that had been a queer little case, where that restaurant had cropped up before.

There'd be arraignments coming up next week—William Linblad, that Parsons who hadn't meant to kill his wife.

The outside phone buzzed at him and he picked it up. "Lieutenant Mendoza, Robbery-Homicide."

"Captain Kettler, Pasadena. Say, Lieutenant, we asked for a

mug shot of that escaped con, Terry Conover. We've now got a witness—he just came to in the hospital—who says it was Conover who pulled a heist here last Thursday night. Liquor store—he got away with about five C's."

"Was he alone?"

"All alone, with a .45 of some kind. The witness is ex-Army and ought to know."

"*Interesante.* And nothing to do about it, but it's nice to know."

"Well, we thought you'd be interested. No make on any car, of course. Any good to get the press to run his picture, you think?"

"If you've been at this thankless job long, Captain, you'll know about the citizenry—*they have eyes and see not.* We can try. You never know."

"What I thought."

"I'll see the papers are called and send over copies. Maybe they'll run them tomorrow. You never know, with the press."

As he put the phone down, Sergeant Lake came in and said, "Mr. and Mrs. Linblad are here, want to see you. They're nice people, just scared and confused."

Mendoza sighed. "Shove them in, I'll talk to them."

Glasser picked up Wanda Larsen at her apartment at noon, and took her to the horse show out at a big fairgrounds. It was her idea; he didn't know anything about horses. But he got interested after a while, the horses were so beautiful, sleek and proud with arched necks. Wanda had brought a picnic lunch. Some of the horses had riders, and some drivers in carts, and some of them jumped fences, and there was judging with colored ribbons.

"I suppose there are different kinds of horses for the different things they're supposed to do," said Glasser, though they all just looked like horses to him.

Wanda looked at him, pink-cheeked and excited. "Oh, Henry. I see I'll have to educate you. I wouldn't go across the street to see the usual horse show—thoroughbreds." She didn't like thoroughbreds, whatever they were. "These are *Morgans,* Henry.

The only American breed there is. Morgans do everything—the most versatile horse there is, and the very nicest."

"Oh," said Glasser.

"Before my father died, we lived on a ranch, you know. Right next to the Bluebell Morgan Farm up in Marysville. I've always loved Morgans. If I could ever own a Morgan, I'd be in heaven," said Wanda wistfully.

Hackett and Higgins had just finished talking to another one off the list of heisters—he had an alibi for Friday night—when a telex came through from the chief of police in Fresno. John Upton had once been charged with assault when he was living there, but the charge was later withdrawn; he'd accused a used-car salesman of palming off a lemon on him, and given him a beating.

"Not much of a charge," said Hackett, grinning. "A lot of people must have had the impulse to do that." There wasn't any other record on him there; he had been employed by a local garage, had a good work-record. The A.P.B. was acknowledged; he had a sister living in the area and she'd be contacted.

A report came up from Ballistics: the S. and W. .22 Landers had handed over yesterday was the gun that had killed the Booths. Hackett told Lake to start the machinery for a warrant on Sid Belcher; that would come through tomorrow.

At one o'clock Dr. Ducharme and his wife turned up; the hospital had released him and they were going home tomorrow, but he'd look at some mug shots now. Landers and Conway had just come back empty-handed from the hunt for the heisters, and Landers took the Ducharmes down to R. and I., lingered talking to Phil until the captain chased him away.

At three o'clock a Traffic unit called in; they had come across a body. It was a wonder, said the Traffic man, it hadn't been spotted before, and maybe it had been and the citizens just not bothered to do anything. It was in the parking lot of the Convention Center at Pico and Figueroa, a young girl, looked as if she'd been raped.

"It always happens," said Hackett. "I told you, George.

Eighty-six on Friday, eighty-eight yesterday, and touching ninety today—the heat wave building up, and it always means more business for us." They looked into Mendoza's office to tell him about it; he was re-reading the autopsy report on Mrs. Branch and just grunted.

At the Convention Center, the black-and-white was parked along Pico; Hackett pulled up behind it and they got out.

"Looks as if she was dumped from a car," said one of the men. She was sprawled out there, just beyond the low planting marking off the sidewalk from the parking lot. She was half-naked—a pair of panties pulled down around her ankles, a knitted sleeveless tunic still on her upper body, sandals on her feet; her long brown hair was tangled, and you couldn't tell if she'd been pretty because she'd been strangled and her face was suffused and dark, with a tongue-tip protruding. Beside her, as if it had been just dropped there as an afterthought, was a cheap white shoulder bag.

There'd be nothing here for the lab; obviously, she'd been killed elsewhere and dumped. They called an ambulance, nudged the purse into a plastic evidence bag and went back to the lab to get it printed. There were a lot of latents on it—it was patent leather —and when Duke had finished lifting them, they opened it and looked at the contents. They were expectable: lipsticks, powder puff, a billfold of imitation ostrich, Kleenex, all the usual miscellany. In the billfold was a single dollar bill, and some I.D. in the little plastic slots.

She'd been, if this was her bag, Stephanie Midkiff, an address on Leeward Avenue. There was a school library card from the same high school the Linblad kid had attended. Snapshots, probably friends, family. "Why hasn't she been reported missing?" said Higgins. "Rigor had set in. I'd have a guess she was killed last night sometime."

"Maybe she has been," said Hackett. "We'd better go and ask."

The address on Leeward was a single house, a big old two-story house that had probably been here longer than any house around. When the front door finally opened to repeated ringing at the bell, a teen-age girl faced them. "We'd like to talk to Mrs. Midkiff," said Higgins.

"Well, I'll see if she'll come—the baby's got colic," she said. "What do you want?" They waited, and she said, "Ma! It's two men want to see you—"

"Tell her it's about Stephanie," said Hackett.

"Do you know where she *is?* I been worried, but I couldn't get Ma to pay attention— Ma! Please come!"

Mrs. Midkiff, when she finally came, looked tired and cross and worried. "I never buy at the door," she said, and Hackett showed her the badge.

"I'm afraid we've got some bad news for you about Stephanie. Is she your daughter?"

"Sure, that's right. You *police?*" She looked at Higgins. "Yeah, I guess so. What about Stephanie?"

"I'm afraid she's dead," said Hackett. There was a good deal of noise coming from inside the house; he had to raise his voice.

"Stephanie? What you mean, she's—"

The girl burst into tears. "Oh, I knew something was wrong! I tried to tell you, Ma, but with the baby fussing and the kids acting up—we should've *done* something when she didn't come home!"

The woman looked at the two big men, stunned, not taking it in yet. She had been a pretty woman once, dark hair and dark eyes. She said, "Stephanie—she'll be at Ruthie's, Linda. You know how often she stays over—she's all right, I don't mind—she just didn't think to say she was, is all. What do you m—" She stopped and went a curious muddy white. "My Stephanie—*dead?* What are you telling me? Oh, my God, how? Was it an accident or—"

"Can we come in?" asked Hackett.

Inside was confusion. There seemed to be twenty kids in the big living room, all ages and all noisy; in the midst of all the other noise a baby howled steadily. The girl, who was about fourteen and seemed to be more on the ball than her mother at the moment—she'd probably been up nights with the baby, both Hackett and Higgins thought from experience—chased the kids out and got her mother settled in a chair. It was an untidy big room, but it felt, indescribably, like a family place.

Mrs. Midkiff listened to them silently, tears coursing down her cheeks. When they'd told her all they knew, she said heavily, "Linda, I'm not up to it—you got to call your father." The girl nodded and went out. "I thought she was at Ruthie's—they've been best friends all through school. I never thought a thing about it—she stays over at the Runnells' now 'n' then, and they're nice decent people, go to our church, it was all right. I thought that's where she was. Now you come and tell me— But she's only sixteen. My oldest, Stephanie. We got eleven, and it's a job, keep food on the table, but I'm a good manager and Steve takes extra jobs—and it don't matter how many you got, every child's as dear to you as if it was the only one—you telling me Stephanie's dead—like *that*—"

The girl came back. She was a skinny little thing with big dark eyes. "He's coming," she said. "He was crying. He said we should help the police any way, and he'd bring Father Michael."

She nodded. "But she was a good girl, my Stephanie," she said to Hackett and Higgins. "She didn't go racketing around—she was raised decent—how could such a thing happen?"

"We don't know yet, Mrs. Midkiff," said Hackett. "This Ruthie—they were best friends? Where was Stephanie yesterday, do you know? Did she go to see Ruthie?"

She looked at the girl. "I been so bothered with the baby—"

"She went out about three o'clock," said Linda. "She was going over to Ruthie's. And she never said about staying over, and she always did if she was going to—I was worried—" Her chin quivered but she'd stopped crying.

"Ruthie Runnells. Where?" asked Higgins.

"On W-W-Wilshire Place, half a block down. Three thirty-seven."

They didn't try to explain about the autopsy, the necessary statements; that could come later. They walked down the block and found the Runnells' house on Wilshire Place.

Ruthie Runnells was sixteen, the same age as Stephanie, and she was a fat blond girl, a flawless pink-and-white complexion her one asset. Her mother was fat too, and blond, and she burst into tears along with Ruthie when they told her about Stephanie.

"And—I—was—mad at her!" sobbed Ruthie. "I knew—it wasn't—her fault—but I was mad! I can't help—b-b-being fat!"

"You saw her yesterday, Ruthie?" asked Hackett. "Do you know where she—"

"I was the one made her!" sobbed Ruthie. "Oh, I deserve to get killed too—it was all my fault! A lot of the girls do it—everybody *says*—and it was—it was—sort of an *adventure!* She didn't want to—it was me made her—and I been scared to tell anybody!"

"Do what?" asked Hackett.

"Darling, if you know anything to help the police—"

Ruthie flung herself into her mother's arms. "Oh, I should've told you! I should've told somebody—but how could I know— It was all my fault! I'm sorry— I'm sorry! Everybody does it—the new fun thing, Rita Marks said and she's a *senior*—it was like an adventure!" She sat up and sobbed and hiccupped. "The boys put their phone numbers in library books at school—like, Tom, and a number—and you call and talk and maybe make a date—"

"Ruthie!" Her mother was shocked. "You know you're not allowed to date boys we don't know! I never heard of—"

"I *know!*" she said passionately. "That was—was why! And —it—all—turned out— I was mad at her, and it wasn't her fault, and now—it was *him,* the one with the little moustache—*he killed her!*"

"Look, Ruthie," said Hackett gently, "if you'd just tell us what did happen, that you know about—" Mrs. Runnells was making shocked noises, incoherent as the girl.

She sat there, a fat kid hiccupping and crying, and she should have looked ridiculous but she said with incongruous dignity, "I *am* on a diet. That the doctor gave me, with the thyroid pills. I've got to stick to it. But—I egged her on, and we called that number, in the biology textbook. It said Rex, and a number. And he sounded sort of nice. Over the phone. He said, meet him at five yesterday—that place a lot of kids go—the Hangout, on Seventh—he'd have a pal along for me—"

"And did he?" asked Hackett.

"He—he—said go take a walk, kid, you're too fat! It was after Stephanie got in his car—and— There was another boy, he didn't say anything—"

"Can you describe them? What about the car?" asked Higgins.

"He was about twenty, I guess. He had a moustache. The other one, I don't know, he wasn't as old. Sixteen maybe. The car—it was new, it smelled new—and it was bright yellow."

8

MENDOZA HAD JUST GOT UP TO LEAVE, THINK-
ing dire thoughts about Scientific Investigation, when Sergeant
Lake came in. "They finally got round to sending you a lab report
on Branch."

"So I may not complain to I.A. after all." Mendoza sat down
again and opened the manila envelope. Scarne had appended a
note: "Sorry for the delay but we were waiting on the Feds. Hope
it was worth the delay."

In a way, it was. It was interesting, and Mendoza's eyebrows
climbed as he read, but there wasn't any real reason for surprise.

There had been a number of latent prints in Mrs. Branch's
apartment, most of them hers; another set had been identified as
belonging to the maid, Agnes Harvey, when she'd let them take
her prints. That, reflected Mendoza, was neither here nor there;
Agnes had a legitimate reason for being there. There were two
other sets of prints at various places in the apartment: nine fairly
good ones lifted from drawers, cupboards, and a china saucer:
probably male prints. There were five others, possibly female, also
picked up from drawers and in the bathroom.

The saucer, one of the regular set in the kitchen, had been used
as an ashtray on the kitchen table. Somebody had smoked about
three marijuana cigarettes there; the ashes had been analyzed.
Good quality marijuana, if there was such a thing. There hadn't
been any hard liquor in the apartment, but there'd been a bottle of

sherry wine, and somebody had drunk some of it out of a teacup. The lab had lip prints from that.

"*Caray,*" said Mendoza to himself, "and that was after he found he had to wait for Perkins to leave the desk." With the body in the next room—

All the prints were unknown to the LAPD files, so they'd been sent to Washington. The kickback had just come through. The possibly female prints were not known, but the others, probably male, had been on file. They belonged to one Alan Keel, who'd been picked up for possession in the company of a twice-convicted seller, three years back, in Seymour, Connecticut. It didn't sound like a very big town, and possibly it hadn't many police officers; at any rate, the prisoners had been brought in and were in the process of being booked in when the other man seized a gun from the booking officer and they escaped the building and eventually the town, in a stolen car. The other man, Webster Niles, had a record elsewhere and had since been arrested, tried and sentenced to prison in Illinois for selling heroin, but Keel had not been heard of again. Nobody knew if that was his real name; but at least, the F.B.I. cross-indexed system could assure S.I.D., LAPD, that his prints were not on record with them under another name. The pair had got away before a mug shot had been taken of Keel, so none was available. He was generally described from that one abortive arrest as Caucasian, middle height and weight, brown hair, eyes blue, about twenty-three.

"*¡Santa María!*" said Mendoza, annoyed. Fingerprints could be very useful sometimes, but at others, he had thought before, the scientific investigation was only tantalizing. Here were some nice fingerprints, and they were no damned help at all. Well, some: identified as belonging to a probable user, as the X who smoked the grass in Mrs. Branch's apartment, waiting a safe time to get out of the hotel. And, appended Mendoza to that, possibly the grass was the reason—aside from getting stuck with a body—he hadn't gone on to more robbery in other apartments there.

He felt frustrated. He clapped on his hat and went home.

There, he found most of his household out in the backyard staring up at the alder tree. Cedric was barking, and the cats lined up on the back porch silently reminding everybody it was time for their dinner.

"He's back," said Alison unnecessarily as Mendoza came down from the garage. "Our little feathered friend. Him and the missus both, all ready to raise another family."

"*¡El Pájaro!*" the twins were shouting excitedly, and the mockingbird, with a flash of gray and white wings, uttered his all-too-familiar war cry, the first four bars of "Yankee Doodle."

"If you want a project for the month," said Mendoza, "why don't you put a phonograph out here and teach that damned bird the rest of it?"

"I wonder if he would pick it up," said Alison meditatively, and Mendoza regarded her with alarm.

Palliser was off on Mondays. He consulted the yellow pages over breakfast and called three contractors to get estimates on the fence. Only one man offered to come and look at the job today.

When Mendoza got to the office, Hackett and Higgins were waiting to give him a verbal report on Stephanie. Wanda was typing up a formal one for the files. "Another stupid thing," said Mendoza. "We seem to see more of it every day. The kids, I know, they haven't the experience, but— So where do you go on it first?"

"I hope," said Hackett, "we may get some news of Rex and his yellow car at that Hangout. If we have to hunt for that book—" He groaned. "Ruthie told us what it was—a biology textbook, *Life in Our World*, and it's a supplementary text to first year biology so God knows how many copies the school library might have. Stephanie copied the phone number—at Ruthie's urging—and took the book back to the library on Thursday."

"So, *buena suerte*," said Mendoza.

"There was another break-in last night—market owner just

called in, and Matt and Tom went out to look at it. If we're going to get with this, George, let's do it."

"And I," said Mendoza, "will be back at the Clark Hotel awhile." But as they came out to the anteroom, Lake was on the phone and beckoning at Grace and Conway at the door. Presently he put the phone down and scribbled. "What's up, Jimmy?"

"That was one of our pigeons," said Lake. "It just came to his notice that there's a reward on those bank heisters. The Feds made them for sure—that teller identified their mug shots. A couple of ex-cons from Chicago, Denton and Walker. This pigeon says they've got a room at the Ambassador Hotel."

"Oh, now, really," said Hackett. "Right under our noses?"

"Well, they don't know they've been identified, I suppose it's possible."

"Anything's possible," said Grace. "We'd better check it out anyway."

"That is indicated," said Mendoza. "We had some mug shots—the Feds sent them over at the time—" The bank job was two weeks old.

Wanda found them and Grace tucked them into his breast pocket. He and Conway took off for the Ambassador, Hackett and Higgins went out, and Mendoza was about to follow them when a big sorrowful-looking man came in slowly, his shoulders stooped, shabby in an old gray suit, and said his name was Steve Midkiff.

"When the police officers talked to me yesterday, they said about—identifying the body. My Stephanie."

"Oh, yes, Mr. Midkiff. I'll take you down." At the morgue, the attendants had cleaned up the body, and looking at Stephanie, Mendoza saw that she'd been a pretty girl, brown-haired, brown-eyed, nice skin. She looked very young.

"I don't understand how this happened," said Midkiff. "Oh, I know about it—the kids and the phone numbers—but it don't make sense. Stephanie knew better than to do a fool trick like that. But

[129]

the kids—" He made a defeated gesture. "Try to raise them right, and just one minute they forget everything they've been taught —and that's just enough. What—happens now? Do you think you can catch the one did it?"

"We hope so, Mr. Midkiff. We've got a couple of good ideas where to look."

"Well, that's good," said Midkiff heavily. "But then what? You put him on trial for murder and even if he's found guilty, the judge gives him maybe a couple years, and then he's out on parole ready to kill somebody else's girl."

"We're only paid to catch them," said Mendoza. "I know, Mr. Midkiff."

"You got a daughter?" he asked dully.

"One of each—twins."

"Oh. Well, you worry. You try your best, but you can't help worrying. But you know, it's funny—this is one thing I just never worried about, with Stephanie. She was a good girl. Sensible— I thought she was sensible."

"Just as you said—the moment's impulse."

"Yeah," said Midkiff. "Yeah. I guess so. People say damn fool things. Our neighbor lady, she come over last night to say she's sorry. She said, but we got ten left. As if— When can we have her?"

"We'll let you know. You understand there has to be an autopsy?"

"Yeah." Midkiff sighed.

On his way over to the Clark Hotel Mendoza thought about that; you worried, all right. About what world Terry and Johnny would grow up to, ten years from now. But there was a saying, the things you worry about never happen. Like hell, said Mendoza to himself.

At the hotel, he started out briskly with Quigley. Quigley had never, he said, heard the name of Alan Keel before. It was no use repeating the description to him, it was too general. "Mr. Whitlow's here," he told Mendoza. "I suppose it's all right? To—clear out the apartment, I mean."

Mendoza reassured him and sought out all the maids. He got no reaction from any of them to the name, and if any of them had recognized it he thought he would have. He went up to the fifth floor and looked for Agnes Harvey.

He found her past the open door of Mrs. Branch's apartment. She was saying, "Oh, I couldn't, sir. It's too much."

"No, really, we'd like you to have it," said Walter Whitlow. "Mrs. Branch thought a lot of you, you know, and we appreciate it that you—took good care of her here." He was a little embarrassed. They both looked round at Mendoza. Whitlow had a long brown mink coat in his hands.

Agnes Harvey's lips tightened a little as she recognized Mendoza. She was a good-looking woman, dark brown, with regular straight features, a fine deep-bosomed figure. She said quickly, "I hope it's all right, Lieutenant—the police are finished here?"

"It's all right."

She looked away from him. "I really couldn't, Mr. Whitlow. It's worth a lot of money, and you've given me so much already—all her nice dresses and good underclothes—"

"You know she thought a lot of you, Agnes, she'd like you to have it."

"Well, I thought a lot of her," she said. There were tears in her eyes; she dabbed at them with one hand. There was a neat pile of clothing on the couch, two suitcases standing beside the door. "If you really think so, Mr. Whitlow—"

"You take it," he said, heaping it into her arms. "Have you—got any further, Lieutenant?"

"We've got a name," said Mendoza, leaning on the doorpost. "Just a name. Alan Keel. Have either of you ever heard it before?" He watched them.

Both of them looked completely blank. "Never," said Whitlow. "Is he the one who—?"

"Possibly," said Mendoza.

"I never heard that name," said Agnes. "I just hope you don't think any of us had anything to do with it now. Coming asking for my fingerprints—"

Mendoza thanked them, asked if Louise Wilding was upstairs. When he retreated down the corridor, Agnes was still thanking Whitlow; and something was teasing at the back of Mendoza's mind. Something about Whitlow—a very brief expression in his eyes—

Upstairs he found Louise Wilding busy in the Bolts' apartment, and got her out in the hall a moment. She was nice-looking too, lighter than Agnes and with a slighter figure. She said she'd never heard the name of Alan Keel. "I understand you refused to tell Sergeant Hackett about any of the men you've dated, Mrs. Wilding."

"Why should I? I'm an honest woman, Lieutenant." She faced him squarely. "It's my private business, and if you think one of them might be a criminal, or even know somebody who'd do a thing like this, you can think again. I like to think I'm respectable. I've had one husband desert me, and I'm not about to rush into marriage again with the first man comes looking. I go out now and then, but you can be sure it's with men who know how to be gentlemen, and not common criminals."

Mendoza grinned at her. "So, stand up for yourself. I'll believe you." But all this was getting nowhere. He hadn't got any reaction to the name; if the man who owned those prints was connected to the hotel in any way, it wasn't under that name.

But as he got back into the Ferrari, it suddenly came to him what that faint expression in Whitlow's eyes had been. Relief.

"¿Cómo no?" said Mendoza to himself thoughtfully. And what did that say?

Landers and Piggott, having looked at the break-in, explained to the market owner that there wasn't much to go on. They could call out a man to dust the door, places where stolen items had been, but it wasn't likely there'd be any evidence. This was a little neighborhood market, and the back door on the alley had been forced; as far as the owner could tell them, what was missing was cigarettes, a few bottles of wine. He said apologetically, "There's a burglar alarm, but it's just to hope I scare robbers off with the noise—it's not hooked up to the police station, it costs too much. I had new locks put on and that cost a fortune. I been thinking of quitting, just go to work for somebody, no responsibility."

"But you know, Matt," said Landers, "that sort of rings a bell with me. I know, the little overnight break-ins, a dime a dozen, how many have we had—but just now, looking at that place, I had the thought—very roughly, it's the same M.O. If you can say there is any."

"As what?" asked Piggott.

"As a spate of little jobs like that we've had the last couple of months. I didn't go out on all of them, but—there've been drugstores, other markets, a gift shop, and that place—I was on that one—that sells all the magic tricks and unfunny practical jokes— If I remember right, there were seven or eight, maybe more, all broken into by the back door and all with a pry-bar. Just the brute strength."

"Not much M.O. about that," said Piggott.

"No, I know, but I just wonder if all those haven't been the same joker." When they got back to the office Landers asked Wanda to look up those files, and studied them. There'd been other break-ins in that time, but there were fourteen that bore vaguely the same earmarks. All small jobs; the loot would add up, but it was penny ante. There were four drugstores (barbiturates taken there), three markets, the gift shop with some expensive costume jewelry taken, the magic shop, and five coin-operated Laundromats with the coin meters emptied. All of those had had their rear doors pried open; not surprisingly, in the downtown area, all of the rear doors had been on alleys. It just said to Landers that it could be the same one, or more than one, who had pulled all those jobs.

And whether it was or wasn't, it didn't much matter because there was no lead on it at all.

The desk clerk at the Ambassador Hotel looked at Grace and Conway in alarm and said, "Some of our guests? Here? Criminals?"

"Well, we had a tip," said Grace, and produced the mug shots

[133]

of Denton and Walker. The clerk looked at them and turned paler; he was a willowy young man in a gray plaid suit.

"Oh, dear," he said. "Yes, I think— I mean, in these pictures they're not dressed up, and one of them needs a shave, but I think—oh, dear, I'd better call Mr. Montague, he's the manager—"

Montague was an older man, competent and brisk. He studied the mug shots seriously and said, "I've seen them around. I think they've been here about ten days, two weeks. I didn't register them in, but—" He thought. "I saw this man over at the travel-agency counter sometime last week." He trailed them over there curiously.

The pug-nosed young man at the travel-agency counter said, "Oh, I remember this one, yes. He bought two tickets on a guided tour—wait a minute, now, it'll come to me—a three-day bus tour to the Hearst castle, it was, with a side trip to Sequoia National Park."

"Do tell," said Grace. "Well, so far as we know, they're new to California, evidently they want to see some of it. What name did he give, if any?"

"It was a traveler's check made out to John Dalton—" Conway yelped in pleased mirth and the hotel men stared at him. "He had identification—"

But that covered so many things, so easily falsified: easy to get a driver's license under any name, the bank-account number, whatever. They looked at the register; the man calling himself John Dalton was registered in a double room with a James Kelly, on the fifth floor. "You don't want me to go with you, do you?" asked Montague.

"No, no," said Grace. At this hour the big hotel was very quiet. They rode up in the elevator and had a little hunt for the room number, down several corridors. When they finally found it, Grace knocked gently on the door, waited and knocked again.

There was a stir and mumble beyond the door. "Who's it?" asked a thick voice.

"Western Union, sir," said Grace.

Another stir, another sleepy voice. "What is it, Dick? Mus' be middle o' the night—"

"What the hell, telegram for me, who the hell 'd be sendin' me a telegram? Just a minute—" It sounded as if they both had hangovers.

The door was pulled open cautiously. Both Conway and Grace had their guns out. "Surprise, surprise," said Conway. "You're both under arrest. Mr. Denton and Mr. Walker, just as our pigeon said."

"Oh, for Christ's sake!" said Denton disgustedly. Walker was still in bed, and neither of them in any state to put up a fight. They got dressed under the guns, and were put into cuffs, and then Grace and Conway had a look around. They found a good deal of the bank loot, two Colt .45's, and a lot of fancy new clothes Denton and Walker had bought.

"You ain't give us our rights," said Denton on the way to the elevator. "You got to tell us our rights." He probably knew that set piece as well as any cop, but it seemed to give him some satisfaction to hear it.

Back at Parker Center they called the Feds to tell them about the capture. The Feds had a warrant on the heisters and came over posthaste to pick them up, and what remained of the loot. The pigeon, who had a long pedigree of petty counts, was at the moment clear of the law, and had spelled out his name carefully; he had a job as bus boy at the Ambassador Hotel.

Hackett and Higgins were a little surprised to find the place known as the Hangout open at this hour. It was hard to say what turned a place into the home-away-from-home of the teen-age kids, but evidently this was one of them. It was a long narrow storefront in the middle of a block on Seventh, not attractive at first glance, the ordinary quick-lunch place. But inside there were little booths with red-checked plastic tablecloths, a long counter with padded stools, a handwritten menu up on the wall behind that. Beyond the space behind the counter, through a square doorless opening, was visible a little kitchen with a grill, stove, refrigerator.

Only two people were there, sitting in one of the booths, a fat motherly looking woman drinking coffee and a fat bald man reading a newspaper. The woman looked up as Hackett and Higgins came in and said instantly, "Here are a couple of cops, Harry."

The man looked up. He was older than they'd thought at first, perhaps seventy. He had a genial round face and a fine even set of store teeth. He got up with great cordiality and said, "So they are, Millie. Morning, what can we do for you? We never had the law visit us before. Excuse me, I'm Harry Hart, late of the Dubuque, Iowa, force. Not that we can claim to be as good as you big-city boys, still we try to run a tight little force there. Sit down. Like some coffee?" He got them settled in a booth and supplied with thick mugs.

"Well, nice to meet you, Mr. Hart. We understand your place is pretty popular with the kids, the teen-agers around here." Hackett manfully drank black coffee minus sugar.

"That we are," said Hart, looking rather amused. "Came out here after I retired, tired of the winters back there, and opened up this place mainly to give us something to do, but I must admit we've kind of enjoyed it." He fetched himself more coffee and sat down opposite them, and the woman came to squeeze in beside him. "It's funny, how we got all the kids coming."

"It's natural," said his wife firmly. "We raised six of our own, I guess we ought to know something about kids. I'll tell you how it was—the first bunches of them came in, I can't say I liked it. All their noisy transistor radios and so on—and it didn't matter to us, maybe losing their business. We set up the rules and regulations, see—they want to come in here, no radios playing, no loud talk, no swearing, no dirty jokes, and they've got to behave decent, not leave the tables in a mess. And you know, kids like the rules and regulations. And so many kids these days, the silly way parents act, afraid to say no, you can't do that—a lot of kids, they've never had to keep to any rules and regulations, it's a kind of novelty, and they like it." She smiled. "Before we knew it, we had the kids around all the time, after school, weekends. But mainly we get the good ones—the really wild ones, they go someplace else. But our kids, our regulars, I like to feel maybe we've done some good here. Why, that Whitney girl came to me before she went to her own mother, and I know most of them, boys and girls alike, they've got different ideas about police from listening to Harry."

"That's good, Mrs. Hart," said Higgins. In a quiet way here, the Harts were making influences felt.

"But what brings you here?" asked Hart. "None of the kids in trouble with the law?"

"We don't know—maybe you can help us, maybe you know this one we're after." Hackett told them about Stephanie. They hadn't known her, she hadn't been one of their regulars, but they were shocked and sobered.

"In a way, it's worse than if she'd been a wild one running with any boy she could pick up," said Millie. "A nice girl, and doing a fool thing like that, but kids— He told her to meet him *here?* Rex— I can't call any Rex to mind."

"No," agreed Hart. "But come to think, boys, if she was a nice girl—and he'd get that, talking to her on the phone—he might've said that to make her think he was O.K., if she'd know what kind of place this is."

"That could be," said Hackett. "He's said to have a new bright yellow car. No idea what make."

"Doesn't ring a bell," said Hart. "She met him here on Satur-day? About five o'clock?"

"The other girl said they didn't come in," said Higgins. "He was waiting outside on the sidewalk with this other boy. He'd told the girls to carry flowers so he'd know them—they'd picked some roses from the Runnells' yard." Millie snorted.

"Now I tell you, you might go and see Eddy," said Hart ruminatively. "Eddy's a great one for cars—an expert, you might say. He's going to be an engineer. He comes in here afternoons and Saturdays, to help out. It's a job keeping the dishes washed up,

[137]

and Eddy's a good worker. Bright boy. He might remember seeing that car—not likely there'd be two like it around at the same time. Not many of the kids come here got cars, it's not like out in the suburbs. And if this Rex was here Saturday afternoon with his yellow car, ten to one it'd be parked in the public lot next door. Not often a place in the street."

"Which is a thought," agreed Hackett. Teen-age boys and cars— "Where do we find Eddy?"

"High school up on Ninth. Eddy Gamino. He's a senior."

"Well, thanks very much," said Higgins. They were both pleased with the Harts: nice people, doing a good job here.

"Any time, boys. Good luck on it."

When they got up to the high school on Ninth there were three black-and-whites outside and a uniformed sergeant with a riot gun on the front steps. "What the hell's going on?" asked Hackett.

The sergeant, taking them in comprehensively as fellow cops, said, "Sodom and Gomorrah. One of the teachers just got raped in her classroom. The other boys are inside chasing him—he's got a knife."

"They can probably use some help—" But as they started in, a crowd of uniformed Traffic men came out with a hulking big black boy yelling obscenities at them. They already had him in cuffs, and took him away in a hurry. An ambulance purred up and the attendants hurried in with a stretcher. The sergeant put the riot gun in the back of one of the cars and drove away.

"A fellow said to me the other day," remarked Higgins, "these are interesting times to live in. Interesting! I could do with a lot less interest."

They saw the boys' vice-principal and asked for Eddy Gamino. He just looked resigned, told his secretary to have the boy brought in. Five minutes later, where they waited in the outer office with its inevitable golden-oak furniture, the secretary busy over her typewriter, a boy came in. He was a sharp-faced, thin, dark boy about eighteen, neatly if shabbily dressed; he had a long nose like Mendoza's, and like Mendoza's it twitched curiously when he saw the badges.

"Say," he said, "is it about Miss Beal? I just heard about it, I've been in the chemistry lab, I don't know anything to—"

"Something else. Mr. Hart thought you might be able to help us," said Hackett.

"Oh, Harry." The boy smiled. "He is the world's greatest, Harry. Did he say how? Anything I can do, Sergeant." Hackett was surprised; he'd only flashed the badge for a second. Eddy grinned. "I've got a photographic memory. It comes in handy."

"I'll bet," said Higgins. Thinking of Steve Dwyer, he looked at Eddy approvingly. Even in the midst of this mess and madness, the chaos of the inner-city schools, there remained the sane ones like Eddy, somehow getting an education. The smart ones you found anywhere, but all too often, here and now, they turned the smartness toward the wrong goals. It was encouraging to find the ones like Eddy still around.

Hackett was explaining about Stephanie, Saturday afternoon, Rex and the yellow car. "Gee, that's bad, if she was a nice girl," said Eddy. "She went here? I didn't know her. At Harry's, about five o'clock, he told her? Well, I was there from about two on, helping out in the kitchen. We're usually pretty busy Saturdays, and the only time I'd get a look at that public lot is when I go out back to empty the garbage, the wastebasket—"

"All we know about the car is, it's yellow and the other girl said it smelled new," said Hackett.

"Along about that time, I probably would be going out to empty the cans— We were busy. Let me take a look back," said Eddy. He'd sat down on the built-in bench along the wall, long legs sprawling, and now he shut his eyes. "There's four aisles of parking, about twelve slots to an aisle. Yeah— I can't pin the time down for you closer than between four-thirty and five, but —yeah," he said, eyes still shut. "I saw it. There were a couple of light cream-yellow heaps—a Corvair, a Rambler—but just the one chrome yellow, real bright. I got it." He opened his eyes. "It was parked on the second aisle over from the back door of Harry's place. It was a Ford Mustang—chrome yellow all over—and sure enough brand new. It still had the price tag on the side window, and it was wearing a temporary license—paper strip on the back bumper. I'm sorry I can't give you that, I didn't look at it, to have it register—just saw that it was a temporary license. But that's probably the car you want."

"You've helped a lot, Eddy." Hackett didn't feel it was enough to say; he wished there were better words.

"Just glad I could help you, Sergeant. I hope you get him."

As they watched him out, Higgins said, "It's kind of encouraging, Art."

"Oh, it is," agreed Hackett. Thank God for the Eddys, still there among the chaos.

They went up to the school library and talked to the head librarian, a thin, dark young woman with owlish spectacles, Frances Giffard. On the library shelves were four copies of *Life in Our World,* and those they commandeered. With Miss Giffard's help, they had a look at every page of all four books in the next hour: among the various marginal notations, including names and phone numbers, they found no Rex.

By the files, the library owned thirty-four copies of that book. The rest of them would be checked out by students. "I could send an announcement around asking them to be turned in," said Miss Giffard, "but whether it'd do any good—"

"Well, you'd better do that," said Hackett. "And as the copies do get returned, you'll hang on to them for us, let us know."

"Oh, I will. That's terrible, about that poor girl— A person gets frightened," she said. "All the violence, all over. Yes, I will, Sergeant."

Landers and Piggott, back to looking for the heisters and bringing in the last one on that list, at two o'clock on Monday afternoon, were greeted by Lake with a telex from San Diego. They had Sid Belcher. He'd been stopped for an illegal left turn, and the Traffic men had spotted the plate number from the A.P.B. There was a girl with him, Jane Alice Adams; the A.P.B. hadn't said anything about her so they let her go. He'd tried to put up a fight, but was presently tucked away in the city jail. Would L.A. send somebody to pick him up?

Mendoza, coming in from a belated lunch to hear that, said, "You'd better go down and ferry him back, Tom. The warrant came through this morning."

"Oh, hell," said Landers. "All right. I'm not at all sure we shouldn't have included that girl on it, you know. She might have been with him when he shot the Booths."

"If so, we may hear about it, when we talk to him."

Landers got out the phone book and called the Hollywood airport to find out about flights down there; it only took thirty minutes.

Most of the papers had run the official mug shot of Terry Conover today.

Poring over all the official mug shots down in R. and I. yesterday, Dr. Ducharme hadn't made any of them as the nice young fellow in the bar.

Hackett and Higgins had just come in from lunch and were telling Mendoza about Eddy Gamino when Sergeant Lake brought in a lab report.

"*¡Qué caso tan singular!*" said Mendoza, glancing over it. "So here they are, *amigos*—your freaks on Blackwood. Now you just have to find them." He handed it over.

"I'll be damned!" said Hackett. The lab had picked up some latents—quite a lot of them—in the Blackwood house. They were all in LAPD records. They belonged to Gilbert Deleavey, Roselle Kruger and William Siebert, all of whom had records of possession, burglary, petty theft; the girl had done a little stretch for soliciting. The lab had considerately requisitioned their packages from R. and I. and sent those along too. By their descriptions and mug shots, three of the four freaky hippies were seen at the Blackwood house on Friday night.

"But that's crazy," said Hackett. "A murder? These small-timers? It doesn't make sense, Luis."

[141]

"The lab doesn't make mistakes, *compadre*. You may have some trouble finding them, these addresses aren't very recent—but you'd better go and look. At least we know, whatever the reason, they were there . . . And I do wonder, about Whitlow—but *casi no es posible*—they were fond of Mother—" Mendoza was sitting on the end of his spine, cigarette smoldering on his lower lip, fiddling with those love beads.

"At least nothing new's gone down," said Higgins, looking at the lab report. "This is a very funny damned thing, Art—"

"Famous last words," said Mendoza.

"—these little drifters, turning up on a murder. But they were there, so I suppose we go have a look for them."

And three minutes later Mendoza's casual warning came true. Robbery-Homicide, on the Central beat in L.A., seldom lacked for business. Usually humdrum business. But this was the day they were presented with that unprecedented thing, the locked-room puzzle. It happened in fiction. And in fiction it was more entertaining.

Sergeant Lake put through the call from Lieutenant Carey at two twenty-eight. "Look," said Carey, "I've got a thing, Mendoza. I think— I'm afraid it'll belong to you eventually. It is a hell of a thing, and so far we can't make head or tail of it, but it could be something nasty. I feel it in my bones. It's a four-year-old missing—apartment on Hooper Avenue—all colored, good middle class, these are all a good type of people—and we've found some blood in the hall. I want to search the building, because she never came out, by what all the witnesses say—"

A four-year-old. You worried, of course. About the hostages to fortune. "Business for Homicide, Carey?"

"I'd lay a bet on it," said Carey. "Damn it to hell—"

9

WHEN MENDOZA SLID THE FERRARI INTO A
loading zone along that block of Hooper Avenue, there was a little
crowd in front of the apartment house in the middle of the block.
He walked back there. Three black-and-whites were around, one
in the drive of the apartment, two on the street; two uniformed
men stood on the top step of the entrance to the apartment, and
Carey was talking to a couple in the drive. The squad cars had
attracted the usual attention of the neighborhood, but along here
it made no difference that most faces were black; it was a neighborhood of ordinary working people and they were interested,
concerned; nobody was calling any names.

A city crew had been putting in a new sidewalk right in front
of the apartment, half of the cement poured, the forms all in for
the rest of it. The crew was standing around desultorily, watching
the police.

Carey had spotted Mendoza, and started to meet him. The city
crew, the couple Carey'd been talking with, all the little crowd
around, eyed Mendoza's dapper tailoring and black Homburg
with deep and passionate interest. Carey drew him over to one of
the squad cars and they got in. "What's all the excitement?" asked
Mendoza.

"Plenty." Carey's pug-nosed round face was grim. "I'll give it
to you short and sweet. Mrs. Blaine, apartment thirty-four on the
fifth floor. She missed the four-year-old, Katie May, about

eleven-thirty. Says she always keeps a close eye on her, the way you do a four-year-old. Katie isn't allowed out of the building alone, and all the neighbors that are home say so too— Mrs. Blaine a good, careful mother. As I told you, you can see this is a good neighborhood, place kept up, they're all good people. She didn't think too much about it at first, went out in the hall looking, sometimes Katie May dropped into one of the other apartments, everybody likes Katie and she's a good little girl— I've seen her picture and she's a cute one, anyway. But, no Katie May. Some of the neighbor women started helping her look, and then they turned up the fact—when it seemed she wasn't anywhere in the apartment house—that she hadn't come out either. Because there were witnesses front and back, and nobody saw her."

"Elucidate," said Mendoza.

"It's—damn it, it's like one of those mysteries where the room was locked and the murderer got out by magic," said Carey. "Look at it. This is a big apartment house but there's only one front door and one back door. You can see the front. Ever since ten o'clock this morning that city crew's been there, working on the sidewalk. Six of 'em. Right up next to the apartment steps. And they all swear that no little four-year-old ever came out that door, alone or with anybody. They've all seen her picture too and they go on saying it. And the back door, at the end of the front hall, leads out to an alley that runs east-west along this whole block. The garages for the apartment are across the alley. And out in the alley, directly across from the back door, one of the tenants, Sam Appleby, and his sixteen-year-old son have been working on a car since eleven o'clock. Also, about twelve o'clock his wife came out and asked him to keep an eye on their five-year-old while she went to market. So he and the son both weren't too absorbed in the car that they had their eyes off the door where the five-year-old was sitting playing. They both swear on a stack of Bibles Katie May never came out that door, and they know her. For what it's worth, the five-year-old, sitting smack in the doorway, says so too."

"*¡Cómo no!*" said Mendoza.

[144]

"Well, to go back. The women were all alarmed by this time and Mrs. Blaine called the police. The Traffic men got interested when they heard the witnesses, and started to go through the apartment, and then they got to thinking maybe it wasn't such a hot idea without a warrant, and they called my office. I got interested when I heard the story, and came down to look at it for myself. The manager's out, nobody knows where, and all we're doing right now is marking time. I've got a Traffic man at back and front and on every floor, and there's no sign of her."

"You mentioned some blood."

Carey gestured, back and forth. "It says nothing. A little smear of it on the wall up on the fifth floor, but it could be where somebody had a cut finger. Only it looks fairly fresh." Carey reached into his pocket and produced a snapshot. Mendoza looked at it. Maybe it had been taken on a birthday or when she was dressed up for Sunday: in it Katie May Blaine was wearing a little pink dress with bows, and white socks and white slippers. She had faced the camera solemnly, a round-faced brown little girl, her hair in two neat pigtails tied with pink ribbon. "A cute one," said Carey. "I'll tell you what it comes down to, Mendoza. It doesn't look as if she came out of the building—but if she's still in there somewhere, she's being held in some way, or she's unconscious, or she's dead."

"I could think of alternatives."

"I have," said Carey. "There's no refuse chute to a basement—the apartments all have garbage disposals. I've been through the place and I can't spot anything that might pose any danger to a child. The neighbors, Mrs. Blaine, her husband—she called him about an hour ago and he came home, he's a dental technician—have been on every floor, calling her—so have all of us. Nothing. And the witnesses go on insisting she never came out. I tell you, Mendoza, I hope to God they're wrong— I hope she got out and is around somewhere. But—"

"Has everybody been hypnotized by the witnesses? Haven't you—"

"Not likely," said Carey. "We've looked elsewhere too. Up at

[145]

the north corner there's a fellow with a little magazine and newspaper stand. He knows Katie May from seeing her go by with her mother. He hasn't seen her today. Down the other way are people who knew her by sight and say they'd have seen her if she went by, especially alone. Woman at the dress shop who's been redecorating the window, fellow at the drugstore on the corner putting up sales notices outside, down at the smaller apartment building two men washing the front windows."

"*¡Porvida!*" said Mendoza. He looked at the snapshot.

"Moreover, the mother says she's an obedient child, not exactly timid, friendly to people she knows, but a little shy. Nobody thinks she'd have tried to go out of the building by herself. And there wasn't any reason for her to run away, she hadn't been punished, nothing out of the ordinary had happened. She's just—gone."

In spite of himself Mendoza was caught by the puzzle. Carey seemed to have covered all angles. This was a crowded street, not a main drag but a busy street, and somebody should have seen Katie—known in the neighborhood—if she had passed anywhere along this block. "You want to go over that building foot by foot," he said.

"I do. I'm waiting for more men. Traffic wouldn't detail me any more, and while all the tenants at home have said a search warrant doesn't matter, I'd like to talk to the manager."

"I'll lend you some men." Mendoza went back to the Ferrari and used the phone in it to call his office. "Who's in, Jimmy?—well, chase them all down here—this might be a thing."

When he walked back to the apartment Carey was talking again to the Blaines. He introduced Mendoza casually; nobody was going to mention Homicide here until they knew a lot more. "There'll be some more men here in a few minutes," said Mendoza. "We want to search the building."

"But how could she be—I've called and called, we all did—" Mrs. Blaine stopped with a little gasp. She was a pretty woman, neatly dressed in a plaid cotton housedress, and her hands twisted together like separate frightened little animals. Her husband, a tall serious-faced man in a dark suit, had his arm around her. People from the apartment were standing close around, with concerned expressions, muttering speculations.

"We haven't got a search warrant," Carey was explaining to Blaine, "but it would take time—if we could reach the manager—"

A subdued clamor rose, from the little crowd. "You can look in my place—" "You don't need a warrant, officer, you just find that baby if she's anywhere here—"

Mendoza went down the drive to the alley. One comprehensive glance showed him the back door—a narrow one, with a single step—and the old car up on blocks just outside the garage opposite, with just enough room for a car to pass between it and the apartment building. It was a narrow alley: the garages in a long row on the other side were mostly open, but three of the doors were closed. "What about these garages?" he asked the Traffic man posted at the back door.

"They weren't locked. We've had 'em all open. This is the damnedest thing I ever—I mean, where the hell can the kid be?"

Mendoza went back to the street just as the little blue Elva pulled up; Grace and Conway got out of it, and a minute later Hackett's scarlet Barracuda came up with Higgins beside him. They all huddled with Carey, hearing the story. Without discussing it, they stood back to let Grace talk to the parents; but all the obvious questions, Carey would have asked.

The parents looked blindly at Grace, slim and dapper as Mendoza, and told him all the things they'd told Carey. Katie May had never tried to run away; she was a good girl. A little shy. She knew she wasn't allowed out of the building alone. She always came when she was called. And she couldn't have got far, and everybody had been good, coming out to help, but when they hadn't found her by now, where could she have— "But she can't be anywhere in there!" said Mrs. Blaine with a frightened sob. "She'd have heard us calling— Oh, Dick!" She grasped her husband's jacket and wept. He looked steadily at Grace.

"You mean—if she's somewhere in there—"

"Now we don't know anything yet, Mr. Blaine. She could have

fallen and hurt herself some way. Maybe in somebody's apartment, and nobody there— Now, I know how you feel," said Grace. "I've got a little girl at home too. We'll be looking."

Traffic had spared them six men. They left two at front and back, and were just deploying the rest to cover every foot of the building they could reach, when an agitated black man came pushing through the crowd demanding to know what was happening. Relieved cries went up on all sides—"Mr. Smiley, it's Mr. Smiley—" "You tell the officers it's all right, Mr. Smiley, we got to find her—"

Smiley was the manager. Apprised of the situation, he said instantly, "You got my full permission, search wherever you want, gentlemen! I got master keys to all the apartments where nobody's home, I'll be right behind you. We just got to find that poor mite, whatever's happened to her—and don't you worry none about it being legal, this place's owned by a big bank and they're not goin' make any trouble over police hunting a little girl lost. Come on, let's cover it and find her!"

They covered it. There were five floors, with eight apartments on each floor. On a week day, most of the tenants at home were women; most of them had been on the hunt with Mrs. Blaine the last couple of hours. There were, it developed, only five men at home in the building; they were all night workers, and they were all cooperative.

The men covered each floor systematically, taking note of the places where they got no answer. They went, in teams, into every room of every apartment, floor by floor, and then they used Smiley's master keys to investigate the places where nobody was home.

And they didn't find her.

At five-forty Mendoza and Carey were talking to the crew again; the crew was slightly annoyed at being kept hanging around, but they were concerned and interested in Katie May too. The boss was white, the rest Negro. They were all firmly positive that she hadn't come out the front door.

"Look," said the boss. "We sat right out here, had lunch on the job. Sitting in the parking there, facing the front door. No kid came out."

Sam Appleby was trailing the detectives, to hear that. "And she never come out the back either," he said mournfully. He was a tall, broad, very black fellow, his old slacks still oil-stained from his work on the car. "I know Katie May—so does my boy Arthur —and we were on opposite sides o' the car, he'd have seen her, him facin' the back door, if I didn't—and I was glancin' up every so often, be sure Jackie was still there playin'—"

The Traffic men went off shift. There wasn't any reason to maintain a guard on the doors; there wasn't anything to guard. The detectives were talking to themselves.

"All right," said Hackett to Higgins, "what are we all thinking about? Five men alone at home here today. Just five."

"But they're all good types," said Higgins. "And if any of them had done anything to her, where the hell *is* she? Oh, I know, appearances—"

They went to see those men again; they all lived in the single apartments with one bedroom.

Chester Felleman lived on the fourth floor. He was a trumpet player in a combo playing at a supper club in Hollywood, and he was a friendly young fellow. He had let them look through the apartment willingly; he said now, "She must've got out and run off, though it don't seem likely—poor little kid." He said he'd been asleep when all the uproar started.

William Reed lived on the fifth floor. He greeted Hackett's reappearance with a silent nod; he was a man about forty, broad and brown and stolid. He was a waiter in a restaurant out on La Cienega, and he was getting ready to go to work now. "I suppose it's all right for me to leave?" he said. They'd searched that apartment too; he shared it with two other men who worked days.

Robert Wagstaff, in an apartment on the third floor, was a night security guard at a manufacturing plant, as was the fourth man, Nelson Procter, in an apartment down the hall. Both the men were young, and seemed concerned about Katie May; the apartments were clean.

Edward Mawson, on the second floor, worked at a twenty-four-hour tow-truck service garage, and he too was due on the job, he said, and he too looked perfectly straightforward, a quiet man about forty, his apartment very neat.

Mendoza hadn't called the lab to come and take a sample of that minute bloodstain for analysis, because it wouldn't be any use. The Blaines didn't know what type Katie May's was; they were Christian Scientists and didn't go to doctors unless it was absolutely necessary.

"¡Diez millones de demonios desde el infierno!" said Mendoza violently. They were standing out on the sidewalk beside the Ferrari, at ten minutes past six. "She didn't vanish into air, damn it! Now what the hell happened here?"

"I don't know," said Carey, sounding subdued, "but I'll make a prediction. I think she's dead. I think she ran into a pervert. Maybe, in spite of all the witnesses, she got out of the building, though I don't see how. But I feel in my bones something's happened to her, or we'd have picked up a trail."

The Blaines had gone back to their apartment, desolate; all the helpful neighbors had dispersed; with the squad cars gone, the little crowds passing didn't know that anything had happened here. "Well," said Carey, "no point hanging around. Tomorrow, we start hunting again. Unless—" He went back to his car and drove off.

"Is anybody taking any bets?" asked Mendoza. Nobody was. In unaccustomed silence they dispersed too, to go home. Wondering where Katie May was tonight.

Mendoza told Alison and Mrs. MacTaggart about it over a shot glass of rye, having inevitably poured an ounce in a saucer for El Señor. "But—the locked room you can say," said Alison. "I don't see how—Luis?"

"Well, cara?"

"Not to teach you your job, but—if the worst happened and the poor child is dead, a four-year-old wouldn't—take up much space, as it were. I mean, I'm thinking of under beds, and the backs of closets, and even garment bags or big drawers—"

Mendoza said sardonically, "That we know too, my love. We looked at all those places. It's just a damned mystery, and locked rooms I prefer between book covers. I just hope to hell Carey isn't right."

"Och, the puir child," said Mrs. MacTaggart. "I'll be putting up a prayer for her." She regarded Mendoza's cynical glance severely. She was fond of her gallant Spanish man, up to a point. But if she'd despaired of immediately coaxing him back to Mother Church, she had, aware of her duty, seen to it that the twins were properly baptized. Long before they'd been of an age to babble Spanish or English, and no reason why their heathen parents need know anything about it, she reflected, warming up Mendoza's dinner.

Piggott, not knowing anything about Katie May, went home and frowned over the baby tetras. "Thank heaven," said Prudence, "they seem to have stopped eating each other. They're all about the same size now—but when I think of what we started with! And all the trouble it's been—"

"Yes, I guess we don't get rich raising exotic fish," said Piggott. Separated as they were in batches in the dishpans, they were a little easier to count; after some concentrating, he made it seventy-two. "That comes to fourteen-forty, at twenty cents apiece. What shall we blow it on?"

The heat was building up; it had gone to ninety-nine today, with the humidity soaring.

Landers called in at eight-fifteen to say there'd been a delay on the flight back from San Diego; he hadn't fetched Sid Belcher back till seven o'clock, and there hadn't been any food on the plane, it being a short hop, and he'd nearly starved to death. "I thought he could cool for a while— I didn't question him." They would leave that for the day watch.

But it wasn't a very busy shift for the night watch. They had an old wino found dead on the street, and a freeway accident with two D.O.A.'s. At ten-fifteen they had a call from Sergeant Barth at the Wilcox Street precinct in Hollywood.

"I saw in the paper that you'd had a couple of heists at the restaurants down there—the good restaurants. We just had one like that, I wondered if they matched up."

"Very possible," said Glasser. "They seem bent on building up a bundle, going at it every other night. What were your heisters like and where?"

"Two of them—descriptions nil except both medium-sized. Stocking masks. Two big guns. They came into a place called The Brass Pheasant on La Cienega, just as it was closing at nine-fifteen. Got away with about seven C's."

"That's our boys," said Glasser.

"I never stopped to think how much cash a nice restaurant would have on hand—"

"No, neither did we. It's a nice M.O.," said Glasser. "And nowhere to go on it."

Fifteen minutes later Traffic called in to report a brawl in a bar, with one man stabbed to death. Schenke went out on it with Glasser; it was Galeano's day off. They left reports for Wanda to type up.

At seven o'clock on Tuesday morning Alison was just getting out of bed when the phone rang. As usual, the livestock, including the twins, had been up for an hour, since Mrs. MacTaggart had padded down to the kitchen, and both Alison and Mendoza had been trying to ignore the happy shouts and barks from the backyard, interspersed with the mockingbird's various calls.

On the second ring, Mendoza bolted out of bed. *"Ahora veremos,"* he said alertly, "and that will be Carey. He felt it in his bones—and damn it, so did I—" He plunged out to the hall with Alison pursuing him with his dressing gown.

"Carey?" he said. "You knew it—so did I. What and when?"

"Damn it, how the *hell* could it happen— Yes, we've found her. Just as I knew we would. One of the tenants there, a Jim Rittenhouse, found her when he went to get his car at six-thirty. I just got here. The alley behind the apartment. Yes, she's dead."

"*¡Santa María y todos los arcángeles!*" said Mendoza. "All right, I'm on my way." He slammed the phone down, picked it up again and dialed. In sixty seconds he was talking to an outraged Dr. Bainbridge, who swore, listened, and said he'd be on the way.

Alison made him drink a cup of coffee. This morning he wasn't choosing a wardrobe with care, but automatically he put on the sharp-tailored dark Italian silk suit, the discreet tie.

It was seven-forty when he got to that block on Hooper Avenue, having used the siren. There were plenty of parking slots on the street. He went down the drive and found a little group just standing around: Carey, the two men from the squad car, Smiley, another black man in work clothes looking shaken and solemn.

"Mr. Rittenhouse, Lieutenant Mendoza," said Carey sadly. "Will you tell me how, Mendoza?"

"*No se.*" He went to look.

Katie May had vanished neatly dressed in a blue cotton dress, blue ribbons on her pigtails, white cotton socks and white shoes, white cotton panties. The dress was missing, and the panties; one bow was gone from a pigtail. The little body lay face down on the old scarred blacktop of the alley, mute and pathetic. There was dried blood on the legs. And the body looked curiously flattened, even smaller than it should have looked.

"I just didn't feel like goin' on to work," said Rittenhouse to nobody in particular.

"The Blaines?" said Mendoza.

"I told them," said Carey. "They came down—well, you don't have to be told, all broken up, their only one. I couldn't let them touch her—anything that's here, we want to know. They're intelligent people, Blaine saw that. They're upstairs."

"There'll be a lab team here but I don't think there's anything to be got." Mendoza was smoking rapidly. "You know why. She was—somewhere—yesterday. After everything was quiet, she was brought here and left. How the hell—how the *flaming* hell—did we miss finding her, Carey? If she was in this building?"

"You tell me—I'm beyond wondering."

Paunchy little Dr. Bainbridge came trotting down the drive, carrying his bag. "Oh, yes," he said, looking. "Very nasty. I can't do much here."

"We'll want priority on the autopsy, Doctor. Can you give us an idea when?"

Bainbridge squatted, felt the body, took his time peering. "Approximately sixteen to eighteen hours."

"Hell!" said Carey loudly. "That puts it within an hour, two, of when she was missed—while all those women were roaming around that place hunting and calling for her! She must have heard them—if she was—"

"We don't know that," said Mendoza. "All right, the witnesses. They can be wrong. It could be she got half a block down and ran into the pervert. And there'll have been a lot of talk along this block about Katie May—could be he thought the safest place to leave her was right here, make us think we missed her here, put it right back to this building." Just as, he thought, that damned front-door key was the link between that X and the Clark Hotel.

"I want to take her in," said Bainbridge. "It's odd— I'd almost say she'd been run over, but there's not enough damage—" He stood up, pursing his lips. "Could have been a motorcycle, maybe along here in the dark without a light—or one of those little Honda cars, though even that'd be heavy enough to— Well, I'll have a look. These damned things make me feel I've lived too long, Luis. I'm getting tired of this place—it seems to be asking for another Flood to drown all the sinners, any day."

"The Lord promised He wouldn't do it that way again," said Carey.

Bainbridge snorted. "It seems to me He's trying to tell us something, with all these earthquakes and volcanic eruptions and tidal waves."

[154]

Two ambulance attendants came down the drive with a stretcher.

As the day watch came into the office, Mendoza briefed them on Katie May. They couldn't do much about it until they heard from Bainbridge. All of them felt a curious outrage about Katie May, not so much for the mere fact of death—as the tough Homicide cops they were used to the violence and death, though nobody ever got tough enough to look at the Katie Mays with equanimity—but because it was impossible that they could have missed her yesterday.

"Where in hell was she?" asked Hackett in frustrated rage. "We tore that place apart, Luis! We looked in closets and clothes hampers and bureau drawers! She wasn't there, that's all. Damn the witnesses, she got out of the building and got picked up somewhere else. Just as you say."

"Those witnesses were damn certain," said Higgins. And whenever a thing like this happened, inevitably they were thinking of their own hostages to fortune at home. Palliser, hearing about Katie May for the first time, looked angry.

"You must have missed her, and those witnesses—they couldn't be absolutely certain—"

"And," said Mendoza, lighting a new cigarette, "before I went home last night I came back to R. and I. and checked all five of those men out. The five lone night workers who were at home there yesterday. And they're all clean. No pedigrees anywhere at least under those names. I asked NCIC."

"Hell and damnation!" said Hackett.

And until they heard from Bainbridge, there was continued business. Somebody had to go over to the jail and talk to Belcher, not that there was much in that: the gun tied him to the Booths' killing. Parsons was being arraigned this morning. No pigeon had called in to finger Terry Conover, no excited citizen to say he'd been seen.

And Miss Frances Giffard, at the school library, had called late yesterday afternoon to say that three more copies of that biology textbook had been returned. If they were ever going to chase down Rex and his bright yellow Mustang, that would probably be the best bet, finding that marginal note.

And then there were the freaky hippies they were after on Blackwood. That autopsy report had been waiting on Mendoza's desk this morning: it said expectable things; he'd died of a fractured skull. The lab would be matching up the blood on that piece of two-by-four to the old man's type.

Gilbert Deleavey, Roselle Kruger and William Siebert—all in records. The addresses for the men had proved N.G.—they had moved on awhile ago. Yesterday, before being called up on the hunt for Katie May, Hackett and Higgins had found Roselle's sister Marjorie, who looked to be much the same type as Roselle, at an apartment on Virgil where Roselle had been living the last time she was picked up. Marjorie had peered at them through tangled brown hair and said, Oh, Roselle'd gone to live with Lorna a couple of months back. She couldn't remember Lorna's last name, but added vaguely that she used to go around with Billy Weber —or maybe his name was Holland—and they used to hang out at the psychedelic coffee shop up on Third. It did seem significant, as Hackett pointed out, that that was in the general neighborhood where the Blackwood house was.

That was as far as they'd got on it. Now Piggott and Palliser went out to the Ninth Street school to leaf through the biology textbooks, and Hackett and Higgins started for the psychedelic coffee shop to see if it was open.

Mendoza went out for some breakfast.

Sergeant Lake, knowing Grace would want to hear, called him at home and told him about Katie May. Grace said sadly he'd been afraid of that, but how the hell had they missed her? He added, "I'll come in. Nothing special to do, and you're shorthanded with Tom and Rich off."

The psychedelic coffee shop was open, surprisingly. There were only two people there, in the little room hung with the violent-colored posters, and the men from Robbery-Homicide looked twice to decide the sexes. Both of them had the shoulder-length hair, but the one with the sideburns and beard would be male. They were both wearing Hawaiian shirts and pink pants, and they were sitting at one of the tables drinking coffee and listening to very loud rock on a tape recorder. They looked up as Hackett and Higgins came up to the table, and the girl reached to turn the volume down.

"We're not open," she said, and took another look and said, "You're cops."

"That's right," said Higgins, and produced the badge. "And the door's open."

"Only," said the male, "to symbolize that our hearts are ever open to peace and love."

"Is that so?" said Hackett. "We're looking for Roselle Kruger, said to be a pal of Lorna, who comes in here with Billy Weber or possibly Holland."

"We have nothing to do with man persecuting man in the name of the law," said the male. "There is no such thing as a criminal, my dear fuzz—only differences of opinion on right action."

"Now that's an interesting theory," said Higgins. He reached down casually and picked up the lofty one's coffee cup. The reaction was instinctive and immediate.

"Hey, that's mine!"

Hackett laughed. But it would be a waste of time, trying to point the moral to them; maybe experience and age would give them a little common sense, or maybe not. "We're not after Lorna or Billy," he said. "Just Roselle, and they might know where she is."

"Oh," said the girl. "Roselle is a young soul. One mustn't hold grudges, but I must say—after she swiped that ring—I couldn't care less. I haven't seen Lorna, about the last month, but Billy—his name's Langendorf if it matters—is living with a lovely group of people right around on Burlington Street. It's called Indigo Meditation—some of them come to our Yoga classes every Monday and Wednesday."

"I suppose," said Higgins back in the Barracuda, "every

generation has its rebels, Art, but this particular point in history seems to be turning out some funny ones."

"That you can say three times."

On Burlington, they idled along looking. On the corner of the third block down was a big ramshackle two-story house with a wide front porch. On the porch railing was hung a big hand-lettered cardboard sign with astrological symbols all over it and the legend *Indigo Meditation.*

Hackett parked in the first place he found and they walked back. They climbed old wooden steps to the front porch and faced two young men sitting on an old-fashioned porch swing drinking what looked to be iced coffee out of tall glasses.

It was going to be much hotter today; the humidity was still building.

"And what does the upstanding fuzz want here?" asked the blond one brightly.

"We're looking for Billy Langendorf," said Hackett.

"Oh, then you are in luck. I am he. In case you're interested, this other free soul is Howard Nutley. What can I do for the fuzz?" He was good-looking, or might have been without all the hair: handsome, rather girlish features, and at that he hadn't quite so much hair as the other one.

"Just a few questions," said Hackett, feeling rather tired of these people.

"Oh, shake not thy gory locks at me!" said Billy. "We are, in this little commune of kindred souls, in the jargon very clean. But clean. The Supreme Court has seen to that, bless their souls. Time was, you know, we free spirits had to resort to the shoplifting and all such undesirable methods of attaining the regular diet. But of late, life is much easier, all owing to these blessed judges. Those big bad reactionary Congressmen tried, oh, yes, indeedy, they thought up a law that anybody getting the food stamps at one address had to be related, but the Court clobbered that one. Unconstitutional! So we're but clean, police. Ask what you will."

"You talk too much," said the other one.

[158]

"Look, all we want to know," began Higgins, and was overridden.

"It's beautiful," said Billy. "But beautiful. You want to know how it works?—the lovely general welfare—so I tell you. I buy thirty-eight bucks' worth of food stamps for fifty cents, and I spend the stamps for thirty-seven bucks and fifty-one cents' worth of the groceries, and get the maximum change allowed—forty-nine cents. I put another penny to it and buy another fifty cents' worth of food stamps— Well, it's beautiful. It snowballs. The fourth week I sell the stamps for fifteen bucks—and what it works out to, in a month I get nearly a hundred bucks' worth of groceries and fifteen bucks cash, no sweat at all." He beamed at them. "Twenty of us free souls in this place, all doing the same, and we live high—very high, I tell you."

"You talk too much," said Nutley.

Hackett and Higgins, who had—what with the hostages to fortune—budgets to figure, stood there silent, because there was too much to say that this free spirit wasn't equipped to understand. Maybe the inevitable end to the free—and worthless—money would teach a lot of people a few basic lessons. Maybe not.

"Do you know," asked Higgins, "where Roselle Kruger is living?"

"Roselle—oh, that dear soul," said Billy. "She found communal life a trifle claustrophobic. She and Lorna made other arrangements—with a couple of kindred spirits I'm not acquainted with. I do recall she mentioned a name. Claude Sharp."

"Thank you so much," said Higgins.

10

BY THE TIME PALLISER AND PIGGOTT GOT OUT
to the school, Miss Giffard reported that two more of those books
had been turned in. They all should be in by tomorrow, she said,
because this was the last week of school; but so many children
were so irresponsible these days, some of them might forget. She
was busy checking files, getting ready for the closing of the
library; they sat down at one of the empty tables and each started
to leaf through a book. It was tedious work, deciphering all the
marginal notes, quite a few of them pornographic; and when
they'd finished this batch, it was nearly noon and they hadn't
found Rex and his phone number.

They went back to the office to see if anything new had come
in, just as Traffic called. Some kids playing in an empty lot down
on Santa Barbara had just found a man's body. "The heat wave,"
said Palliser. "Business always picks up."

"No, by what they say it's been there awhile," said Lake.

Piggott said he'd go and look at it, and just then a lab report
came up, so Palliser took it into Mendoza's office to hear if
Bainbridge had called.

He hadn't. Mendoza was sitting there rapidly shuffling the
cards, looking annoyed. Glancing up to see who it was, he said,
"And I'll tell you something, business picking up or not, we're
going to get a rundown on every soul employed at the Clark
Hotel—relatives, boyfriends, financial status, personal problems

and so on, however long it takes. That key is a direct connection—"

"We didn't find Rex," said Palliser. "If all those books don't get returned before school closes, we may never find him. Has Bainbridge called?"

"No." Mendoza opened the lab report. "So they finally get round to telling us," he said a moment later. "That flashlight the Bryan girl gave you—they picked up some latents on it. Enough. The prowler was Lester Watson, quite a pedigree. I had that autopsy report an hour ago—Elsa Short. She died of shock and multiple knife wounds. Here's his package—you name it, it's here, assault, D. and D., possession, pushing, assault with intent, resisting arrest."

Palliser took the package with some interest. Watson was tersely described as Negro, male, six one, one hundred fifty, black and brown, various scars, forty-two. Palliser didn't ask why he was walking around loose, with a record like this. "The address is fairly recent."

"And he's still on P.A.," said Mendoza. "Come on, let's justify our existence and go pick him up—clear one away at least." Mendoza stood up, yanking down his cuffs, reaching for his hat.

The address was one of the government-erected huge apartment complexes, down on Seventy-first. As with most of these places, where few of the tenants were earning the money to pay the rent, or had many personal standards, it had deteriorated rapidly in the couple of years it had been up, and there was garbage strewn around the halls, stains on the walls where plumbing had been wrecked, and various smells. They got no answer to a knock at the door of Watson's apartment, and when Palliser knocked again the door across the hall opened and a woman looked at them briefly. She was slatternly, ungracious, smelling of cheap wine.

"Either you gents Mr. Tucker? Mr. Watson he tole me to say, tell Mr. Tucker as he's out lookin' for a job does he come, 'n' he be back sometime. I was jus' to say." She shut the door.

"Tucker being his parole agent, I suppose," said Palliser. "What do you suppose he was doing uptown last Friday? All hopped up?"

Mendoza shrugged. "Met the supplier somewhere up on our beat. Doing what comes naturally. I get tired, John. I also want some lunch."

Piggott looked at the new body, wondering just how it had got here. This wasn't an empty lot exactly; it was a huge bare plot of land on a corner of Santa Barbara Avenue, completely enclosed with a high board fence about twelve feet high. There were no signs on the fence to indicate ownership or intent to build; something had evidently been torn down here, but the earth was overgrown with weeds and wild mustard, and the tearing down had left mounds and hillocks and depressions here and there.

There was a gate in the fence, on the side street, with a padlock on it; but you could always trust the kids to find a way in to an intriguing off-limits playground. The two eight-year-old boys out there by the gate with the other Traffic man and a couple of mothers were scared now, but they'd been getting in here lots, they said, only they never noticed the body before.

By law there had to be an emergency number posted on all locked public premises. The Traffic men had called it. This lot was at present controlled by a realty company in Beverly Hills, and a very annoyed clerk had appeared just now to unlock the padlock. The Traffic men, young and trim, had climbed the fence where the boys had, at the rear where it adjoined an alley, but Piggott hadn't felt inclined for the exercise.

The body had been here awhile; he couldn't guess how long. It was male, good-sized, with dark-blond hair, and dressed in ordinary sports clothes: gray slacks, a dark jacket, striped shirt. There didn't seem to be any blood anywhere, or any bullet holes visible.

Piggott went out to talk to the boys. "How long have you been getting in here?" he asked mildly.

They looked defiant. "Since about last week, week before—we didn't hurt nothing. But we never went over to the front side before. We thought it was a bundle of ole clothes or somethin' there. Wasn't till we got close enough to see—"

The mothers were agog with interest. "A murder!" said one of them to the other. "And my Bobby found it! Wait till his dad hears—"

"Aren't you supposed to be in school?" said Piggott.

"Aw, it's only the last couple days, it don't matter."

There wasn't much to do about it but send it to the morgue, have the doctors and lab look at it and take its prints, and hope it would get identified. Piggott saw it off in the ambulance, and stopped halfway back to the office for lunch; from there he called Sergeant Lake. "You might tell the lab to go get the prints. It's been dry and hot, and I don't think he'd been there that long—they can get some."

"Will do," said Lake.

Hackett and Higgins, following the routine that so often breaks cases, went back to S.I.D. looking for some traces of Claude Sharp. Surprisingly, he didn't show up in records.

"Maybe a newcomer to L.A. and hasn't been picked up for anything yet," said Higgins. "So where next?"

"I can just hear what Jase would say," said Hackett. "Him and his simple mind." He asked for a phone book and looked in it, and there he was, on Savannah Street in Boyle Heights.

"Oh, no," said Higgins. "It can't be the right one, Art. Running with these drifters and dopies? In the phone book?"

"Well, no harm checking it out," said Hackett. They drove over there; the address was another of the old apartment houses like so many in this downtown area, and the mailbox numbered four bore the handwritten name of Sharp.

They went down the hall and found it. "I still can't figure this one, Art. These small-time junkies and a murder. It doesn't fit." Higgins pushed the bell. After a while he pushed it again.

"Nobody home," said Hackett. But a moment later the door opened slowly and somebody asked sleepily, "Whatcha want?"

It was a girl. "We're looking for Roselle Kruger," said Hackett. The light was very dim, and they couldn't see her well enough to compare her mentally to the mug shot.

"Whaffor? Come around in the middle o' the night," she said, yawning.

"It's eleven o'clock," said Hackett.

"Who notices clocks? Whatcha want with Rosie?"

"Are you by any chance Lorna?" asked Hackett gently.

"Yeah, thass me, why?"

"Suppose we come in and tell you," said Higgins. She went back inside, leaving the door open, so they went in.

"Hey, Rosie, some guys want to see you. Maybe that dude promised to let you have the barbs—"

It was a bare, dirty little place, clothes strewn around, a portable TV in one corner, no carpet. In here it was much lighter, with the curtains pulled aside; one glimpse past the door at the left showed them a kitchenette in a wild clutter of dirty dishes and food standing around. In the other direction was the half-closed door to a bedroom, presumably.

Before they saw Roselle, a man came out of there, also yawning: William Siebert, one of those they wanted. He would be the black one among the hippies noticed so apprehensively by the neighbors. He was clad simply in a pair of white shorts, and he was scratching his chest lazily. He stopped short on noticing the two big men, and suddenly yelped shrilly, "They're cops! Lorna, you damn fool, they're cops!" He turned in panic to run and Higgins got hold of him.

"You just calm down—" They hadn't expected to find a bonus. The next minute, with Siebert flailing at Higgins, Gilbert Deleavey appeared from the bedroom and with one horrified look ran for the door. Hackett grabbed him and groped for the single pair of cuffs he had on him, but before he got them on, the two girls were there, screaming and trying to scratch his eyes out.

"Take it easy, damn it—" One of the girls raked his left cheek painfully, and Deleavey got loose and tried for the door again. Somebody out in the hall asked loudly what the hell was going on. Hackett got Deleavey pinned against the wall and fastened the cuffs on him. Like a horse in halter, he calmed right down. Hackett went to help Higgins and they got the cuffs on Siebert.

In the next few minutes, they wished they'd put them on the girls instead. The girls put up quite a fight, but eventually Hackett managed to get his gun out, and pull the bigger girl off Higgins, who yanked his out too. The girls subsided sullenly onto the sagging couch and started to call them dirty names. The arrest warrant had come through this morning, with the nice lab evidence, and Hackett had just pulled it out and was about to recite the little piece about their rights when a hard hand snatched the gun away from him and a hard voice said, "What's going on here?"

One of the neighbors had called the police.

The uniformed men apologized. "All the screaming and yelling, you can understand— Say, you're both bleeding, did you know? You'd better get patched up when you take these birds in. You Narco?"

"Robbery-Homicide," said Hackett, feeling his cheek.

"No kidding? They don't look like killers, though they did a little job on you." The patrolmen were amused. They supplied extra cuffs and obligingly ferried the prisoners in.

Before they talked to them, Hackett and Higgins went down to First Aid where the nurse washed off the blood and said dryly stitches wouldn't be necessary.

They got Siebert and Deleavey into the second interrogation room and for openers asked them who Claude Sharp was. It seemed he was a fellow they'd met somewhere who was taking off, somebody after him, said Deleavey, and he'd let them have the key to his place. That was all they knew about him.

"And I heard what you said to the other fuzz. Like, homicide. That's murder, man. We never killed nobody."

"What about Mr. Blackwood?" asked Higgins.

"Who's he?"

"The old man," said Hackett patiently, "whose house you broke into last Friday night. It'd be interesting to hear why, almost anybody could have guessed there wasn't anything of value there, but we know it was you. About eight o'clock at night." Still broad daylight, and all those neighbors giving the accurate descriptions. Just how stupid the little punks could be—

Deleavey and Siebert looked at each other. "Oh. We never found a thing," said Siebert mournfully. "There wasn't nothing worth a buck even. That old man, he let us in, but I guess he was expectin' somebody else, when he saw us he kept sayin', get out—"

"It was all Rosie's notion," said Deleavey. "Might've known it'd turn out a real nothin', she's a know-nothin' chick all right."

"So you hit him with a piece of two-by-four," said Higgins. "You must have brought that with you just in case. You knocked him down and killed him, if you're interested."

They looked at each other. "Is he *dead*—that old man?" asked Deleavey incredulously. "Man, nobody meant him to be dead! It was just a li'l tap, stop his noise while we looked for the loot—"

"I dint do it," said Siebert hurriedly, "Gil did."

Deleavey turned on him wrathfully. "You damn liar, it was you hit him!"

"It wasn't my idea—"

Hackett and Higgins got tired of listening to that; they'd probably go on saying it all the way up to and including the trial. They went to talk to the girls in the next interrogation room. Lorna was sullen until she heard that Blackwood was dead, and then started to cry.

"So it was your idea?" said Hackett to Roselle. "Why? What gave you the idea Blackwood had a lot of loot there?"

She looked at them foggily, a mousy little thing with the usual stringy brown hair parted in the middle, tangled around her shoulders. "How'd you know it was us there, anyways?"

"You left some nice fingerprints all over the place," said Higgins.

"We did?" She looked at her hands. "I still don't get it. There shoulda been a lot of money there."

"What made you think that?" asked Higgins.

Insofar as her rather dull eyes showed any expression, she was surprised at the question. "Gee," she said, "we was all surprised there wasn't nothing there. Nothing! He'd just sold that house, it said so on the sign out front. Houses, they cost an awful lot of money—thousands of dollars. And he'd just sold it to somebody."

Hackett and Higgins looked at each other. "My God in heaven," said Hackett.

They called up another squad car, ferried the four of them down to the jail on Alameda, and drove up to Federico's for a belated lunch.

They found Mendoza and Palliser sitting at the big table in front drinking coffee and awaiting food. "You're not going to believe this, Luis," said Hackett, sitting down beside him. "I know a lot of the people we deal with are fairly stupid, but anybody that stupid—" He told them about the hippies.

"You coined the phrase, Art—the stupidity and cupidity," said Mendoza. "We've got the prowler identified, at least, if we ever find him home. And there was another telex in from the chief in Fresno. John Upton's sister hasn't seen or heard from him for a couple of weeks, since she had a letter from his wife. It's—mmh—a little *extraño* that A.P.B. hasn't turned up a trail. If he was a pro with a pedigree, used to running, I wouldn't be surprised, but he's not."

"Has Bainbridge called yet? . . . And you know," said Higgins, "whatever he tell us, where do we go from here on that? However the hell we missed Katie May yesterday, there's only one way to go at it. Ask R. and I. for the records of all the perverts—and there are hundreds in the files—sort out the ones in this area, as well as we can pin them down, and go out to find them one by one."

[167]

"*Seguramente qué sí,*" said Mendoza, putting out his cigarette as his steak arrived.

"And," added Hackett to that, contemplating his dieters' special sourly, "how many of them are around who haven't accumulated records, Luis? While we chase our tails at the routine, he could be somebody—in that apartment or somewhere on that block—looking upright as hell, and nothing to show."

"*Pues sí.* Frustrating," said Mendoza. "And I'm also feeling frustrated about Harriet Branch. Nobody knowing Alan Keel. As I told John, we're going back to take a long close look at all those hotel employees."

"With everything else on hand? There's also Rex," said Palliser, "and a new body—I haven't heard about that yet."

"Just an unidentified body," said Mendoza, who had called in while they waited for lunch. "Matt thought, a couple of weeks old." Even in the crowded city, there were places a body could stay unnoticed.

"Which reminds me of Carlos Masada," said Higgins. "Nothing to do on one like that."

"What we didn't tell you about," remembered Hackett suddenly, "was Billy. Billy and the food stamps—"

Mendoza, hearing about that, went on laughing for some time. "Is it that funny?" asked Hackett. "I thought it was pretty damn sad myself. Living on other people's money, the money forcibly taken away from people who work, and the damn fool doesn't even know that."

"It's funny, Arturo, in a sinister kind of way, and I use the word advisedly," said Mendoza. "Yes— Mrs. Whitlow's shrewd father, and the insurance agent thought he was crazy—but what's fifteen C's a month now? Don't worry, *compadres.* What this benighted country needs is a damn good depression, and— *¡Ay de todos políticos!*—are we going to get one! The ride on the merry-go-round comes to an end eventually, for all the Billys."

"Ancient Rome," muttered Higgins.

"Let's go back and try Bainbridge's office," said Palliser.

[168]

At the office, they found Jason Grace talking to Lester Watson's parole officer. Coming in to help out at the odd jobs, on his day off, Grace had heard about that from Lake and called around to find Tucker.

Tucker just made a defeated gesture to questions about Watson. "Look, it's impossible to do anything for that kind. What is there to do? Keep an eye on him while he's on P.A.—and the kind with any mind left, at least they'll mind their p's and q's while they're being checked on, but the Watsons can't even do that—as witness your evidence. He's been on the hard stuff since he was sixteen, and it's a wonder to me he's still alive. Now he's killed a woman, just for nothing. His mind blown by the H or whatever, running berserk. I hope now they'll tuck him away at Atascadero, but I take no bets. Did you hear about the proposal to close all the insane asylums? Nothing said about what to do with the inmates. I think most politicians are crazy themselves."

"Maybe we wouldn't notice," said Hackett wryly, "if they did just turn the lunatics loose. Enough walking around that way now. We'll try to pick Watson up before he goes berserk again."

Tucker just shook his head and went out.

Sergeant Lake was plugging in a call. "It's Bainbridge, Lieutenant." Mendoza fled into his office, with the rest of them on his heels, and put the phone in the newest gadget he'd acquired, the amplifier. "Yes, Doctor?"

"Well, she was raped," said Bainbridge abruptly. "The actual cause of death was manual strangulation, but she was knocked around a little—not enough to do any serious damage, before death. I pinned it down to between noon and two P.M. yesterday."

"But that's—damn it," said Hackett, "just when that hunt was under way—"

"In the apartment," Mendoza reminded him. "This might have been half a block away."

"Those witnesses—" muttered Grace.

"So, go on, Doctor."

"When you give me a chance. There's something rather funny,

Luis, and I don't know what caused it. I said at first it looked as if she'd been run over—well, I suppose it could have been done that way, a motorcycle or— But the body, the torso that is, has been oddly compressed in some way, some of the internal organs bruised, as if she'd been—oh, damn it, all I can say, as if something heavy had been on top of her for— What? No, that was after death."

"*¡Vaya por Dios!—¿Cómo dice?*" Mendoza bounced upright in the desk chair. "Compressed? Listen, Bainbridge—could that have been done when the body was hidden somewhere, maybe pushed under a couch or—*un momento,* I've got an idea coming—behind a trunk in a garage or—"

"That's quite possible," said Bainbridge. "There's no evidence to say. I had Scarne and Horder here, a minute examination of all body surfaces and all the clothes. There's nothing. And no fingernail scrapings."

"But a four-year-old couldn't put up much of a fight," said Mendoza. "And the dress was missing. Is that it?"

"That's it. I could probably pin the time down closer with an analysis of stomach contents."

"I don't think that's necessary. Thanks very much." Mendoza replaced the phone and lit a cigarette.

"Right up in the air," said Hackett disgustedly. "Nothing! She could have been a block away from the apartment—"

"I don't think she was," said Grace slowly. "I think those witnesses knew what they were talking about."

"Then why the hell didn't we find her, Jase? My God—weren't we all thinking of those five men living there, at home in the daytime? I looked at two of those places—Reed's and Wagstaff's —and I mean looked," said Higgins. "In hampers and garment bags and bureau drawers and the back of the closet shelf—places not really big enough—she couldn't have been—"

"I think she must have got out of the building," said Hackett. "Just as you said, Luis. Ran into the pervert down the street."

"And," said Mendoza, blowing smoke like a dragon, "was

grabbed up off the street while nobody saw it or did anything? The people out who knew her?—or anybody else? I never said I thought that happened, Art— I said it could have."

"It's got to be the answer. And it puts us right back to Records and the Goddamned routine. There's no other way to go."

Suddenly Grace said, "The elevators— I know we looked, and there's no place to hide a mouse, but if the lab had a look for traces of—"

"*¡Media vuelta!*" said Mendoza loudly. "*¡Pedazo del alcorno qué—!* Me, the blockhead to end all— The roof! My God, the roof!"

They stared at him, and were all on their feet the next minute. With no wasted words they fled for cars in the parking lot. Grace tumbled into Palliser's Rambler with Higgins, and the siren on the Ferrari started to howl as they turned out to Los Angeles Street.

Twelve minutes later the Ferrari braked in the loading zone outside the apartment house, the Rambler behind it; they ran in to find Smiley. He was just coming out of his own front apartment on the ground floor.

"Gentlemen—" He looked a little surprised.

"The roof!" barked Mendoza. "Is there access and where? From inside?"

"My sweet Jesus Christ!" said Smiley. A look of horror came into his eyes. "We never thought about the roof—my God! That's where it must've—acourse there's access inside, got to be for the elevators and air conditioning. The housing's on the roof, they got to get up there to do any repairs. We had an elevator stuck"—they were hurrying along, he leading the way, toward the elevators —"about two months back, the men were here two days fixing it. It—"

"My God, what fools we were not to think of—but if there's a trapdoor, why didn't any of us notice—"

"It's pretty near invisible," said Smiley, pushing the button for the top floor. All of them crowded into the tiny space, they rode slowly upward, impatient. "It's one of those counterbalanced things," said Smiley. "Door's built in the ceiling and when you pull it the ladder unfolds right down. There's a space there for insulation, and a trap to the roof." The elevator landed and they all piled out and followed him down the hall.

"And at least the male tenants probably guessing that," said Mendoza.

"Lieutenant, everybody here'd know about that after the time we had gettin' that elevator fixed back in April," said Smiley.

"Q.E.D.," said Hackett.

"There you are." Smiley pointed. In the ceiling at this end of the hall, nearly invisible unless you knew it was there, was inset a square board painted the same off-white as the ceiling and walls. There was no visible handle, but Smiley reached to the ordinary red fire extinguisher hung on the wall there and produced from behind it—"It's kept right here handy"—a short steel rod something like a boathook. Reaching up, he engaged the hook in a tiny aperture in the board and pulled. Silently the board swung down and following it came a folding ladder just reaching to the floor.

"Wait a minute," said Hackett. "We don't want to ruin any lab evidence, Luis."

"We've got to see what's up there. Jase, take it easy and don't fall down and break a leg." Mendoza regarded the ladder dubiously.

"Straight up," said Smiley, "and right over your head's the other trap. You can only open it from inside. But that space's only about three feet high, be careful."

Grace went up the ladder with his own handkerchief in one hand and Hackett's in the other. He was excitedly convinced that this was the answer to the locked-room mystery, and why none of them had thought of it— Reaching the space above the ceiling and discovering that it was floored solidly, he had another thought. There wasn't another building on this block over four stories high, and even in the unlikely event that anybody had been on another roof along here, they couldn't have seen—

Little Katie May, with her pigtails and solemn eyes, in this place—maybe with somebody she knew from the apartment, someone Mommy and Daddy knew—

He reached up and pushed cautiously, and the other trapdoor went up silently at about the level of his waist, and he straightened up through it. The hot sun struck glaring on his face after the air conditioning inside, and it was a moment before his vision cleared.

Three feet ahead of him was the housing for the elevators and air-conditioning mechanism, about seven feet by ten. And all around him, as he slowly swiveled to examine it closely, was the roof: the rough synthetic slate, in this dry summer climate, covered with the accumulation of thick dust untrammeled by any mark at all.

"Damnation," said Grace softly to himself. He reached out an arm's length and put his hand down on the roof. When he took it away, there was a distinct palm print in the dust. If anybody had been up here since the elevator had been repaired two months ago, they'd have left a plentiful trail of footmarks. But nobody had been. Nobody at all.

Resignedly, the rest of them went back to the office to get started on the routine. Grace said he wanted to talk to the Blaines, he'd get a cab back.

There wasn't, of course, much to say to them. They both looked haggard. Grace didn't know much about what Christian Scientists believed, he'd been raised an Episcopalian himself, but he supposed any religion taught that there wasn't such a thing as death being an end to a person. It wasn't logical, anyway. He figured that people on the other side were taking care of Katie May, but he didn't quite know how to say that to the Blaines.

"If only we could have bought that house," said Mrs. Blaine. "If we hadn't been living here—"

Blaine said heavily to Grace, "You see, I only just graduated and started to work regular six months back. I was in school up to then, training. We haven't been able to save much. There was a house in

Leimert Park we liked, but the down payment was pretty steep, we couldn't—"

"I can't have any more babies," she said. "Something went wrong. If only we hadn't been living here—"

"Have you—got any idea about how—?" asked Blaine.

"We'll be looking," said Grace. He thought there might be something he could do for the Blaines. He gave them his warm smile. He said, "You know, my wife can't have any either. At least, no luck yet. But we adopted one—her mother and father got shot by a lunatic when she was only three months old, and there wasn't anybody to take her. So Ginny and I pestered the County Adoption people and finally got her. She's just over a year now. Would you like to see her picture? Her name's Celia Ann."

"I'd like to, Mr. Grace." Mrs. Blaine looked at the snapshots of Celia Ann, in her bath and with the big furry gray cat the Lieutenant's wife had given her to celebrate signing the adoption papers, and cried a little, and said, "She's a darling."

"And I know you don't want to think about it now," said Grace, "but sometime later on, well, you know, there's always babies left with nobody to look after them. And they—get to be your own, however they come."

"Thank you, Mr. Grace," said Blaine. "We'll—sort of think about that."

Predictably, the computer turned up a large number of the known sex perverts from the LAPD files. And on one like this, as Mendoza said, there were no hard and fast rules: you could sensibly reckon that a pervert living, say, within a mile-square radius of the crime was more likely to be X, but a man might have wandered up from Santa Monica or the Valley, for whatever reason, and just have been there at the wrong time for Katie May.

It was going to make a lot of legwork.

Mendoza had had a long day, and was just starting home at five o'clock, when Lake stopped him in the anteroom and indicated Horder.

"Here's a funny thing," said Horder. "This new body—the one

in an empty lot somewhere. I went and got its prints—nice clear set. And I'd been looking at the other ones fairly recently, and I thought where had I seen that tented whorl before, and so I checked. The prints match a lot of the prints we picked up in that Park View Street place, Lieutenant. The Upton girl."

"*¿Cómo no?*" said Mendoza, astonished. "But—" The unidentified corpse, of course, could conceivably be a suicide, he thought suddenly. They didn't know how he had died. John Upton, that hot-tempered man, lashing out and feeling sorry afterward. "That's funny all right. But the A.P.B. hasn't turned up a smell of the husband. He had a little arrest record in Fresno—they probably printed him. You'd better check and see."

"O.K. I thought it was a very queer thing," said Horder.

"Which we do sometimes get," said Mendoza.

Landers and Conway took their girls out to The Castaway, that nice restaurant in the hills above Burbank, where there was such a fabulous view out over the metropolitan area. And Landers enjoyed the evening, but taking his girl home, little blond Phil O'Neill, he felt vaguely dissatisfied; he'd rather have had Phil to himself. He'd asked her to marry him twice, and she said she was still thinking about it. Maybe third time was lucky, but he felt this wasn't an auspicious occasion. She'd enjoyed Rich Conway's jokes a little too much. And Margot Swain was a nice girl, but—

That night the restaurant heisters hit the Tick-Tock restaurant in Toluca Lake, and the night watch had the Burbank force calling to match the M.O. and descriptions. It looked like the same boys.

They had heard something about Katie May from the news on TV and the grapevine; the locked-room puzzle. It was an offbeat one, and they kicked it around a little.

Glasser was still driving the loaner, and feeling annoyed at the garage; they'd said he could have his own car back today, but it hadn't been ready and the old Plymouth had developed a noisy muffler.

At nine-thirty they got a call: two men attacked and robbed on the street by two j.d.'s, one seriously hurt. Glasser and Galeano went out to look at it, and found the squad-car men holding one suspect. The ambulance had come and gone.

"We were just on our way to the parking lot," said the uninjured citizen, dazed, talking compulsively. "We both work at the post office, Bob and I've known each other fifteen years—Bob Thatcher—we'd been overtime on account of everything piling up—the Goddamn standards lowered so much, you get all these illiterates can't read, the mail piling up, and— But some of us are still conscientious—we were just on the way to the lot, Bob talking about all the damn inflation and prices— Those two came running up behind us and knocked Bob down, grabbed me, they got my wallet, the one that got away—he had a knife—but I got hold of the other one, that one, and—"

His name was William Spears, a middle-aged man, lean and gray, ordinary looking. He had held on to the other one, and dragged him back into the post-office building and yelled for help and cops. The other one had got away.

They looked at the one they had. He wouldn't say anything, sullen; but surprisingly he had a Social Security card on him. His name was Raymond Halley, and he was about twenty. He wouldn't tell them about his pal. They stashed him in jail for the attention of the day watch.

The hospital said Thatcher was in serious condition. They had to notify his wife.

On Wednesday morning, with the office back to full strength, Mendoza came in late at eight-thirty and read the report Glasser had left on the assault with intent. At least they had one in jail. He might be persuaded to tell who the other one was.

Hackett had gone over to talk to him, said Lake.

At nine o'clock the lab called. "This is a queer one, Lieutenant," said Scarne. "This new body—Horder said he called you about it—we've made him. We asked Fresno for Upton's prints last night and they sent 'em right down, it was the first thing I looked at. It's Upton all right, the body."

"*¡Cómo no!*" said Mendoza. "You don't tell me." The body there, maybe, since the night he'd killed his wife. Maybe suiciding in remorse. But how the hell and why had he climbed over that fence to do it in such a funny place? "So, thanks very much." He told Lake to call Bainbridge's office, see if there'd been an autopsy yet; at least they might give him the cause of death.

Everybody was out on the inevitable dogged routine.

"Excuse me, Lieutenant," said Sergeant Lake formally, at the door ten minutes later. "Mr. and Mrs. Whitlow would like to see you."

Mendoza looked up, and what Mrs. MacTaggart said was his second sight fingered a little cold line up his spine. "Oh? Shoot them in, Jimmy."

11

THE WHITLOWS CAME IN RATHER HESI-
tantly. Mendoza had stood up beside his desk, and greeted them
with veiled curiosity. They both looked ghastly. Mrs. Whitlow
was in a plain gray dress, her hair untidy, and no makeup on;
Whitlow correct in a dark suit, but his eyes were tired.

Mendoza waited for them to open a conversation; the little cold
finger was still edging up his spine. He asked them to sit down,
and Whitlow guided his wife to one of the two chairs in front of
the desk, took the other. He got out cigarettes and gave one to her,
lit it, lit his own. Mendoza sat down again and picked up the gold
desk lighter. "Have you thought of something you haven't told
us?" he asked at last.

"Yes," said Whitlow flatly. "That's a way to put it. I'm sorry,
this isn't easy. My wife—thought of it first, and we've talked—and
I do see that it could possibly—might just possibly—have—
something to—do with Mother. That we should tell you."

She raised her eyes from her cigarette. "It's hard for Walter to
say it, Lieutenant, because he—we've cut all connections now.
There wasn't anything else to do— I tried—we both tried so hard,
for such a long time, but I came to see it—it was a waste of time."

"I can tell him, Edna. You see, our daughter—our daughter
Harriet—"

"We'd been married ten years before she was born," said Edna
Whitlow, "and you can imagine how we felt. She was such a

pretty baby—we named her for Mother, you see. And maybe—it's a thing parents do—maybe we spoiled her, indulged her. Too much. Believed all the—the jargon about not punishing or—" She shook her head blindly. "And we thought afterward—if we'd sent her to the private schools instead—but I guess we'll never know about that." She put out her cigarette, took a tight grip on her handbag, and said, "And I suppose—the police—hear the same story from a lot of parents these days. Don't they? How could she, how did we go wrong, what can we do? Oh, God, the times we tried to reach her, the ways we tried— But you know what I'm telling you. We found she was taking drugs when she was still in high school. Then she dropped out, and we didn't know where she was for six months. Then she came home asking for money. We—"

"Call that a synopsis of the last eight years," said Whitlow, "and leave it at that. As my wife says, we tried. That psychiatrist, after I'd listened to him half an hour I thought he was on drugs too—another waste of time, we didn't send her there. She wouldn't have gone anyway. I don't know and after all this while I don't care all the places she'd lived, the men she's lived with, since she left—some of those communes, the cheap rooms, the— At first we didn't like to think of her going hungry, and when she came we gave her money—we thought as long as she came, it was a link, sometime we might reach her, might— But in the end I saw we never would. She's lost, she's gone. It's as if she'd died, Lieutenant—or been possessed by that—that slut of a drug-ridden—"

There was a long pause. "You see," she said painfully, "it was that key. I heard you talking about it that day, and I asked Walter about it, but he wouldn't tell me. Because—he'd already thought what it might—"

"Oh, my God," said Whitlow tiredly, "how far can a man rationalize? Yes, I'd seen it was no use—she can't be reclaimed. But to think of—anything worse—"

"I think," she said, "women are inclined to look at these things a little straighter. When he did tell me, I saw it right away, and I

[179]

thought we'd better tell you. You know how long Mother'd lived at the Clark. I used to take Harriet with me, to see Grandma—she used to like that, especially all that time back when the hotel was busier, all the people. That's—when she was quite a baby, three, four. And Mother would come downstairs when we left, we'd talk to Mr. Quigley and— Well, that doesn't matter. But the first time Harriet came home—I thought it was going to be all right, she was going to do everything she promised, get off the drugs and straighten up. She stayed home three months that time. And Mother had been—so distressed over it—I took Harriet to see her, we were all so happy that she was home. And you see, that was the very day—that Mr. Quigley came to explain—how they were going to start locking up at midnight, and gave Mother that key to the front door. She put it on her ring right away."

"¡Ca!" said Mendoza softly.

"She'd—remember that," said Edna Whitlow. "You said to Walter, somebody knowing about that key, and the hotel being locked at midnight, made you sure it was one of the hotel people. But I never thought any of them would have—anything to do with—what happened to Mother. And I just saw how it could be. Mother 'd never given up hoping she'd come home. Be good. I—we never told her about some of the men we saw her with, coming asking—or the places she'd lived, we used to go begging her— But if she'd come—and asked Grandma for help—" She stopped.

"And doesn't that fall into place," said Mendoza, fitting jigsaw pieces in his mind. "Yes. I'll have to ask you if you know where she's living now."

"She's probably in your records, Lieutenant," said Whitlow. "I don't know if she's still at the address we had two months ago. It's on Howard Drive out in Monterey Park, I've never been there. I don't know if she was there alone or how she was getting money for the junk, for food. I said she needn't come to us again—we were finished. And she laughed at me." He got up. "So we've told you. Edna—"

"It's easy to say, isn't it," she said to Mendoza, "that I'll never forgive myself I didn't make Mother move away. If Harriet hadn't known—and about that monthly check too—"

"We don't *know*," he said. "It's just possible."

"Oh, I know," she said. "I've known ever since I heard about that key." She nodded to Mendoza; they went out quietly.

And the jigsaw pieces fitted better this way than the other. Mendoza got up and went out to the anteroom; Hackett was just coming in shepherding a man before him. "Who have you got?" asked Mendoza.

"One off the list of perverts, what else?"

"Stash him away," said Mendoza, "or let somebody else talk to him. We're going calling." He told Hackett about this on the way downstairs. They stopped at R. and I. to see if they had Harriet Whitlow in the files. She was there, from five years back: possession, soliciting, several counts. She'd served a single three-month sentence in the County Jail. The latest address in their records wasn't the same one Whitlow had given Mendoza.

"So we try there first."

They had a little hunt for the address, over in east L.A. When they found it, it was an old stucco four-family place looking ready to fall apart, and there was a sheriff's notice posted that it had been condemned. "*¡Condenación!*" said Mendoza, but they went in to see. They got no answer at the right-hand door on the ground floor; the place looked deserted, but they went to try the left one.

It was jerked open suddenly from inside as they got to it, and a man appeared talking over his shoulder loudly. "And you can damn well put up or shut up, you little bitch! When I get back with the john, you play up or I'll give you a working— Who the hell are you?" He brought up against Hackett's bulk solidly. Mendoza had the badge out. The man swore obscenely and expressively, but Hackett had a grip on him.

He was about twenty-eight, medium height and weight, dark-haired. "Now I wonder," said Mendoza, "if this could be Mr. Alan Keel."

The man went tense and quiet under Hackett's hand, and just as a precaution Hackett patted him down and got his own gun out. Mendoza pushed the door farther open and they went in.

This was Harriet Whitlow; they'd seen her mug shot now. She was twenty-four, and she looked twenty years older. She'd been a pretty girl once, blond like her mother, but the years of drugs had blotched her skin and puffed bags under her bloodshot eyes and the hard living had marked her. She was dirty, and thin, and sloppily dressed in shorts and a filthy terry halter, and she stared at Mendoza and Hackett in dull surprise.

"Cops," she said wearily, eyeing the badge. "On account the building's gonna be torn down and we got to get out."

"Cops," said Mendoza, "on account of your having the little brainstorm about visiting Grandma a week ago tonight when you were short of the money for junk."

The drugs, of various types, did nothing at all for the user's brain; she was surprised, and hadn't any quick defense, even automatic denial. "How'd you know about that?" she asked stupidly.

"Oh, we generally get there," said Mendoza. "And I rather think this *hombrate* was with you. Have you got a name?"

"Go to hell," said the man.

"His name's Alan Lord."

"And you shut up!"

Mendoza glanced around at the bare dirty room where they'd been camping out. Odds and ends of clothes, packages of potato chips, cheese crackers, soft drink bottles. Among the miscellany on a rickety table was a woman's handbag, shabby white plastic. Mendoza eyed it; legally, he couldn't look inside it without a warrant unless they resisted arrest.

"You're both coming in," he said.

Suddenly she came out with a string of obscenities, as it reached her that she was going to be taken in, away from the drugs, whatever she was on at the moment. She grabbed up the bag, first thing to her hand, and threw it at Mendoza clumsily. Instinctively he ducked, and the bag flew open and scattered things around him on the floor—lipsticks, a compact, an aspirin bottle full of red barbs, a hypo in its own box, a shower of small coins—and a key.

"¡*Qué mono!*" said Mendoza. "Thank you so much, Miss Whitlow." It was the Yale key for the front door of the Clark Hotel.

"Goddamn you"—she turned on the man—"I bet you left some prints—you thinking you're so damned smart—"

"Shut up," he said automatically.

"You're both under arrest," said Hackett, and began to recite the set piece about rights.

The jungle, thought Mendoza, looking at the girl. "Grandma opened the door to you right away, did she? Quite possibly she'd have given you money if you asked nicely. Just why did she have to be killed?"

The girl's mouth was sullen; she jerked an indifferent shoulder at him. "This creep had to be along—she didn't like his face or something, started to raise a fuss. She was old and ready to die, what the hell? And then when that damn snotty little night clerk went off, the damn emergency door—"

"But you remembered the right key," said Mendoza. "Yes." He went out and used the phone in the Ferrari to call for a squad car. When it came, they handed them over to be ferried in. What the girl had said would make a statement of sorts if she'd sign it; but it had probably been the man who'd killed Mrs. Branch.

Mendoza was curious about him, and they questioned him at the jail; they got nothing out of him, not even a name. "Lord will do," he said flatly. When they processed him in, Mendoza asked for the prints to be sent to the lab, and eventually they were identified as those found in that apartment, tied to the name of Keel. Maybe neither was his right name; conceivably they'd never know.

Mendoza applied for the warrant; it would probably be called murder two and conspiracy.

* * *

Landers had gone over to the jail to talk to Raymond Halley on that assault last night. The second post-office employee, Bob Thatcher, was listed in critical condition at the receiving hospital; he'd been stabbed several times.

Halley was about twenty, and Landers felt that he'd talked to so many like him in the last few years, all the faces blended into one. First, Halley was sullen and silent. When Landers told him about Thatcher, he suddenly saw the light—he was in jail and his pal wasn't. "Listen," he said to Landers, "Pat had the knife, I didn't. I just knocked that one guy down and took his wallet—it was Pat—"

"Pat who?" asked Landers.

"Uh—Pat Norton. See, we been living in one of these communes, over in Hollywood, only Pat got fooling with some girl and her old man clobbered him— I tried to help him and we both got thrown out, and those Goddamned thieves stole all our food stamps!" said Halley indignantly. "We didn't have nothing but about thirty lousy bucks I got—" He stopped.

"Got where?" asked Landers.

"Well, uh, I grabbed a purse from a dame in the street—night before last, I guess. We got a room to sleep in and then that damn fool Pat hadda go and blow the rest of it on speed! So we—"

"Where's the room?" asked Landers. "Do you think he went back there?"

"How the hell would I know? All the clothes we got are there." He gave Landers the address; it was on Temple.

Landers went back to the office to give that to Wanda for typing. Higgins had gone out hunting Lester Watson again; everybody else was busy at the routine, hunting for the perverts off that list, when they found them bringing them in to question. Conway was just emerging from a session in an interrogation room, and Landers suggested that they go look for Norton together. He still had the knife, presumably, and if he'd been riding high on the Methedrine— They found the address, an old rooming house, and went in. An indifferent fat woman downstairs said there were two young fellows had rented her second back a couple days ago. They went upstairs.

They found Pat Norton sitting on the bed, taking off his shoes. He was about Halley's age, with the long hair and a scruffy little beard, and he looked dazed and unwell, his eyes shot with red. "Cops?" he said. "What do the fuzz want? Where's Ray?" He looked around as if suddenly aware of something missing.

"In jail," said Landers. "You remember ripping off those two fellows last night? On the street? One of them grabbed Ray. He told us where to find you."

"Oh," said Norton. "Oh. What'd you say we did? I just found my way back here awhile ago— I don't know where I been." Absently he started to take things out of his pockets, and the first thing he brought out was the knife—about an eight-inch blade, still stained. Landers took it away from him. The second thing was a wallet, with a few bills in it, bulging otherwise with I.D., snapshots. Landers looked at that; it was Thatcher's wallet.

"Do you know that the man you stabbed is in critical condition, that he may die?" asked Conway.

Norton stared at them open-mouthed. "I don't remember stabbing anybody. But I don't know— I been on speed. A real high ride, man. I don't remember anything Ray and I did all yesterday. Like I say, I just got back here awhile ago—don't know where I been—"

They took him in, and would be applying for the warrant. As they handed him over to the jailer, he turned to Landers and said seriously, "Did I do that? Stab somebody? I honest to God don't remember. Say, you think if you give me one of those—you know—lie-detector tests, it'd say for sure?"

It was getting on toward one o'clock when Mendoza and Hackett got back, and found the office humming quietly. A piece of routine legwork like this was tiresome, but it kept them busy. In the natural course of events, the kind of men they were hunting were sometimes elusive, usually loners, often drifting around—they wouldn't find all of them on that list. Lake said Higgins hadn't found Watson yet, and was out on the other thing. Grace had just brought in another one to question; they were both interested to hear about Harriet Whitlow. Having talked to Landers, Grace passed on the news about Norton and Halley, and just about then the switchboard flashed and Lake plugged in. "Robbery-Homicide, Sergeant Lake . . . Thanks for letting us know. . . . The hospital. Thatcher just died."

"Well, convenient timing," said Mendoza cynically. "We were going to ask a warrant for assault with intent. Now it'll be murder two." He wondered if he ought to call the Whitlows, and decided against it: Edna Whitlow knew, and had it to live with.

"That's funny," said Wanda suddenly. The mail had just been delivered, and she'd been going through it. She held up a long envelope. "It's for Sergeant Palliser. A personal letter, and we're not supposed to get personal mail at the office—"

Mendoza took it and looked at it idly. In the upper left-hand corner of the envelope was a little black-and-white cut of a dog's head: a German shepherd. The return address was Langley Kennels, For the Finest in Shepherds, M. Borman, Tempe, Arizona. It was addressed in typescript to Palliser at LAPD headquarters. "Now I wonder what that's about," said Mendoza. "Leave it on his desk. I guess you and I have lunch alone, Arturo."

Palliser, coming in at two-thirty with one Wilbur Sullivan from the list of perverts, took one look at the letter and groaned. He had known that Madge Borman, a nice woman, wouldn't forget that promise. Better know the worst: he slit the envelope and brought out a friendly effusion from the nice woman. —Don't know what I'd have done, so far from home and laid up in the hospital, so kind, seeing that Azzie was looked after. Marla's pups born on April first, ready for new homes at the end of June or first week in July. And, remembered what you said—watchdog for the baby—shall have one of the girls, a very nice little girl registered as Trina. And, you can pick her up at the airport, let you know when—

Palliser felt uneasy; that was so definite. Well, nothing to be done immediately. If he found Robin in a good mood tonight, break the news gently.

Higgins had just come back after another abortive look for Lester Watson; they teamed up to talk to Sullivan.

And they complained about the endless routine: on other cases, reduced to finding the possibles out of Records and bringing them in to question, they had spent days at it only to come up with nothing. But sometimes the routine paid off right away.

All of a sudden, it looked as if that was going to happen here too, and Palliser and Higgins felt a little excited. If Sullivan was X on their locked-room puzzle, they might hear some answers in a minute.

He was a tubby man in his forties, going bald, and his eyes were furtive. He had a record of child molestation, one count of child rape that hadn't stuck; there'd been some legal hassle, as often happened, and with everybody knowing he was guilty he'd gone free. The third time he was picked up for molestation he'd been sent to Camarillo; he'd been out of there for a year. He was living with his mother at an apartment on Crocker Street, and he had a job in a men's store on Vernon Avenue, about three blocks up from Hooper.

And after forty minutes' session with him Higgins said, "I like him, John. I like him a lot, on Katie May. He's got the right record and all the wrong answers. Let's hear what Luis thinks."

Mendoza rather liked Sullivan too, just at first. Sometimes they got lucky and turned up an ace on almost the first draw.

Sullivan said he'd been at work all day Monday. He hadn't done anything bad like that, he was all cured of wanting to do like that since he'd been in the hospital. They asked if the store owner would back that up. He shuffled around and said Mr. Brown had been out about noon, to the bank, but he'd been in the store all the time. Higgins had gone out to see Brown, who said he'd been out of the store, leaving Sullivan there alone, from noon to one-thirty, and he was damned annoyed and about to fire him, because a good customer had come in just today and said he'd been there about one o'clock on Monday and the store was empty, no clerk there. Leaving the place open, said Brown, for shoplifters; just walking out—

That was definitely interesting, and Mendoza went back to the interrogation room where Sullivan was sitting huddled miserably in the little chair. "Mr. Brown's found out about your leaving the store open on Monday and just walking out," he said conversationally. "Where did you go, Sullivan?"

"Oh, hell, I was scared he would," said Sullivan. He was a mixture: a hint of some Oriental in his eyes, and he was a light saffron color. He said earnestly, "Honest, I don't—I don't want to do that to kids any longer. I never did that to that little kid. Honest."

"Where did you go on Monday?" asked Higgins.

"Oh, hell," said Sullivan. "If it isn't one thing it's another. Now I got to tell you and I get in more trouble. Oh, hell. I went out to put a bet on a horse. That's all."

"Where?" asked Palliser.

"Oh, hell," said Sullivan unhappily. "I don't see nothing wrong, put a bet on a horse. Don't see why it should be against the law. Now you close up that place, and everybody blames me. Oh, hell. It's Sam's Bar and Grill down the block. There's a racing board up in back."

"*Se comprende*," said Mendoza amusedly in the hall. "Out of the frying pan—"

"See if it checks out," said Higgins.

"And just how do we go about that?" asked Palliser.

"There are other specialists in the building," said Mendoza. He went into his office, told Lake to get him Vice, and laid the phone in the amplifier. The desk sergeant answered and he asked, "Is Perce there? Mendoza." In a minute he was talking to Lieutenant Andrews. "Perce, we've just heard there might be a horse parlor in the back of Sam's Bar and Grill out on Vernon."

"Is that place open again?" said Andrews. "Between you and

me, Luis, I don't see that it's very logical it should be legal inside the fence and illegal out, but that's what the law says and we're paid to enforce it. Besides, those operations take quite a cut. The last time we closed that one up was six months ago, thanks for the tip."

"Well, we've got a rather important alibi hanging on what—mmh—Sam and his cohorts may have to say." Mendoza explained and Andrews laughed.

"Yes, I see—unlucky for Sullivan. Well, we're sort of at loose ends here, some of us may as well go down there and pull a raid. I'll get back to you, Luis."

"And until we do hear, we hold Sullivan," said Higgins. "Just in case."

"I think so. The neighborhood's suggestive, but I also think"—Mendoza leaned back smoking meditatively—"I have the feeling, George, that the answer isn't that easy. That simple. Sullivan is obvious—and incredible."

"You just lost me."

"He was so handy—right there, a known pervert, a couple of blocks away. Did he suddenly get the urge and wander off his job looking for any child? Did Katie May run away, something she'd never done before, get out of the building unseen by all those witnesses, and just fortuitously meet up with Sullivan two, three blocks away? How? And if it was that far away, how did he know where she'd come from, to put her back there? And—"

"All right, I'm caught up," said Higgins, rubbing his prognathous jaw. "But I still want to clear him out of the way."

"*Conforme.* We'll be hearing what Vice picks up."

At five o'clock Sergeant Lake, with an incoming call, glanced around the office for somebody to take it. Three interrogation rooms were in use, and nobody but Wanda visible, but as he turned back to the phone Palliser came in with a young Negro fellow who was protesting that he was clean, real clean. "Oh, John."

"Anything new?"

"It's that librarian—Miss Giffard."

"Oh." Palliser took the phone and said his name.

"There are only six more of those books have been returned, Sergeant," said Miss Giffard. "Really, the students are so irresponsible—and I doubt if there'll be any more, goodness knows where they'll be. It's the last day of school tomorrow, graduation exercises Friday night, and only a handful of them will be here tomorrow, probably none coming in here. And then we're closed till September—oh, summer school starts in two weeks but—"

"Yes," said Palliser. "Well—" That was another piece of routine, where the tedious work was the only answer. If they were ever going to identify Rex, it would probably be by finding his name and phone number in one copy of that damned book. Ruthie Runnells had said he was too old to be in school, and that chrome yellow Mustang with its temporary license plates might have been sold by any Ford agency in Greater Los Angeles; sometimes people shopped around. "I'll come over and get the books. We can return them to the school when it's open again."

He left the suspect—a rather unlikely one—under Lake's eye and went to pick up the books, giving Miss Giffard a receipt.

Lieutenant Andrews called back just as Mendoza was about to leave the office. He said that Sam's horse parlor had been closed down. Sam and three of his cohorts were under arrest, and had resignedly backed up Sullivan's story: Sullivan had been there from half-past twelve to half-past one on Monday.

"I knew it couldn't be that easy," said Higgins. They let Sullivan go; if Andrews wanted to pull him in, let him. Mendoza could never get excited about the gamblers; it was a human foible, and there were others who did a lot more harm.

The day watch was drifting out. The routine would go on, on Katie May. Maybe one of those biology texts was the one with Rex's name in it. And sometime they'd pick up Lester Watson; there was an A.P.B. out on him. The restaurant heisters hadn't hit in their territory again. And there'd be other things coming along.

At which point, hat in hand, cigarette snuffed out in the ashtray,

Mendoza uttered a sharp yelp and said, "*¡Mil rayos! ¡Dios me libre,* I'm going senile! I'm—"

"What hit you?" asked Sergeant Lake, hand on the door.

"Upton!" said Mendoza. "John Upton! And it went out of my head completely, I never—" He manipulated the switchboard and called Bainbridge's office, but nobody was there. "Remind me in the morning to find out if he committed suicide or what."

However, they were to have other things to think about on Thursday morning.

On Wednesday, his day off, Glasser spent an hour or so solemnly reading a juvenile book Wanda had given him, *Justin Morgan Had a Horse.* She'd also given him a magazine all about Morgan horses, and the photographs were nice. Beautiful creatures, she said fondly. Glasser liked the Morgans all right—they were very handsome. But he liked Wanda better, and if she was interested in horses—

He could hear her saying, Not horses, *Morgans.*

Mendoza was just getting undressed at eleven-thirty, wandering around the bedroom and looking approvingly at Alison sitting up in the king-sized bed, red hair shining in the lamplight, doing her nails. "You look very fetching, *enamarada.* It's a pity you've got an idiot for a husband. Forgetting that entirely—but at least we know, on Mrs. Branch—and what a hell of a thing for the Whitlows." And the hostages to fortune—you never knew how they'd turn out. You tried, you hoped, but you didn't know.

Their particular hostages right now had progressed to the last lesson in the first McGuffey Reader and were demanding a hen so they could gather eggs "like *los niños* in the story."

"That stray tom was around again," said Alison, "and speaking of idiots, you know El Señor—he hasn't the least idea how to put up a fight, and he's too proud to run. The last time he got bitten there was an abscess the size of an orange and Dr. Douthit said—"

The phone rang in the hall. Mendoza, shirtless, went to answer

[191]

it. Two minutes later he came back and reached for his shirt. "*¿Qué occure, amado?*" asked Alison.

"I'll tell you when I've heard."

Bill Moss and Frank Chedorov, on routine tour, had come on shift at six o'clock. It had been a quiet night. They'd handed out a couple of traffic tickets and brought one drunk in to the tank. At nine they knocked off, Code Seven, for sandwiches and coffee at an all-night place on Broadway.

At ten-fifty they were cruising down Hope Street; there wasn't much traffic now, no freeway entry near. They were talking desultorily about politics—fortunately they both shared the same opinions—and rather looking forward to the end of shift. It had gone up to a hundred and two today, and only dropped to about ninety after dark. In June, the heat wouldn't last; it should start to cool off tomorrow or next day.

"Hold it," said Chedorov suddenly. Moss, who was driving, braked.

"What's up?"

"That drugstore on the corner—there were flashlights inside. Just as we passed."

Moss grunted and swung the squad car around to the side street, which was much darker. The drugstore backed up to an alley on the side street, as all that block of buildings would; they stopped at the mouth of the alley and peered, not wanting to use their own flashlights. "There's a car up there," said Chedorov. "Right up from the back door of the drugstore, Bill."

Moss grunted again. They were both experienced cops; they didn't have to discuss what to do. Moss took the squad car past the alley and parked it quietly along the curb; they both got out. They didn't take the shotgun until they knew what they had here. Flashlights in hand, they went down the alley to the rear door of the drugstore. Chedorov flashed a light briefly on the lock. It was an old building, and the door was a wooden one, not especially strong. There were pry marks all around the lock and the door was a couple of inches open. They listened and heard cautious voices from inside, shuffling steps.

Chedorov made a move toward the door, but Moss gestured him back savagely. "They're on the way out," he muttered, "wait till they come." They both fell back down the alley, guns out, ten feet apart.

The door creaked and two vague dark forms came out, down the step to the alley. Moss and Chedorov switched on their flashlights simultaneously and Moss shouted, "Police! Hold it! Freeze!"

The two ran instead, dropping a large bundle by the back door; in the split second the light had been on them, all Chedorov had taken in was dark clothes, two white faces. They ran up the alley toward the car parked there, and Moss shouted again, and fired the warning shot in the air. The flashlights roamed up the alley, an engine started to life with a great roar, and Chedorov fired straight at the sound. Then, in the glare of the two flashlights, he saw, as if the moment were frozen in time, the top of the hood, the car coming straight for them, he saw clearly the little circle and three lines inside, a Mercedes, it was a Mercedes—

He leaped to the side of the alley desperately, dropping the flashlight. Moss, nearer the center of the alley, didn't make it. The fender caught him as he jumped, and threw him between the wheels. The car roared by, and Chedorov swung with it and emptied his gun after it. Moss's flashlight, still switched on, had fallen pointing toward the mouth of the alley, and its beam just caught the fast-receding license plate and burned three figures into Chedorov's mind.

"It was a blue and gold plate," he said to Mendoza, at the hospital. "I know that. I saw it. I didn't get it all, just the first three numbers. It was zero-one-one. I'd swear to that."

"There's no way to check a partial," said Mendoza. "I don't have to tell you."

"No, sir. But they knew what they were doing—we'd warned them. They saw us—Bill. Listen, we rode a squad together four years, Lieutenant. They don't come any better than Bill. Listen, he hasn't got any family—there's nobody. His folks got killed in an airplane crash last year, and he's not married. There's nobody to care." He sat there on the vinyl couch in the hospital corridor and looked at Mendoza dumbly, a young man with a square bulldog face, and he said, "I ought to—we had two hours to go, end of shift—"

"Forget that," said Mendoza. "And there are people to care, Frank. Because he is a cop." It would be assault with intent at least.

"Assault with intent," said Chedorov. "Unless— Look, they've had him in there hours, when the hell will they tell us—"

"Presently."

"It was a blue and gold plate. Zero-one-one," said Chedorov. To make matters a little more confusing, there were two kinds of California license plates now. Since last year, the drivers who wanted to pay extra could get plates in the state colors, gold on blue; if they wanted to pay more extra, they could buy the vanity plates like that, make up their own. The regular plates in the new colors had the three numbers first, three letters second. The old ones, still a lot around, orange on black, were just the opposite: letters first, numbers second.

"It was a Mercedes," said Chedorov. "I saw the insignia on the hood—you know it—sticking up from the hood, a circle with three lines."

And their treasure Mrs. MacTaggart, the Highland Scot only transplanted here a few years, had once presented Mendoza with the curious information that that insignia was the heraldic arms of the Isle of Man. He wondered how it had got transplanted to the Mercedes manufacturers.

And how many thousands of Mercedes, old and new, might be tooling around L.A.—

A doctor came out eventually. "Well, we've put him on the critical list. He's got both legs broken, a broken pelvis, one arm—compound fracture—internal injuries, fractured skull. He's lost a lot of blood—"

"Type O," said Chedorov. "I'm Type A. But a lot of the fellows would— I mean, they don't come any better than Bill."

"We're managing with plasma," said the doctor. "We won't know just yet. Say by sometime tomorrow. He's got a very sound constitution and everything on his side."

"Yeah," said Chedorov. "Yeah. That's it for now?" He got up, bulky in his uniform. "So we just put up the prayers, Doctor?"

"It's a factor," said the doctor. "It is indeed."

"Yeah," said Chedorov. He looked at Mendoza blindly. He said, "One thing, they close the Protestant churches at night. Ours, no. I guess you'll want a formal statement, Lieutenant. In case you ever get them—for a trial. It was a Mercedes—I saw the insignia. And the plate started zero-one-one. I better take the squad car back to the station—"

Before this all erupted, Mendoza had been reading Mr. Kipling. He liked Mr. Kipling—a sane voice in the wilderness. He thought now, wry and sardonic, *And there is no discharge in that war.* The ultimate war all cops saw so close, every day.

12

"WE POSTED A COUPLE OF MEN THERE IN CASE
they came back for the loot, but it was a waste of time." Mendoza
was briefing the men on Thursday morning; they had all come in
more or less together. "The lab's got all the collection they
dropped, and let's hope there may be some latents—and if so, that
they're in our files. There'll be a team at the pharmacy now, it's an
independent and we notified the owner, he'll be taking stock in
case they didn't drop all they got."

"Moss?" asked Palliser.

"He's holding his own, we can hope he'll make it. I'll remind
you all that Art Hackett was worse off once, and all of us doing the
worrying, and look at him now."

"Back on the diet." Palliser grinned. "We can hope."

"And didn't I have a little idea about that," said Landers rather
excitedly. "When we went out on that break-in the other day,
Matt, remember? If a lot of those little break-ins haven't been
pulled by the same ones—maybe this pair. Because if you can say
there was an M.O., it was the same." He turned to Wanda,
listening with a troubled expression. "Those files I asked you to
pull—remember?" She nodded and went to get them again.

Mendoza looked them over interestedly. "And you could be
right, Tom. But anonymous, *absolutamente*—just like the one last
night. The same M.O. all right, the pry-bar to the back door
overnight. These are small-timers, and if they were the same ones,

I think they panicked last night. It'd be a charge of assault with intent, if we catch up, but I don't think it was, technically."

"And just what chance in hell have we got of catching up?" asked Conway savagely. "The first three numbers on a plate, and the make of the car? It's nothing to work on. We can't check a partial, and how many Mercedes are there around?"

"So we hope there are some latents," said Mendoza. "Or something." And there was still a lot of the routine to get through—they hadn't got halfway down the list of perverts. The six biology textbooks Palliser had got from Miss Giffard yesterday were still unexamined. The A.P.B.'s hadn't turned up either Lester Watson or Terry Conover.

It would be a while before they heard from the lab. The hospital had been asked to call in any change. It was Frank Chedorov's day off; he came in to make a statement, and repeated all that about the plate and the car, for what it was worth, which wasn't much.

Lake had called Hackett and Higgins, who were off today, and they both came in about ten. Hackett had been going out to price a new suit, and Higgins to lay in some film and magnetic cubes to get pictures of Laura at the graduation ceremony tomorrow night; but with all the routine piling up, the office shorthanded, they came in.

Palliser and Grace sat down with the biology texts, and everybody else went out on the perverts. Mendoza, more on the ball this morning if somewhat short of sleep, called Bainbridge's office.

"That corpse"—from an empty lot somewhere?—he didn't remember seeing a report on that but there must be one—"that got identified as John Upton." He hoped somebody had remembered to cancel the A.P.B. "Have you looked at it yet? What's the cause of death?" He was talking to one of the young surgeons down there; Bainbridge wasn't in yet.

"Oh, that one. We haven't posted him yet, as a matter of fact I was just getting to it, but what he died of, without much doubt, was a bang on the head," said the surgeon. "A hefty bang on the back of the head—deep depressed skull fracture. I'd say he'd been dead about ten days. Call it a week last Monday or Tuesday."

"*¿Cómo dice?*" said Mendoza. "I'll be damned. That's very funny. You'll let me know more when you've looked." Now what the hell was this? Five minutes later Landers, coming in with a likely looking prospect and finding nobody else there to help lean on him, looked in to find Mendoza talking to himself. He told Landers what the surgeon had said.

"It's funny enough that it should be Upton," said Landers. "Do we deduce now that somebody murdered both of them? But it looked like the perfectly straightforward thing—husband losing his temper, knocking her down, and running when he saw she was dead. When Jimmy told me the lab had identified the corpse as Upton, I thought he'd probably committed suicide."

"*Ya lo creo.* Where's the first report on the body?" Mendoza searched the tray on his desk and found it, where Wanda had carefully filed it and he hadn't, in the press of business, bothered to read it. "Santa Barbara Avenue. *¡Caray!*—a high board fence. And just how— What the hell is this, Tom? If somebody killed both of them at more or less the same time, why move Upton's body?—and to such a peculiar place? I don't like this—there's no sense in it."

"It's funny all right," said Landers. "I wasn't on that—were there any other latents picked up in the house?"

"No. The wife's, that's all. And damn it, if there was any lab evidence that anybody else had died there, or any other evidence at all, we'd know it by now. I can't make this out at all—there's no shape to it," said Mendoza. Untidiness always annoyed him, and this funny business was untidy all right. He couldn't think of anywhere to look on it, any questions to ask anybody, but it nagged at him. He told Landers to have fun with his prospect; the routine had to be done, but he didn't think they were going to find the X on Katie May by the routine. He got his hat, went downstairs and drove down to Santa Barbara Avenue to look at the place where Upton had been found.

He remembered absently, walking back from the parked Ferrari, another body behind a high fence, awhile back. But that one— He stared at the high board fence. What a place to put a body, he thought. And why? Or had Upton actually been killed on the spot—and how? The fence was at least twelve feet high, and Upton hadn't been a small man. Why go to all the trouble?

The answer, of course, was that A.P.B. It had, as Landers said, looked straightforward; if Upton hadn't been found and identified, they'd still be thinking of him as on the run after killing his wife. Somebody else with a motive for killing Cicely Upton? Who?

And where was his car?

Mendoza, his long nose twitching, walked around the fence down the side street. The fence was just as high there; it enclosed this whole huge corner lot down along the next street running parallel to Santa Barbara. He turned down that. In the middle of the length of fence here, however, was something new. Piggott's report had said some kids had found the body, and here was how the kids had got over the fence—a tall mound of earth had been left outside the fence when the old building had been torn down, and the kids, or somebody, had laid a couple of planks from it to the fence top. Fastidiously, Mendoza tackled the climb and peered over the fence. On the other side another couple of boards had been laid, at a low angle to the ground: easy enough to slide down, or pull yourself up again. Kids? That, he'd take a bet on; but they'd have to find out. And somebody—the X on the Uptons—had known about it. How?

He found a public phone and called the office for the names of the kids who had found the body. They both lived on the other side of the street across from the back of the fence. He only found one to talk to, Bobby Starling, but that was enough. Sure, Bobby said, him and Tim had fixed those boards to get over the fence. Nothing over there they could hurt, he didn't know why the ole company had to put up a fence anyways. And of course now, thought Mendoza, hopeless to expect the lab to find any of X's latents on those boards, the fence.

"¡*Mil rayos!*" he said to himself. He couldn't make head or tail of this at all. He started back across the street, to head for the Ferrari, and was nearly cut down by a small olive-green truck whizzing round the corner. He wondered how Bill Moss was doing.

None of the biology textbooks was the one with Rex's name and phone number. "We find ourselves doing some pretty queer things in this job sometimes," said Grace, shutting the last one, "but this is about the queerest piece of detecting I ever did, John. Seems to be the only way we're going to locate him, though."

Palliser agreed. They sat there a moment, somnolent, after the tedious peering at pages; they could hear the office humming at work all around. Two interrogation rooms were in use; Hackett and Higgins had just turned a man loose after questioning him and were talking to Lake before starting out again.

The list of perverts being what it was, this routine hunt could go on for days. "I suppose," said Grace, "we'd better get back to the legwork on that list. The rest of these books aren't available, you said."

"Miss Giffard said. Irresponsible kids forgetting to turn them in. Summer school open in two weeks, a few may show up then."

Just as they got up, Lake gave them a hail. "I just had a pigeon call in on Lester Watson. He's said to have a job washing dishes at a short-order place on Jefferson. Here's the address."

"So let's go see if he's there," said Grace.

He wasn't. The owner of the place, a very black fellow even bigger than Hackett, with an amiable smile, said his name was Soames. He'd never seen Watson before he showed up two days ago in answer to the sign in the window offering a job. "But one day is enough," said Soames. "Man, that boy is so punch-drunk he's walking around in a dream. You can't trust him, carry a plate across the room, I tell you. I told him to get out, yesterday. Paid him five bucks, and it was worth it to get rid of him."

When they asked him to call in if he spotted Watson anywhere around, he asked, "What's he done, anyway? I wouldn't think he'd have brains enough to shoplift a candy bar."

"Murder," said Grace.

"You got to be kidding," said Soames. "Him?"

"Him. He stabbed an old lady to death. He's punch-drunk on too many years of heroin," said Palliser.

"I will be Goddamned. Listen, gents, I sure call in, let you know, if I see him. I sure will."

They thanked him for the intention, and went on to lunch at Federico's. Palliser called the office; Lake had checked with the hospital, and Moss was holding his own, very slightly improved. "I hope he makes it," said Palliser.

He was still feeling uneasy about Madge Borman's letter, reposing in his breast pocket. When he'd got home last night, Roberta had been breathing fire; the third man had appeared to give an estimate on putting up the fence, and said the best he could do was three hundred and fifty dollars, it was a big yard. Outrageous, she had said, and why Palliser insisted on such a high one—three feet would be plenty. Palliser had held his peace, and offered to give the baby his bath while she got on with dinner. He'd see how she was feeling tonight, if it seemed auspicious to break the news to her about Trina.

"You know," said Grace thoughtfully, "Katie May's funeral is tomorrow. I was thinking I might go. Those are nice people, the Blaines."

At one-thirty, with Mendoza talking to himself about Upton and pacing his office, they had a harried call from Traffic. As if to celebrate the end of the school semester, there was quite a sizable gang rumble going on up on the playground of that Ninth Street high school. The gangs were Negro and Mexican respectively, and there were knives around, quite a few, and clubs, and chains; three Traffic men had been injured and one Negro boy was dead. There could be others. There were eight squad cars and a couple of uniformed sergeants with riot guns there.

"Happy, carefree school days," said Hackett. He and Higgins went out to look at that; by the time they got there the fighting was just about over, and the ringleaders in cuffs ready to take in. The dead boy was Sam Safford; the school supplied his name and an address for him. He'd been stabbed in the heart.

The Traffic men had confiscated seventeen knives, twenty-six improvised clubs and assorted lengths of chain. In all the confusion of the melée, it wasn't at all clear who had stabbed Safford, and probably never would be. The autopsy might pin down a particular blade.

They tried to talk to some of them at the jail, and got nowhere, of course. To this kind, confused aimless kids so easily stirred up by a good many real and some imagined grievances, police were the enemy, and they just growled sullenly and repeated all the familiar names.

They gave up after a while, and Hackett dropped Higgins back at the office to give Wanda a first report on it, and went down to Twenty-fourth Street to break the news to Safford's family, if any.

It was another old apartment building, the little strip of ground in front bare of grass. Hackett went in and looked at the mailboxes; Safford was the first floor left rear. He walked down the hall and pushed the bell. Nobody enjoyed bringing the bad news, but it was another job cops had to do.

The door was opened, but he didn't attempt to break the news. The man leaning on the door was incapably drunk, about ready to pass out. As Hackett hesitated, he folded to the floor; the little shabby old apartment was empty except for him. Hackett found the door marked *Manager* and a sharp-faced middle-aged Negro who said merely, "Sam drunk again? It beats me how that woman puts up with it. Her, she'll be at work—they couldn't meet the rent, wasn't for her. What'd you want?" Hackett told him. "Oh. Him. Well, his ma'll be sorry, but between us he was a worthless little bastard. Chip off the old block. Well, I'll tell her."

*　　*　　*

The legwork had turned up quite a few of the perverts now, and none of them had looked remotely possible, after Sullivan, until Landers brought in the young fellow this morning. He worked for a furniture company on Jefferson, driving a delivery truck, and a little questioning revealed the fact that he'd made a delivery to the apartment on Hooper last week. There were two counts of child molestation on him; it was possible he'd seen Katie May there, marked her. Somehow enticed her out of the building?

With some elementary follow-up on that, it fell to pieces. He'd been on the job last Monday, and they placed him at a lunch counter way out on Atlantic between twelve and one, vouched for by four witnesses.

"Witnesses," said Grace, lighting a cigarette after the fellow had taken off in a hurry. "I don't get past those witnesses."

"They've got to be wrong," said Hackett, stretching and massaging his neck muscles. "There's no way it could have happened in that building, Jase. After we thought of the roof—"

"Well, we didn't think of it right off. I just wonder if there isn't something else we haven't thought of," said Grace.

"Reaching for the hunches—better leave it to Luis," said Higgins.

"He's trying for one on the Uptons." Hackett laughed. "You know, that is a hell of a funny thing—the Uptons. It looked so—basic. Simple. And then it turns out—but by all we heard, who could have wanted to kill both of them? Why? Except for his temper, Upton seems to have been well liked enough, and she was—as Mrs. Cohen said—quite the homebody, quiet young woman minding her own business." He yawned. "Say, I wonder if anybody remembered to tell Fresno about Upton. Somebody ought to tell his sister he's dead."

He went to ask, and found Mendoza sitting up at his desk shuffling cards, cigarette in one corner of his mouth. "This is the damnedest thing we've had to nag us in a while, Arturo. What? —yes, I thought of all that. And damn it, I've got a little feeling—just a vague little feeling, *extraño*—that there's something

I ought to remember, just on the top of my mind—something about something—and it won't come. *Eso es lo peor.* Damn it— What?"

"His sister. Up in Fresno." Hackett regarded him rather amusedly. Mendoza in the throes of trying to have a hunch was never very coherent.

"*Dios,* no, I didn't—you'd better send a telex up to the chief."

Hackett saw to that. Conway and Landers had just brought in another man to question. It looked like the long way around to go, but as Shogart always said, it was so often the routine that broke cases. And the types they were after here were apt to be chancy characters, ill-balanced, and the guilty one might come apart as soon as they looked at him. And then they might get some answers to the locked-room puzzle.

Hackett, who was not frequently given to hunches, frowned suddenly as he thought that. Something vague just floated across the top of his mind—and floated away. Something—something about locked-room mysteries—no, it was gone. Whatever it had been. If it was anything important it would come to him eventually.

At five-thirty the hospital called. Moss had been conscious, and they were saying now he'd make it; there would be a while of convalescence, but he'd be quite all right. Everybody was pleased about that.

"And just what kind of a chance do we have of getting that pair?" said Palliser, coming in to hear that and joining in the general relief. "Has the lab got anything?"

"We don't know yet," said Mendoza. "They picked up a lot of latents off the loot—they'd gone in for the drugs mostly this time, cigarettes, some liquor. We don't know they belong to our pair, but it's a good chance, the places they were picked up. But they're not in our records."

"Didn't I say it," said Landers. "The small-timers—and on jobs like that, just as I said to that fellow the other day, hardly worth our time to look for prints, there's never any solid lead. They could be just starting out, never been picked up at all."

"And I wonder how many of the new plates start out zero-one-one," said Higgins.

"Well, you know," said Hackett, "I had a little thought on that—" And the switchboard flashed and Lake plugged in. A minute later he turned.

"Traffic's picked up Lester Watson," he said succinctly. "There's a unit in pursuit now."

"In pursuit? Watson hasn't got a car—"

"He has now, evidently," said Lake. Hackett ran into the sergeants' office and switched on the monitoring radio tuned to their frequency. In thirty seconds it came on—"All units, K-one-ninety is in pursuit of stolen car. K-one-ninety on Jefferson Boulevard approaching Central, all units—"

They listened, following the pursuit. There was carnage on the way: the stolen car, driven very erratically to say the least, by the terse descriptions of the men in the squad car after it, struck a group of pedestrians when it mounted the sidewalk along Central, somehow ploughed on back to the street, and hit ninety m.p.h. in the next block.

The end came at Central and Ninety-second, where the car failed to negotiate a right-angle turn and went through the front window of a bar. After a brief hiatus, there was a call for an ambulance; a moment later, for another.

"His P.A. officer did say," commented Hackett, "that he hoped we'd pick him up before he did any more damage. We'd better go and find out just how much—leave a little work for the night watch for a change."

The two Traffic men said they'd spotted Watson along Jefferson, on the street, and when they left the car to take him he'd jumped into a car just starting up at the curb, shoved the driver out. The owner of the car, a respectable citizen who'd just stopped to buy a pack of cigarettes, was mad: the car, a year-old Impala, was a total loss.

Watson was dead of a severed artery from the broken glass; five people in the bar and four more in that group of pedestrians were seriously injured, and one baby was dead.

They left all the information for the night watch, but undoubtedly they'd come in for some of the statement taking too.

Mendoza went home, locked the garage and went across the backyard to the kitchen door, not even casting one baleful look at the happily yodeling mockingbird in the alder tree. In the back porch Cedric was slurping from his bowl; he looked up and offered a polite paw which Mendoza didn't see.

In the kitchen there was an appetizing smell of baked ham. It hadn't been quite as hot today but the air conditioning was on, gratefully cool after the still strong sun outside. Alison was shredding lettuce at the sink and Mrs. MacTaggart just opening the oven.

"Busy day, *amado?* How's that patrolman?"

Mendoza said, "What patrolman? Oh, Moss. He'll be all right." The four cats were weaving in and out between legs, reminding people that this was usually the time they had dinner. "I need a drink."

"You look as if you'd already had some. Something," said Alison unerringly, "is trying to come to you."

"I don't know," said Mendoza, his eyes unfocused. "Damn it, I can't put a finger on it. That is the most shapeless damned thing—it makes no sense. *Pues sí.* The hot temper—and how many people have? Other than that, the ordinary young couple—"

"You need a drink," said Alison, and got down the bottle of rye. El Señor, forgetting about dinner, floated up to the counter top and uttered indignant wails as Mendoza poured his own without getting out a saucer. Alison supplied him and El Señor lapped.

"Dinner in ten minutes. I hope it comes to you," she said. "You're really not *compos mentis* when a hunch is trying to come through."

Palliser, coming in the back door of the house on Hillside Avenue, found his household more serene than last night. Roberta looked quite peaceful, setting the table; the baby was asleep or at

[206]

least silent, and the coffee was just perking. He told her about Moss, and the tiresome day at all the routine, and she said, "Poor darling. Just for once, how about a drink before dinner?"

"That's a good idea," said Palliser. And five minutes later, when they were sitting relaxed at the table and she'd had a sip or two of gin-and-tonic, he began cautiously, "You remember that thing last January—the freeway accident, and the dog?"

"Um, that's rather nice," said his Robin. "Oh—yes. The dog with the funny name. Azzie. A great big black German shepherd. What about it?"

"Well," said Palliser, "I didn't mention it at the time because—well, I just didn't. She might have forgotten all about it. But she didn't."

"Didn't what? You made these awfully strong, John," said Roberta.

"Well, she was so grateful for my getting the dog taken care of while she was in the hospital—it wasn't anything, but she was—and just as I suspected, she didn't forget. I had a letter from her yesterday, and the fact is, that dog—Azzie, you know—he's a show champion, she said—the fact is—"

"How many drinks have you already had?" she asked. "The fact is what about Azzie? And of all ridiculous names—"

"Well, you see, she breeds them. Little Azzies. Only it's a she."

"John Palliser," said Roberta dangerously, "you're trying to tell me something, so just go ahead and do it."

"Well, she's giving us one. Of Azzie's latest pups. At the end of the month. I've got to go to the airport to pick her up. Her name's Trina. Miss Borman says the females are better watchdogs," said Palliser baldly.

Roberta stared at him over her glass, aghast. "A—one of those? A—good heavens, John!"

"They're nice dogs, and good watchdogs," said Palliser. He gave her the letter.

Roberta read it and took another swallow. "You know," she said, "that's really very nice of her. She needn't do that. I know they're nice dogs. And people do—keep them in the city, I mean. And it's a big yard, once we get the fence built— And I suppose a pup from a good kennel like this would be terribly expensive."

"You don't mind? You said a dog, but— Well, after all," said Palliser, much relieved, "if we're going to have a dog, it might as well be a dog that is a dog, Robin. If you know what I mean—"

"I think we're both a little tight," said Roberta. "No, now I think it over, I think it'll be fine to have a real dog. Only we'd better get that fence up, if you have to build it yourself."

"That's too much like work. We'll find somebody to build it."

The night watch had heard about Moss, and were relieved to know he'd make it all right. They didn't get any calls until ten-thirty, which was just as well: Glasser and Galeano went out to see some of the witnesses on that spectacular pursuit and crash that afternoon; there'd be inquests, and the evidence had to be gathered, pointless as it might seem. The remains had to be legally tidied away.

"It just occurs to me," said Glasser, "any cop might have a few vices, Nick, but that's one thing none of us would take up—we see too much of what it does. The dope."

They took Galeano's car because the loaner Plymouth was now belching black smoke out of its tailpipe. "Haven't you got your own piece of junk back yet?"

"They say I can have it on Saturday," said Glasser gloomily.

At ten-thirty they had a call from a sheriff's detective out in County territory in Hollywood. He said one of the good restaurants along Sunset had just got hit by heisters as it was closing, and it sounded like the same pair Central had first sounded the alarm on. Medium size, stocking masks and big guns. They'd got away with nearly three thousand bucks. "I never realized how much an expensive restaurant might—"

"Have on hand at closing time," said Glasser. "That sounds like them. I don't know what we can do about it."

"Well, we thought you'd like to be kept up-to-date," said the sheriff's man.

Friday was Piggott's day off. After he'd had breakfast he got the extra tank, that they'd got to try the tetra-breeding in, all ready and heated to proper temperature, and with a net he fished all the baby tetras out of the dishpans and transferred them to it. Any amount of water was astonishingly heavy; he panted downstairs with it and got it into the back of the Nova and drove out to the shop called Scales 'n' Fins on Beverly Boulevard.

"Oh, my," said Mr. Duff who owned the shop, "you've done very well, Mr. Piggott. Especially for the first time. How many did you have to start with?"

"All I can say is, you might have warned me," said Piggott feelingly. "More than three hundred and fifty, I made it."

"Well, I did. I said you'd need to separate them as some grew faster."

"Grew faster by eating their brothers and sisters."

Mr. Duff dipped the baby tetras out with a net and transferred them to one of his tanks at the back of the store. There were seventy-three. "That's very good," he said. "Congratulations." He paid Piggott fourteen dollars and sixty cents out of the cash register.

When he got home, Prudence had the living room straightened up. "My heavens," she said, "isn't it peaceful, to be back just watching the pretty grown-up ones sailing around?" The original tank, full of the beautiful exotic fish, looked tranquil indeed, the lovely little fish in their bright colors wandering among the foliage. "But, Matt, what on earth are we going to do with all those dishpans and screens?"

When the day watch came in on Friday morning, they found a new one to make the paper work—not much of a thing. At five o'clock this morning, long after the night watch had gone home, a

Highway Patrol unit had happened across an accident, with a D.O.A. in it, at the entrance to the Harbor freeway. The report said it looked as if the car had gone out of control and rammed the central divider. The D.O.A. had been a young woman, sent to the central morgue. Her handbag and personal effects would be there too, but the car had been registered to Ernesto Moreno at an address in Santa Monica, and in her handbag was identification: she was Loretta Moreno of the same address.

Mendoza, looking even sharper than usual in a new silver-gray Italian silk suit, had come in, looked at the overnight report, and got out the deck of cards. He sat there stacking the deck, to practice the crooked poker deals, and he said to Hackett, who had come in with the news that Moss was conscious and swearing a blue streak because there wasn't any lead on the pair in the Mercedes, *"Pues sí.* Mrs. Whitlow's shrewd father—the ride on the merry-go-round has to end sometime. *¿Para qué? Nada más.* Just in case, with the hostages to fortune—" He began to deal rapidly. "And somebody knew the way over that damned fence. How? And, for the love of God, who? And why?"

"The Uptons," said Hackett. "Who indeed. The hunch hasn't come through."

"The lab," said Mendoza, "sent those latents from the breaker-inners' loot to the F.B.I. and NCIC. Scarne just called. NCIC doesn't know them at least."

"Oh, great," said Hackett. "Just as Tom said, they've never been picked up. Small-timers. Well, at least Moss will make it. I noticed the restaurant heisters are still on the take."

"A very profitable M.O.," agreed Mendoza. He contemplated the dealt hands, gathered them all in and began to shuffle.

"There's a proverb in Spanish," said Hackett. " 'Patience, and shuffle the cards.' "

"I'm familiar with it," said Mendoza. "Damn it, there's something—some little thing—I can't put a finger on. What gets me, Arturo, is—why move one and not the other? And, *Dios,* where's Upton's car?"

"It's shapeless all right. He didn't give himself that bang on the head."

"*Obvio.*" Mendoza squared the deck. He cut it once, to the king of spades. Twice, to the king of diamonds. Three times, and turned the king of clubs. Four, and the king of hearts.

"That's very pretty," said Hackett, "but it butters no parsnips."

"Go away and do the legwork, Arturo." Mendoza lit a new cigarette. "I'm busy working." Suddenly he discovered those love beads on the far side of the ashtray, and without comment dropped them into the wastebasket.

The routine forever came up to be done. That morning, before setting out on the routine on the perverts, Landers looked up the number and called Ernesto Moreno to break the news about Loretta. As the citizens so often were on these occasions, Moreno was dazed and incredulous. "Dead?" he said. "Loretta's dead? An accident?"

Landers explained about the formal identification, about the accident. The car had been an old heap, a fourteen-year-old Chevy; possibly the brakes had failed. Moreno said in a fading voice that he understood. "You kinda knocked me for a loop," he said. "I been sitting in an all-night poker session with some fellas. I guess I'm not exactly— Where'd you say I should come?"

Landers repeated the address, and Moreno said he'd be down.

Grace went home to View Park at ten-thirty and picked up Virginia, and they went to Katie May Blaine's funeral. She was buried at the Rosedale Cemetery. Grace introduced Virginia to the Blaines afterward, and of course Virginia found the right way to say things. "You don't want to worry," she told Mrs. Blaine simply. "She's being looked after, the other side. She'll be all right." And whether or not that was what Christian Scientists believed, the Blaines nodded and seemed grateful.

Ernesto Moreno showed up at ten o'clock, and Landers happened to be in so he took him down to the morgue. Moreno was a little man, dark and thin, about thirty, and he looked at the body in the cold tray and licked his lips and said, "Yeah, it's Loretta. My wife. I mean, it's such a *surprise*—when you called—"

"There'll have to be an autopsy, sir. And an inquest." All the tidying away in legal terms.

"What's that? Oh, yeah—whatever the law says," said Moreno dully. "That's O.K."

"We'll let you know when you can have the body," said Landers. "It's just a formality, Mr. Moreno."

"Yeah, O.K.," said Moreno.

The five men from the list of perverts they had found and brought in that morning were all N.G. Two of them had alibis for Monday, and the other three were—as so many of them were—inconclusive. Possible, not very probable.

Sid Belcher was due to be arraigned in court at ten o'clock, and Palliser went to offer the brief police evidence on that. After they had worked a case, it was the necessary nuisance to take time off something new, to contribute to the legal machinery, often cumbersome and slow, occasionally venal, always there.

But Palliser was feeling relieved, and rather looking forward to meeting Trina, their very own real dog-that-was-a-dog, daughter of that quite imposing creature Dark Angel of Langley. The champion.

He got back to the office at twelve-ten, to find Hackett, Higgins, Conway and Landers just leaving for lunch, having just let the latest two go—more inconclusives.

Mendoza came out of his office looking preoccupied. Evidently the hunch hadn't jelled yet.

"We've been talking about all the pros and cons," Lake was saying to Higgins. "Everybody says electric stoves are cleaner, and last longer. Even now. But Caroline says about the energy shortage, maybe there'd be gas when there wasn't power. And they're cheaper."

"Well, we've got an electric one," said Higgins, "and Mary

likes it better, she says. It doesn't get the walls as dirty. I don't think there'd be much difference in price now, Jimmy."

"Well, the other thing is, you call the city for service on the electric ones, and it isn't so expensive. The gas company—"

"*¡Diez millones de demonios negros desde el infierno!*" said Mendoza loudly. "*¡Válgame Dios!* By God, the gas company— And what the hell was his name, what the—"

"Don't tell me the hunch has finally arrived?" Hackett was interested.

"It nearly ran me down—a gas company truck— And he was supposed to go bowling that night— What the hell was his name?" Mendoza stared into space for thirty seconds and said, "Chet Dickey. At the gas company— And he said, take turns driving —and she was a nice girl— But why the hell should he—"

"Who?" asked Conway, muddled.

"Wait for it," said Higgins. "Something's coming through, anyway."

13

"BECAUSE THAT WAS THE NIGHT—" SAID MEN-
doza. "But what possible reason— It was in George's report, I
remember— On the other hand—" He was staring at the wall
raptly. Slowly his eyes focused and he swung around. "But just in
the event that I'm not seeing ghosts, it won't do any harm to go
and ask a few questions. Let's go."

"I'll hear about the hunch later," said Higgins. "I'm starving
and I'm going to have some lunch." But Hackett and Palliser,
always interested to see the boss's second sight in operation,
trailed along, and in the lot he said they'd take Palliser's car.

"We're bringing back a passenger?" said Hackett.

"*No sé*. Maybe."

Palliser said, "It's all right with me, but where are we going?"

Mendoza told him: that gas company station on Santa Barbara.
He remembered the names from that report; when they got there
he asked for Rodman. The dispatcher was on the phone, a stack of
papers before him. He looked at the three men in faint surprise, at
the badge with instant excitement, and put the phone down.
Mendoza introduced himself. "Couple of different fellows. You
were here the other day," said Rodman to Palliser. "Have you
found Johnny Upton yet, Lieutenant? I haven't seen anything
about it in the papers—"

"Yes, we have," said Mendoza. "Is Chet Dickey around? We'd
like to talk to him."

"Chet? I'll check and see—he and Bill were out repairing a line but they ought to be back now—" Rodman was fired with curiosity, hesitant to ask questions. He used the phone and said, "He'll be right up, just got back. I didn't see anything in the papers about you arresting Johnny."

"So you didn't," said Mendoza. They waited, and a minute later Dickey came in. It was the first time Mendoza had laid eyes on him, and he remembered the terse opinion in Higgins' report: "Liked Upton, liked wife, ordinary casual friend." Like that, thought Mendoza; exactly what Dickey looked like. He was only middle height but stocky and heavy-shouldered, with a non-descript unhandsome face and rather cowlike brown eyes, short dark hair.

"More cops, Chet," said Rodman. "They want to talk to you."

Dim apprehension came into the brown eyes. "Oh." He stared at Mendoza, who introduced himself again.

"And Sergeant Hackett, Sergeant Palliser. We found John Upton, Mr. Dickey."

Dickey licked his lips. "You did."

"And identified him by his fingerprints."

"Oh," said Dickey, and looked ready to cry.

"Could you tell us anything about it? Because it was that Monday night, wasn't it? A week ago last Monday night."

Dickey looked around wildly and dropped the hard hat he was carrying; it rolled and bounced off a leg of Rodman's desk.

"It just occurred to me," said Mendoza, and his long nose was twitching, "that you told Sergeant Palliser Upton called you that night and said he wasn't going bowling, but did he really? You just said so."

"Oh, my God," said Dickey. "I—how'd you come to find him? I thought—"

Rodman was staring.

"Some kids climbed the fence."

"Well, that just shows you," said Dickey. He sounded faintly indignant. "I know the police got a lot to do, and not enough men, but I made sure that cop was going to stop that. One of the squad cars along there, I hailed him and told him, kids getting over there and it was dangerous, and he said he'd talk to 'em. I sure thought—" He bent and picked up his hat. "Oh, hell," he said miserably. "I guess I got to tell you all about it. I'd just as soon not—" He looked around, avoiding Rodman's eyes, and now he looked merely embarrassed.

"Suppose you come back to headquarters with us," said Hackett. They left Rodman looking after them with an expression compounded of excitement and incredulity. He was reaching for the phone.

In an interrogation room at the office, Dickey sat on the straight chair looking forlorn and said, "I don't know—it's been on my conscience awful and maybe I'd've come to tell you even if you hadn't—because God knows I didn't do anything awful wrong —and way I was brought up, a person's supposed to have decent burial even if I come to think it's not so all that important—and God knows Johnny was a nice guy, except he had a temper, you know."

"We've heard," said Mendoza.

"Well—well—" He was stuck, and Hackett helped him get started.

"Upton didn't phone you that night?"

"No, he never. I went to pick him up—for the practice bowling—at seven o'clock. They lived in one side of this duplex, you know, and when I came up to the door I could hear they was having an argument. Now I guess we all got a few faults," said Dickey anxiously, "but I got to say, about Johnny, he wasn't mean. It wasn't that. I rang the bell, I thought maybe they'd stop when I came in, and Cicely did, but he didn't. Seemed she'd got a new dress and he thought it cost too much and told her to take it back, but she wouldn't. Like I say, Johnny wasn't mean, but he was worried about expenses—like everybody else—and he didn't like running charge accounts. Well—that was what it was about."

"So?" said Mendoza.

"Well, he was going on at her, time he got ready to go with me, see. She went in the bedroom, and he was banging around in a temper, like, all over that fool dress, and pretty soon I heard Cicely give a sort of little scream and there was a bang, or a thud like, and then Johnny says to her to get up, damn it. I went in there and she was lyin' half on the floor by the end of the bed, and Johnny picked her up and laid her in the bed and says she just been knocked out, she'd be O.K. Well, look"—Dickey looked around at them earnestly—"I didn't like that. Way I was brought up, a man just don't go hitting women, specially his wife, and I said to Johnny he shouldn't've done that, and he says to mind my own business, she'd be O.K., and were we going to bowl or weren't we. So we got in my car and went out to the bowling alley, out Beverly, but all the way I was thinking we ought to've made sure Cicely was all right. That was a terrible thing to do, knock her down like that. And when we got out in the parking lot—we were already late then—I said to Johnny, about that—maybe phone and see if she was O.K.—and he got mad at me. He said his wife was his own business and I said sure she was but he hadn't got no call to knock her around and I wanted to know was she all right. Well, that made him madder, and he landed one on me and knocked me down, and that made me mad."

"Very natural," said Palliser.

"You bet it was. I'm not as tall as him but I can hold my own all right, I got up and swung on him, and all I can figure is I musta caught him off balance. He went right over, back against the car, and folded. Look, I didn't believe it. I thought he was just knocked out. I tried to bring him to, must've been five minutes I worked on him, and God's mercy nobody else drove into that lot. I got a flashlight from the car, I—but my God, he was dead. He was dead! I never meant to kill Johnny! I couldn't believe it, but he was dead!"

That deep depressed skull fracture: a very accidental homicide.

"Well, my God, I didn't know what to do!" said Dickey. "I was scared as hell. I'm not a murderer! I didn't know how the law might look at it, I was mad at him when I hit him—well, I was scared. I just thought, have to cover up somehow. I—I got him in the trunk of my car, and I went in the bowling alley. I was awful late then, I had to tell the other guys I had trouble with the car. And I said how Johnny'd called me.

"And then when we was bowling, I thought, my God, Cicely knows that's not so. She'll say. And look"—he gestured helplessly—"they was really in love, even if they got mad at each other, Cicely'd be awful upset about Johnny being dead—and I wasn't bowling so good anyway that night—"

"I bet," said Hackett. Mendoza leaned on the wall smoking.

"So I just took off early, and I had a kind of idea about going and telling Cicely how it had happened, so I went back there. Only I couldn't get her to come to the door, and finally I found Johnny's keys and got in, and—my God—there she still was on the bed, and she was dead too! Look, I really got the shakes—I don't know anything about the law, about how cops do—I mean, I know you guys try to do things right, but my God, how did it *look?* I could see right off how anybody might think, my telling that story—and already told a lie to the other fellows—my God, you'd think for sure I'd been messing with Cicely and Johnny'd found out and—maybe you'd think I killed them both! I could see that—"

"What made you think about that fence?" asked Mendoza curiously.

"I was scared just silly," said Dickey. "But after a while my brain started to think again and I thought if you just found her and not him, you'd think he killed her and run away. Which maybe he would've done, when he found out he killed her—I don't know. But I thought about that place—my God, Johnny and Bill and me 'd been workin' on a line on the street right behind it the last two days—and everybody knows about that lot where the old bank was. It's all tied up in the courts—some legal trouble about who really owns it, a couple of lawsuits and all—it might be years before it all got untangled and anybody come to build anything there. And we'd seen the kids getting over, with those boards. So

I—so I just drove out there, it was late then and nobody around, and it was a hell of a job but I got him over that fence and way over across by the other side—the kids seemed mostly to play by the back there. But I thought wouldn't be any harm, speak to that cop so he'd warn 'em off. Just in case. I—"

"What the hell did you do with his car?" asked Hackett.

"Oh—I thought about that when I was lugging him over the fence. There's a junkyard out on Third, and no fence around part of it. You never see anybody around there, and I figured who'd notice one more old heap."

"Shades of the Purloined Letter," said Palliser.

"I had his keys, I drove it out there and stripped it—make it look like just another pile o' junk," said Dickey simply. "I got to thinking it's lucky I'm not married, live alone—it was four A.M., time I walked back where I'd left my car, and went home. And I been scared ever since. I don't know if you believe me, but honest to God that's how it happened. Johnny didn't mean to but he killed her. And I didn't mean to, but I killed him. And—" His eyes were anxious.

"Accidental homicide, Mr. Dickey," said Mendoza, "and thank you for all the answers. Now all the pieces fall into place— Yes, I think we believe you all right. And if you'd just come and told us what had happened—"

"Well, but I knew how it *looked*—"

"Some of us have some imagination, and God knows experience of human nature," said Palliser; but he laughed.

Dickey relaxed a little. "What—what'll happen to me?"

"Well, I should think the D.A.'ll call it accidental homicide and let it go. There's a technical charge about concealing a corpse, but that won't come to anything. If I had to give an educated guess, you'll get a suspended sentence," said Mendoza, stabbing out his cigarette.

Dickey looked incredulous. "Is that a fact? I'll be damned—" Huge relief settled over his face. "I been so worried and scared about it—"

[219]

"We'll have to book you into jail right now. But you'll get a lawyer, and make bail. Don't worry about it. I'm just damned relieved," said Mendoza, "to have this little mystery off my mind."

They were all, they realized suddenly, also starving. They ordered lunch for Dickey from the canteen and drove up to Federico's.

They could send a lab team out to that junkyard, to find Upton's car; there were probably more latents on it.

When Grace and Higgins let the latest pervert go, at four o'clock on Friday afternoon, Grace said it wasn't good enough. The time-tried routine, but he still thought, on Katie May, that those witnesses knew what they were talking about. There were all the other men at that apartment, he said, besides the five night workers: had they all really been at work that day? Vouched for? Could one of them—a single man, or even a married man whose wife was out—have been there at the apartment? A man known to Katie May?

Higgins was tired of hunting the perverts too; he shrugged and said he'd play along. They made a start on it then, collecting all the names of those male tenants, where they worked. They wouldn't get to check any of them today; that took them to the end of shift, and some of the places wouldn't be open tomorrow, but they'd check where they could.

At four-thirty Landers and Conway went out on a new call, and a new body. There had been a heist in broad daylight at a dairy store out on Wilshire, and a woman shot dead. The more they listened to the witnesses, the more they thought this was one they wanted to drop on fast.

"But he was just a kid!" said Howard Knisely, the manager of the store. He was still dazed, incredulous. "I couldn't believe—he didn't look a day over fifteen, and young for that! And there were other customers here—Mrs. Piper there, she must have thought he was kidding— *I* thought he was—and he said it's a stickup, and I saw the gun, Mrs. Piper tried to grab it from him, and he just—he just shot her! It was so fast—I didn't believe—but then I opened the register, and he—"

The woman, Evelyn Piper, who lived in the neighborhood, had been shot in the chest. They called up an ambulance, started to talk to the witnesses. Nobody could give them a complete description, except that the heister was—or looked—so young.

Mrs. Ellen Shaw said to Landers, "Like you, young man—you don't look old enough to be a policeman. Not that you look as young as *him*—not a day over fifteen like Mr. Knisely said, and—I think he had on dark pants, a blue shirt or maybe gray—"

Miss Jean Anderson said he had on jeans and a white T-shirt. "But it was just a minute—don't seem possible, that poor woman shot right before our eyes! I didn't believe it was real—"

Baby-face, as Landers and Conway were already calling him mentally, had got away with a hundred and eleven dollars. He'd been alone, and none of them had seen him get into a car, hadn't in fact noticed which way he went, taken up with Mrs. Piper—but with all the traffic passing, he could have had a pal waiting in a car around the corner. Nobody could say what kind of a gun it was: Ballistics would tell them.

"I've got a feeling, Rich," said Landers, "that this is a mean one—hair-trigger." And everybody had said he hadn't touched anything in the place, so it wouldn't be any use to call out the lab to dust for prints.

By then it was getting on to end of shift, and they went back to the office and left notes for Wanda to type in the morning, and for the night watch, in case Baby-face showed up on something of theirs.

They went home, and Landers phoned Phil and asked her to go to dinner with him on Tuesday night. "I'm a little fed up with all these double dates," he said frankly. "Maybe Rich wants protection from the karate expert, but—"

Phil laughed. "As a matter of fact, maybe he does, Tom. Margot says she's given him every hint she can think of, in a ladylike way, but he's still shy of the marriage license."

"How about you?"

[221]

"I'm thinking about it," said Phil with a smile in her voice. Landers felt fine when he hung up; it was going to be all right, eventually he'd get her. His mother and his sister Jean kept asking him when they were getting married; they liked Phil, from when they'd met her last year, on that funny case where she'd done the detective work and got him off the hook with I.A. Darling Phil, thought Landers fondly. Everything would be fine.

"When you know what happened, how very simple," said Mendoza. "But the general effect left behind was so damned shapeless—"

"At least you're acting human again," said Alison. "And I think that stray tom has moved in with those new people down the street. He was sitting on their front porch this morning and I saw her patting him. I hope to goodness, if he has, they have him neutered." She was encumbered by Bast and Sheba; Mendoza had Nefertite, and El Señor was brooding on the credenza. Cedric was stretched out properly at his master's feet.

"Pues sí. And I do see what Jase means. Those witnesses on Katie May—we might turn up something— Most of what we see in the jungle is simple—if sordid—and follows a pattern, which is why routine pays off. But sometimes there's a wild card in the deck. And damn it, I'd like to get those small-timers who nearly killed Moss, but there's no possible lead—"

"Bringing the office home," said Alison.

That McGuffey Reader was really a wonderful book, said Angel. Hackett agreed with her. His darling Sheila wasn't of an age to take to the printed word, but their bright boy Mark was mastering it by leaps and bounds. Cunningly putting off bedtime, he sat in Hackett's lap and showed him how well he was learning.

"See, Daddy, it says O, O, John, the sun has just set. I can read it all. There are a lot of ooohs in this lesson," said Mark.

"A lot of what?"

"Ooohs, Daddy. Big round ones," and Mark pointed. "When

[222]

they're together they make oooh, but all alone they're in front of one."

Hackett looked at Angel, nonplussed, and she laughed over her sewing. "It's that chart I got for his room, Art. With all the numbers on it, and a zero first."

"A—for God's *sake!*" said Hackett suddenly. "For God's—now I will be damned eternally!"

"Art, you know how he picks up everything—"

But Hackett was staring at all the oooohs in the McGuffey Reader.

On Saturday morning, with Lake off and Farrell at the switchboard, Hackett collected Higgins as he came in and marched him into Mendoza's office. Mendoza was sitting smoking over the night watch report; it had been a quiet night, two accidents at the Stack where all the freeways came together, another brawl in a bar.

"Look," said Hackett. He filched a sheet of paper from the left top drawer, took out his pen. "What does this say?" And he put down the three marks, large and plain. 0 1 1.

"The first three numbers of that damn plate," said Higgins, yawning. Last night had been a big one: the graduation ceremony with Laura Dwyer officially graduated from elementary school, and Higgins had shot up a good deal of film, she'd looked so pretty in the filmy pink dress—she was going to look a lot like Mary, with her mother's big gray eyes. Well, Steve said they were lucky Higgins had been there to look after them, when Bert was shot. Higgins hoped he was doing a good job by Bert's kids, and so far he thought he was.

"And also what?" said Hackett. "Letters too—*¿cómo no*, Luis? Oh-el-el."

Mendoza sat up. "Meaning? Oh—I do see, Art. Oh, yes. Isn't that pretty? If, of course, it was."

"Was what?" said Higgins.

"It took a little child to make me see it, so to speak. Look—" Hackett sat down, the chair creaking with his weight, and lit a cigarette. "It happened fast. It was dark. Chedorov's a trained man, used to noticing plate numbers too, riding a Traffic unit. But he'd just jumped clear of that Mercedes himself, he'd seen Moss run down, and he wasn't thinking just so clearly as he might have been. The car lights weren't on—he caught a glimpse of that plate by Bill Moss's flashlight, he saw it was gold on blue—"

"So, knowing how the new plates read, numbers first, he registered it as the numbers oh-one-one," said Mendoza. "I like that very much, Arturo. *¡Qué mono!*"

"For God's sake!" said Higgins. "It's either one. Numbers or letters. And if it was letters—"

"If it was letters, it's a vanity plate," said Hackett. "Somebody's own private plate number."

"With a couple of small-time pros in the car?" said Higgins.

"Now don't throw cold water, George," said Mendoza. "It could be. There are the hell of a lot of them around."

"And some damn queer ones too," said Hackett. "You know how the rules read—no more than six letters, but any number up to six. A lot of people have used their initials, or a first name and a last initial, or vice versa. Or a company name, or—you name it. We've all seen them around. I passed GLORIA the other day, and one that said YLB 2. Funny ones—we've all seen them."

"And I'll tell you something else," said Mendoza, "and that is, if that was a vanity plate it had six letters. Because the first three were in the position where Chedorov expected to see them. Vanity plates with only three initials or something like that, the letters are centered."

"That I hadn't thought of, but you're right," said Hackett rather excitedly. "And I'll remind you how those are handed out. There aren't any duplicates. If you think up a combination you want on a vanity plate and somebody's already got it, nothing doing. And I'll bet you there wouldn't be many around that start out oh-el-el."

"That I wouldn't bet on," said Higgins, "with the number there are out. But I guess it'd do no harm to ask."

Mendoza was studying the three letters interestedly. "I'll agree, some damned funny ones," he said, flicking the desk lighter, "but oh-el-el— I don't know, it could be any damned thing. What about oh-el-i? Or oh-h, come to that—"

"Look, let's start out with what we have, not guesswork," said Hackett.

Among the marvelous machines they had to help them now was the direct hookup to the D.M.V. in Sacramento. A partial make on a regular plate number was no use to them; there were too many possible combinations on too many cars, in California. But a partial on a vanity plate could be fed into a computer.

They sent up the enquiry: any vanity plate starting out O L L. They waited; this would take a little time. "Where's everybody else?" asked Higgins.

"Checking out a brainstorm of Jase's. I rather like it," said Mendoza; but then he was not so constituted that he enjoyed the routine, either.

The first reports came back. There was a plate OLLY M registered to an Oliver Manning in San Francisco. A plate OLLOVE registered to an Olaf L. Love in Alhambra. A plate OLLY registered to an Oliver DuBois in Bakersfield. "Well, Alhambra," said Hackett. The machine clicked over slowly and spelled out another: OLLER, registered to Richard Oller in Santa Monica. That, it seemed, was all.

"Well, it's possible," said Hackett. "The one in Alhambra—"

"Let's just ask," said Mendoza, and sent up the enquiry: how about vanity plates starting out O L I? They waited.

"I mean, it was just an idea," said Hackett. Mark and his ooohs . . .

The machine clicked and spelled out an OLIVER registered to Oliver Goodis of San Mateo. And OLIFFY registered to an Osbert Liffy of an address in Boyle Heights.

"Take your pick, but I know which is likeliest," said Mendoza softly. "Alhambra, Boyle Heights—given Tom's little idea that this same pair has been out on a number of jobs like that, the same general M.O. They were all around that side of our beat—"

"Let's check it out," said Hackett energetically. "By God, I'd like to get these punks."

They tried the nearer one, Boyle Heights, first; as Mendoza said it was the likeliest. It was an address on Murchison, a block of single old houses. Hackett was driving, Higgins looking for house numbers, and as he said, "It's this side of the street, couple of houses down," they both saw it at the same time.

There was an old gray Mercedes sedan sitting in the drive.

"My God almighty!" said Higgins. "You called it, Art."

"Give the credit to Mark," said Hackett. He parked the Barracuda in front of the old frame house. As they went up the walk, they checked the plate: a vanity plate, gold on blue, OLIFFY.

The man who answered the bell was paunchy, nakedly bald, relaxing on a warm Saturday in shorts and white T-shirt. He looked at the badges and said, "Anything wrong?"

"Is that your car in the drive, sir?"

"Yeah, that's right. I'm Osbert Liffy." Suddenly he looked alarmed. "Now don't tell me that fool kid was in some mix-up with it and never told me! There isn't any damage to it—say, I thought twice about letting Jerry drive it, but that heap of his just died on him, and he's usually a careful driver. My old Merc there, it's near twenty years old, and still perkin' along just fine. I'm some proud of that car. Was there some trouble about—"

"Would you know who was driving it last Wednesday night?" asked Hackett.

"Wednesday—well, yeah, Jerry had it then. He and Jim wanted to see a show somewhere uptown, I let him—"

"Jerry who?" asked Higgins. "Jim who?"

"Say, what's this about? My boy Jerry and his best pal Jim Slayback. You want to see them? Cops? What for? They're out back in the garage workin' on Jerry's car, but I think that heap's laid down for the last time—"

They were too surprised—not quite pros as yet—to be dropped on, to put up much defense. On the ride back to the office, the pair was dumb. Jerry was about twenty, stocky and inclined to stoutness like his father, with a wild mop of dark hair; Jim was about the same age, wiry and blond.

The first time one of them opened his mouth was when Hackett and Higgins stood back for them to pass under the sign, Robbery-Homicide, into the office. Jerry turned to Hackett, wetting his lips. "Did—did that cop die?" he asked.

"Suppose you go on worrying about that a while longer," said Hackett.

Mendoza's cold dark gaze completely demoralized them. "So we catch up to this pair of little sneak thieves," he said, blowing smoke through his nostrils. "You've been on that lay for some while, haven't you?"—and he succinctly enumerated all the break-ins they'd tied together, on Landers' little idea. Jerry and Jim looked astonished.

"How'd you know—that was us did those?"

"Because you are a stupid pair of little louts," said Mendoza. They flushed.

Jim tried to bluster. "Say, you can't talk to us that way—we got rights, you got to—you can't—"

"Everybody's got rights but cops," said Hackett. "You knew that was a police officer you ran down last Wednesday night. You ran him down deliberately."

"It was an accident!" said Jerry, going green-white. "My God, my God, don't you lay a hand—I know how you big apes feel about anybody hurts a cop! Don't you— My God, why else was we doing like that, real careful about there not bein' anybody around, don't take any chance we have to hurt anybody, I always said to Jim—then even if we do get caught, it's nothing, no kind of charge, just little stuff—"

"We have taken the trouble to add up the value of all the little stuff you got away with," said Mendoza. "Whatever you got for it. It comes to some four thousand three hundred bucks' worth—"

"Jesus!" said Jim blankly. "I don't think altogether we got about seven hundred, sellin' it—"

"Of," said Mendoza, "private property. Somebody's private

property. But they don't teach you—mmh—young inheritors of freedom about private property any more, do they?"

And Jerry said, a lesson learned and memorized, "Human rights come before property rights. Like they say—"

"Oh, you Goddamned stupid little bastards," said Mendoza. "I do get tired of looking at you. Too damned many of you. Take them out of my sight, Arturo, before I forget I've got a fairly clean record with this force."

They got a statement of sorts from both of them; they took them over to the jail. At the processing desk, the sergeant told them to empty their pockets, and confiscated a pocketknife from Jerry and a nail file from Jim, counted and put away the money on them.

"Hey, that's mine!" said Jerry and Jim simultaneously.

Hackett and Higgins just looked at each other.

On the way back to the car Higgins asked, "Have you read that thing, Art—very interesting—*Territorial Imperative?*"

"Oh, yes," said Hackett, grinning. "And it's slightly encouraging to reflect, George, that just like the old tag says, the truth is mighty and will ultimately prevail."

"I suppose so, eventually," said Higgins, "but sometimes I doubt if I'll live to see it, Art."

"Cheer up, *compadre*. At least we got them. Let's go tell Bill Moss how."

At the hospital, Moss was half sitting up, some color in his face, all tied up in traction but very much himself and complaining about the nurse who'd stolen his cigarettes. "She's one of these Goddamned idiots who think they're dangerous," he said crossly. "And my God, talk about a censored press—I saw that report in print just once, a couple of years back, all the research at some big hospital saying no proof it's got a damned thing to do with lung cancer, but all the scare tactics—" Grinning, Hackett and Higgins contributed the half packs on them, and he was duly grateful.

"We just thought you'd like to know we dropped on them," said Higgins. "The punks who ran you down." They told him how, and he was amused and resentful.

[228]

"So you give that boy of yours a pat on the head for me," he said to Hackett. "But damn it, I'll be here for six weeks and then a month at home before I go back on the job! Damn it, just a pair of small-time punks—"

They couldn't blame him for being annoyed.

They heard about Grace's project at lunch. Grace, Palliser, Conway and Landers had made some headway at it even on Saturday, leaving Piggott to get all the statements on Baby-face and that heist yesterday.

Some of those men, day workers, who lived at the apartment on Hooper, worked at places that were open on Saturdays. There were fifty-five men living there who worked regularly eight to five or some such hours. This morning they had checked fifteen of them, and all fifteen had been proven to have been at their regular jobs, all day last Monday.

"I just have the feeling," said Grace, "that it comes back to that apartment house."

"I won't say you're wrong, Jase," said Palliser thoughtfully. "But they're all such upright citizens. And from what you told me—if it does, where the hell *was* she? If she didn't get out of the building? You said you were all pretty thorough."

"Sherlock Holmes," said Grace, lighting a cigarette.

"What about him?" asked Higgins.

"I can't quote it exactly. About what's left after you've removed the impossible must be the answer, however improbable it looks. I just think we ought to rule out everything we can. Then what's left—"

"If those witnesses were right, the locked room," said Palliser.

But locked room or not, it wasn't exactly a puzzle on paper to them. Because of that small corpse in the dirty alley—Katie May with her pigtails and solemn dark eyes.

That afternoon they traced down nine more men resident at that apartment. Some of the tenants were like Blaine, professional men just starting out, in five-day jobs; the ones they had checked today were delivery-truck drivers, barbers, one bartender, bus drivers, a clerk at a travel agency, market checkers, salesclerks. All nine men had been where they were supposed to be last Monday, vouched for, innocent.

"We'll clean them up on Monday," said Grace. "Know for sure."

Ballistics called in the middle of the afternoon. The slug from Evelyn Piper's body had come out of a Colt .45.

At five-thirty Saturday afternoon Glasser called Wanda Larsen and said, "You'll never guess what just happened."

"What?"

"I won a new car in a drawing," said Glasser. He still sounded surprised. "They just called to tell me. I don't have to buy anything or—there aren't any strings, I wasn't even there. They say I can pick it up tomorrow, at the agency."

"Oh, Henry!" said Wanda. "How exciting! And of course just what you need—what is it?"

"Well, it's one of those Gremlins—American Motors. I don't know anything about it," said Glasser. "But of all the damned lucky breaks—a new car is a new car. I never won anything before in my life!"

"Oh, Henry, you'll love it," said Wanda. "Phil O'Neill down in R. and I. has one, and she's crazy about it. She says it gets marvelous mileage, and it's fun to drive—what color is it?"

"I don't know, I haven't seen it. Is that so?" said Glasser. "Well, it's a damned lucky break, is all I can say. Look, I'm supposed to pick it up in the morning. I thought I'd come by about two and we can take it out on the freeway, see how she rides, and maybe out to dinner up the coast somewhere."

"Fine," said Wanda. "I'd love to, Henry." She was pleased about the good luck; she spread the news through the office.

Sunday morning saw Mendoza in late; the heat wave was departing and the smog level down. He read the statements on that heist and Baby-face. A big gun. *Dios,* this was one they'd like to pick up in a hurry, he thought, shooting from the hip like that—hair-trigger. They had had a formal identification from the husband.

Robbery-Homicide always had business on hand, and always more coming up. He wondered why he was still here.

The phone buzzed at him and he picked it up. "Mendoza."

"Bainbridge. I'm sorry, Luis, but your office tagged it a traffic accident. Why? I just came to look at it five minutes ago. This Loretta Moreno."

"What about her?" asked Mendoza.

"It wasn't an accident," said Bainbridge. "Whatever it looked like. She was stabbed in the chest. With a very thin knife."

"*¿Qué? ¡Por Dios!* And what the hell—stabbed? That was Landers' report—what the *hell?*" said Mendoza blankly. "Thanks very much for another mystery." He got up and went out to the hall. "Where's Tom?"

14

"STABBED?" SAID LANDERS, STARTLED. "IT looked like a simple accident. I thought she'd probably been thrown against the dash. The husband came in and identified her. He didn't seem too bright, but I put it down to shock, you know."

"Well, we are going to ask Mr. Moreno some questions *pronto,*" said Mendoza forcefully. "What's the address?"

"It was down in Venice somewhere, it'll be in the report." Landers found it, rummaging. They took the Ferrari, and Mendoza stayed on surface streets. At this hour on a warm June Sunday the freeways would be thronged with people heading for the beaches.

It was a poor section of that old beach town, when they found the address, the house a tiny old frame at the back of a narrow lot. As Mendoza and Landers walked up the cracked sidewalk to a low step, a minute sagging porch, they heard sounds of altercation inside, men's voices raised. Landers pushed the bell and the voices quieted at the loud buzz. In a minute, Moreno came to the door, the little man he remembered, dark, with slightly pockmarked skin, a rather stupid expression, dull eyes. He looked at the badge in Mendoza's hand. "Lieutenant Mendoza—Detective Landers. We'd like to talk to you, Mr. Moreno. We've just found out that your wife's death wasn't an accident. She was stabbed." Sometimes the shock value of direct talk was useful.

Moreno's expression didn't change. He said mournfully, "Yeah, I know. How'd you know?"

"The doctor—"

"Oh," said Moreno. "I never thoughta that. It wasn't my fault, it was that damn fool Joe."

"I think we'd better come in," said Mendoza, and Moreno just nodded. He was a sad little man. He turned and went into the room ahead of them, a square and bare little room where two other men were standing. Both were bigger than Moreno, about his age, in the thirties, one Negro and one white.

"The cops found out," said Moreno.

The other two looked merely downhearted. "Gee," said the black one, "I guess we blew it. I'm awful sorry, Ernie. It was just—"

"Suppose we hear some names," said Mendoza. "And some answers to questions." His nose was twitching again.

"I guess I got to tell you," said Moreno. "Nothin' else to do. See, we been on the welfare since I got laid off. I useta work with Joe and Nat. That's Joe—" Sanchez, it transpired, the white one, and Nat Foster. "For the city, pickin' up garbage. But I got laid off and Loretta, she went and saw this movie." He sniffed dolefully. "About some guy pretended his wife got killed and there was a lot of money from a thing called insurance. She said we could do like that. And she looked up a place in the phone book, get it fixed so if she dies I get a lot of money. But nobody meant it to happen for real— Loretta and me, we got on just fine, I thought a hell of a lot of Loretta!" He was faintly indignant now. "I had to have the damn fool notion, get Joe and Nat help out on it."

Neither of them looked very bright either. Joe said, "Well, it just never come to me till we was there, Ernie. We was just helpin' Ernie and Loretta out," he explained to Mendoza, sounding helpless. "An' glad to, we was friends. Nat came along, drive Ernie's car, on account Loretta she can't drive."

"And you never noticed there wasn't a driver's license in her handbag?" said Mendoza to Landers.

[233]

"It wasn't me. The Highway Patrol."

"Ah, I might have known," said Mendoza darkly. "And?"

"And Ernie said, get a chicken or somethin' and put blood all over. Fix the car like there was a accident. See, Loretta was along because we was goin' to take her to her mother's up in San Luis, so nobody'd know she wasn't dead," said Nat. "And I'm sorry, Ernie. Maybe I shouldn'ta said it. But it just come to me, after we got the car fixed against the fence and all—it was me said do it real late so nobody around—it just come to me, the cops wasn't going to think Loretta was dead 'less there was a body."

"And when Nat said it, I kinda saw that too," said Joe. "It never hit me till he said, and then I kinda saw he was right. And Loretta says what did we mean, and it just come to me, there wasn't no other female around to be a body for Loretta, so Ernie gets all the money."

"¡Caramba!" murmured Mendoza, awed.

"And I said that to Nat, and Loretta she started to scream and holler and I tole her shut up, but she didn't, and I just thought, if Ernie's gonna get all that money there has got to be a body in the car, so I stuck my knife in her and then she shut up—"

"I never had no such shock in my life as when you called me," said Moreno. "In the movie the guy made like an alibi, stay with people all night, and I dropped in a gamblin' joint down the pier, I ain't so much on cards but I did, and me thinkin' Loretta was up at her ma's! And then you call me, and she's dead! I called Nat soon as I got home, and he says how it happened, and I was just wild! That damn fool Joe! Well, I got to say it never crossed my mind about it not lookin' right if there wasn't no body— I kinda saw that—but he needn't have gone and killed Loretta! I was good and mad!" said Moreno.

"But there wasn't no other female around, Ernie," said Joe humbly.

"Yeah, and I been tryin' to get him come explain it ever since, him duckin' me because he knew how—I thought a hell of a lot of Loretta, she was a good woman—"

"I tole him you wouldn't like it, Ernie," said Nat. "But you know Joe, he gets an idea in his head."

"Tom," said Mendoza, "I have the feeling we've got into Looking-Glass country. You'd better go phone for a car." Without a word Landers went out to the Ferrari and called in for a squad car. This one was hard to believe, but even in the supposedly superior technological civilization of the twentieth century, the Ernies, Nats and Joes were still to be found.

They all looked surprised to be told they were under arrest. "I didn't have nothing to do with it," said Moreno, still indignant. Very likely he wouldn't know the meaning of the words, conspiracy to defraud. They were to find that there wasn't an insurance policy; he'd just signed an application. The other two were just downcast. They all climbed meekly into the black-and-white, and Mendoza and Landers followed it back to the jail to book them in. They'd apply for a warrant; this one was going to provide some amusement in the D.A.'s office tomorrow.

It provided some more at the office when they got back and told everybody else about it. "All those books," said Grace laughing, "about the shrewd master criminals—"

"You have to live with the thankless job," said Mendoza, "to realize just how stupid the little ones can be. *¡Dios, vaya historia!*"

The office never saw Piggott on Sunday until after church. As he came into the living room putting on a tie, where Prudence waited all ready, she said, "Look, Matt. There's something different about one of the tetras, that lyretail one. It's all puffed up. It looks just like that other one when— I do believe it's another female full of eggs."

"Oh, no, you don't," said Piggott. "Get me into all that again!"

"I wasn't even suggesting it, heaven forbid," said Prudence.

"Let her drop her eggs and everybody else in the tank eat them," said Piggott firmly. He ushered Prudence out the door and banged it after them.

*   *   *

Today, unable to go on checking on Grace's project, they were back hunting the perverts; but nobody had any deep conviction that they were going to get anywhere at that routine. Landers and Conway went back to the dairy store on Wilshire and talked to Knisely again, and the people in the stores on each side: one was a drugstore, one a newsstand, both open on Sunday. But with the normal amount of traffic passing, only the man at the newsstand had heard the shot, and thought it was a backfire; neither had seen Baby-face come out.

They went to talk to the witnesses again; sometimes after a witness had a chance to calm down, think about it, more would come out. In this case it didn't. And they both had a feeling that the sooner they dropped on this one, the better.

"He could have been hopped up, Rich," said Landers. "Going off hair-trigger like that."

"All too likely," agreed Conway.

When they got back to the office the others were taking a break, and Higgins had some snapshots to show; not the colored ones he'd taken with his Instamatic, he wouldn't get those back until Tuesday, but the black-and-white ones Steve Dwyer had shot on Friday night, and carefully developed and printed himself.

"Say, he's pretty good, isn't he?" said Grace. "They look like a pro job."

"Well, he wants to go into the lab end," said Higgins. "I think he's pretty good all right." And the rest of them had been a little amused at Higgins' humble pursuit of Dwyer's widow, but they were all thinking now that Bert would be pleased at how he was taking care of them all. And remembering that Grace had come to them as a replacement for Dwyer; Grace hadn't known Bert.

At two o'clock, with most of them just back from lunch, they had a call from Traffic. There'd been a brawl in a bar out on Third, and there seemed to be a D.O.A. Resignedly Higgins went to look at more of the stupidity. The Traffic men were holding a short skinny little man who had had a few drinks and was feeling no pain. The D.O.A. was lying quietly on the floor of the bar, and—it looked like a normally respectable place—everybody else had backed off and was watching silently. There were only a few customers, a fat bartender.

"So what happened?" asked Higgins.

"The bartender called us when they started to argue, disturb other people," said one of the uniformed men. "This one's Alfred Warner."

"He started it," said Warner. "He hadn't no call. I was just standing there at the bar, have a quiet drink or two, he come up and started laughing at my clothes, he said I looked funny. He hadn't no call. It's my own business, my clothes."

Higgins looked at the Traffic men, who were grinning. Warner, on this warm but not hot day—the heat wave had definitely departed—had chosen to don a pair of royal blue shorts, white tennis shoes, a striped canvas baseball cap and a sleeveless white T-shirt with the simple legend emblazoned on it in scarlet, back and front, KISS ME QUICK, I'M A CZECH! Almost anybody might have shared the deceased's opinion, but he needn't have said anything about it.

"I picked it up by mistake," said Warner, looking down at himself. "It's my wife's, see. The shirt, I mean. She's Czech, and her sister sent it to her—thought it was cute. I never realized I had it on till that guy come up makin' the snide remarks."

Higgins turned a laugh into a cough and said, "Did he take a poke at you, Mr. Warner?"

"Nope," said Warner. "I took a poke at him. And then he pulled a gun on me, after I kinda shoved him and knocked over his drink. He hadn't no call make snide remarks about my wife's shirt, nor he hadn't no call to pull a gun on me. But I wasn't about to get shot, I tried to grab it away from him and the bartender come and tried to get it away from both of us, and then it went off."

Higgins bent and looked at the dead man. The gun was lying on the floor beside him, an old S. and W. .45. "Well, well. Nemesis," said Higgins.

[237]

The dead man was Terry Conover, by the mug shot in circulation.

He straightened up. "You should have recognized him by the mug shot," he said to the uniformed men. "There's been an A.P.B. out on him for nearly two weeks—he got over the wall at Folsom."

"I'll be damned. We had that too— I hadn't looked at his face."

Conover had been shot in the body and shed a lot of blood. At least he'd be off their minds now. Warner would probably be charged with involuntary manslaughter and get off with a suspended sentence, but Higgins took him in now, resisting the temptation to advise him to wear his own clothes from now on. They let him make a call, and he called his wife.

Higgins was still there, getting down notes for a report, when she came. She looked upset, a little dark woman in a smart blue pantsuit, but when she saw Warner she doubled up in mirth.

"Alfred, what on earth are you d-doing in my shirt?" she demanded between whoops. "I never saw anything so ridiculous—if I could have a picture—"

"Well, you put it on top of my clean ones," said Warner.

Higgins explained matters to her, and she took it calmly. In a way, he thought, starting back to the office, it was just as well it had happened. With no dealth penalties getting handed out, and Conover the wild one. At least he'd be making no more trouble.

About four o'clock on Sunday afternoon, Sergeant Lake swung around from the switchboard and said, "Art! Somebody wants you or George."

Hackett shoved the right button on the phone and said, "Hackett."

"Say, Sergeant, this is Eddy Gamino."

"Oh." Hackett focused his mind back to that. Stephanie Midkiff and the damned biology textbooks. They'd expected to let that one lie until summer school opened and hopefully some more of those books came drifting in—hopefully the one in which she'd found Rex's name and phone number. "What can I do for you?"

"Vice versa," said Eddy tersely. "I'm down here at Harry's place, and I just spotted that yellow Mustang—it's parked up the block in front of the drugstore. Oh, it's the right one, temporary license plate in the same spot and all. I just thought, if you'd like to find who owns it—"

"Thanks very much!" Hackett banged the phone down and called to Higgins. They ran, and took Higgins' Pontiac. When they got down to Seventh he went round the block to get on the right side of the street, and they saw the blinding chrome yellow car up there at the corner. But as Higgins slowed, two male figures came out of the drugstore and got into it and it took off. They passed Harry Hart's place, with Eddy standing in the doorway, and followed the Mustang.

Evidently the driver didn't notice the Pontiac. The Mustang went on up Seventh, turned on Coronado, and slid to the curb in front of a small stucco house. Higgins parked behind it, and they got out in a hurry, converged on the pair just out of the Mustang. "Is this your car?" asked Higgins, getting out the badge; but warm satisfaction spread through him as he looked at one of them. Here was Ruthie Runnells' young man too old for school, with a scrubby little dark moustache. He looked about twenty, and he was almost six feet but slender, and he had a weak girlish chin. The other one, younger, was enough like him to mark them as brothers. They were both dressed in sharp flashy sports clothes. When the younger one saw the badge he started to cry weakly.

"I knew they'd find out— I knew they'd find out—"

The older one said, "Shut up." He looked around as if for a place to run.

"Don't try it," advised Higgins.

"It was all your idea—get to know girls—I didn't want to," wept the younger one.

"So let's hear your names," said Hackett. No reply forthcoming, he went to look at the registration in the Mustang. "Rex Hubbard—that's you?"

"So what if it is?" the older one said in a thin voice.

A door slammed and a strident voice called. "What's goin' on out here? Who are those guys, Rex?" She came striding at them like a man; she wasn't very tall but she had a deep-bosomed figure, grayish-white hair in an uncompromising knob on top of her head, and a harsh loud voice. She had on pants and a man's sweat shirt. "What you want with my boys?" she demanded.

Hackett showed her the badge. "A cop!" she said, taken aback. "Listen, my boys wouldn't do nothing wrong! Their dad just scalp 'em, an' so would I, they snitch anything or talk back— Jimmy, what the hell you cryin' for? I'm always tellin' you not to be such a crybaby—"

"How do you happen to be driving an expensive new car, Rex?" asked Higgins. He had been a little curious about that; this neighborhood didn't say money. The question fired the woman up again.

"What business is it of cops, we wanta give Rex a nice car? My husband, he makes good money—he's a plumber—and if he wants to—"

"Is he drunk again?" asked Rex, sounding very tired, and she turned on him.

"And so what if he is? He works hard all week, it's a dirty hard job, and if he wants get drunk on Sundays what's it to anybody? I still don't know what these cops are after— Did you get me my aspirin? Where is it? And the change from that five bucks—"

He took them both out of his pocket and handed them over.

"You're both under arrest," said Hackett, and the woman began to jabber astonishment, anger and incoherent questions. "For a start, homicide—we'll decide the degree later."

"I didn't want to do it," sobbed the younger one.

They left Mrs. Hubbard still talking into the air after them, and they wondered if maybe it was a relief to Rex and Jimmy to get away from her. They were pleased about this unexpected bonus; they'd thank Eddy better later.

[240]

Except that Rex was a little surprise, quiet and meek and gentle, it was much the sort of story they could have expected. Mendoza sat in on the questioning.

Rex was twenty, Jimmy sixteen. Jimmy went to the high school on Ninth, and knew about that latest thing, the phone numbers in margins. They didn't get much out of him but tears and remorse. Both the boys were shy, loners, hadn't any close friends, unsure how to make any. But it had been Rex's idea to put the phone number in that book—maybe get to know some girls. It had been way last month Jimmy'd done that. And then when a girl had phoned, they didn't know exactly what to say—

They finally got Rex to open up when they took Jimmy away to wait in another interrogation room. And he didn't say much.

"I'd never—had a girl friend," he told them. "I didn't know what to say. When they met us—at that place. But that one was pretty. The other one wasn't— I don't like fat girls. I wanted the other one—kind of to myself. I made Jimmy get out—and I—just drove around—we didn't talk much—and I finally parked—just up by Echo Park. I didn't know what to say to her—so I tried to kiss her—and she started to fight me—and I guess I don't know what happened after that. Except—she was dead. I don't know."

It was an easy way to kill anybody, without meaning to. And it was a sad and stupid thing, this—the damned fool kids, one wanting adventure, one possibly queer one going out of control. It was anybody's guess what would happen to them, what the charges would be. No malice aforethought, and Jimmy was a juvenile. But Stephanie Midkiff was just as dead.

Nothing else new, at least, came in on Sunday. Tomorrow they'd finish Grace's project, checking out those upright male citizens living at the Hooper Avenue apartment. And so far they had all been proven shining-bright-innocent, and nobody felt that the list of perverts was going to give them X, so where did they go then?

They didn't know, as Higgins said afterward, that Mendoza's capricious *daemon,* for some reason, was about to take up brief residence in Hackett's subconscious mind.

*   *   *

When the night watch came on, they all asked Glasser about the new car. "Oh, she's a very nice little girl," said Glasser, beaming. "Very nice indeed, boys. I had her up the Malibu road forty miles, and she can skedaddle, for all she's a baby. But I'm still feeling surprised— I never won anything before in my life." He was full of statistics about the Gremlin and what a nice little girl she was. They'd given him a lime-green one with white rally stripes. "Do you know, that little thing's only two and a half inches longer than a VW, but its turning circle is three feet less, and it weighs as much as a Dodge sedan—really built, and drives like a Cadillac—" He had the advertising folder to hand around.

At ten-fifteen they discovered that the restaurant heisters had come back to their beat. The Brown Derby out on Wilshire was held up just as it was closing. They heard the same descriptions—stocking masks, big guns, two men medium-sized. They had got about four thousand bucks.

"Fast and furious you can say," said Galeano when he'd filled out a report on it.

"And this other heister—Baby-face, Tom calls him—sounds like one we'd like to get too," said Glasser. "Maybe hopped up. But not a smell of a lead on any of 'em."

"Sometimes," said Schenke, "we get lucky."

Palliser was off on Mondays. He'd picked up a copy of the *Herald* on his way home last night, and after breakfast he called three men who advertised offering to do carpentry and odd jobs. One said he had too many jobs on hand now to take on another; the second wasn't home but his wife said she'd have him call back. The third came over to look at the job. He was a lean stringy fellow in his sixties who said his name was Nethercott. He said he'd got a load of old lumber where a school had been torn down, he could put up a good stout fence for about seventy-five dollars.

Palliser closed with this offer instantly; he could always paint the fence himself if he had to. Their benefactor said, "Got all my tools in the truck, might 's well start now."

"Darling," said Roberta, bouncing the baby soothingly as he objected to all the hammering and sawing, "aren't you smart to have thought of the ads. Really, now it's decided, I'm dying to meet Trina."

It was, as a matter of fact, the Pallisers' real dog which triggered off the *daemon*.

On Monday, Grace, Piggott, Landers and Conway had gone ahead checking out all those men, while Hackett and Higgins had a look for the perverts on the list they hadn't found yet. The routine did break cases. By lunchtime seven more of the apartment residents had been cleared, and even Grace was feeling that this little idea wasn't about to come to anything.

They all went up to Federico's in a body, which sometimes happened. Mendoza was still talking about Moreno and his cohorts; he'd been at the jail with one of the D.A.'s deputies, getting full statements, and that really was one for the books, stupidity hardly to be believed.

The tall waiter Adam came and refilled their coffee cups, and Hackett sat back feeling slightly smug. The low-protein diet had removed five pounds so far, and his pants didn't feel so tight.

Mendoza lit a new cigarette. "Did you hear about John's dog? I'd forgotten that freeway crash last January—"

"Oh, that," said Piggott. "The dog with the funny name, yes. They're nice dogs, but I should think pretty big for the city."

"Besides, dogs will dig up things," said Grace. "Flower beds. Ginny says she'd like to get a Siamese cat. Of course, I can see anybody wanting a good watchdog these days."

"As a matter of fact," said Mendoza, "Siamese were used as—mmh—watch-cats in the palaces, and I understand they can be trained as guards. Of course, being cats, how faithful they'd be at it might depend on their current mood. I think—"

[243]

"Is that a fact?" said Grace, interested.

"Not all dogs dig up things," said Higgins, thinking of well-mannered little Brucie. "I think it depends on the breed—some do and some don't—"

Suddenly Hackett leaped up and let out a shout. "BEDS!" he yelled. They all looked at him in alarm, and Higgins half got up. "What—"

"BEDS!" said Hackett loudly. "But where does he sleep? Two other men—and only one bedroom with twin beds—" He was convulsed by a sudden light from heaven, but only he could see it.

"*Se conoce*," said Mendoza, concerned, "he's drunk—what the hell are you talking about, Arturo?"

"Beds," said Hackett, breathing rapidly and still staring unseeingly at the far wall. "Only two beds—and there was a couch— I can see it plain as day—and it's got to be a daybed. *A daybed!* That opens out—"

"Art—" Higgins was worried. "Calm down and make sense. What are you talking about?"

Slowly Hackett's eyes focused; he gave a little gasp. "By God, it just hit me—out of the blue. I just *saw* it. In that apartment—up on the fifth floor—three men sharing it, and one of them works at night—and only one bedroom, so that couch in the living room must be—has got to be—a bed-davenport. And that's where—"

"*¡Válgame Dios!*" said Mendoza very quietly, and was on his feet like a cat.

"William Reed," said Hackett. "One of those five night workers."

"Oh, my God!" said Higgins. "You mean he put her in—" And they were all remembering that autopsy report now. Grace was on his feet too.

"Come on," said Mendoza. "We'll go look at it, Art. The rest of you'll know soon enough."

They found him there; he opened the door and let them in without protest, a dark stolid man about forty. Hackett remembered that he was a waiter somewhere. They didn't ask him any questions before they went to look at the couch in the living room. It was a bed-davenport, and Hackett found the lever and heaved it open with one yank, and of course there was nothing the naked eye could see, but the lab would find anything that was there, and there would probably be traces there.

"Was that where you put her?" asked Mendoza.

After a moment he nodded. "I been real sorry," he said simply in a soft voice. "I don't know what makes me want to do like that. I hadn't—in quite a spell. Since I come out here. But I went out—that day, 'bout noon, go down see if was any mail. She was—"

Hackett interrupted him and recited the piece about his rights; they wanted to nail this one, all legally tied up. He just waited, and nodded.

"She was in the hall, she'd just fell down and bumped her nose, it was bleedin'. She was—just awful cute," he said. "She knew me—seen me around. And I—just—had to—do that. It's like a devil inside me, I had to. And she was scared then—and I had to stop her cryin'—"

"And then you heard her mother—and the other women—calling her," said Mendoza.

A slow nod. "And then—when the policemen came—and all of you—I was scared. I see they was all looking—every place. It just come to me, I hadn't made up the bed yet, and I put her in it and folded it up, was all. And nobody looked. And I left for work same time, but then I come home, other two fellows asleep then, I just took her down there. I put her dress in a trash can up the street."

And Hackett thought back, queerly, to that bank robber who had killed Bert. They'd wanted, all the while they were hunting him, to commit mayhem on him: and then when they found him, they were just sorry for him. This was a little like that.

"I don't reckon," said Reed sadly, "they oughta let me out, when I do these things. Seems like I can't stop myself."

Mendoza called the lab; a team would come out. They took him in, and booked him. When they took his prints, they sent them to

[245]

NCIC, and were shortly informed that he was William Chale, originally from Atlanta. He had a long pedigree of attempted and completed child molestation charges there before he raped a five-year-old in Pittsburgh eighteen years back; he'd got a ten-to-twenty and been out in four years. Five years later he had raped a nine-year-old in Erie, Pennsylvania, and been put in again, and was out in three years. There would be others he'd never been tagged for. He'd got off his last parole in Pennsylvania two years ago, and come out here. He said this was the first time he'd done anything here; they didn't know whether to believe that or not.

The two men who had shared the apartment with him were shaken and astonished. They were both the upright citizens, working for a big construction company. They'd met him last year, they said, at an employment agency uptown. Both of them were saving up to get married, and Reed getting a night job in that restaurant, it had seemed a pretty good arrangement. They hadn't seen much of him, but he'd always seemed like a nice, quiet guy.

"I feel, damn it," said one of them, "like I brought a rattlesnake in this place. Not knowing. That poor baby. I wouldn't know how to look Mr. and Mrs. Blaine in the face."

And Mendoza said, "I've known you to have a little hunch now and then, Art, but that was a spectacular one—*¡Pues hombre!*"

There weren't any leads on Baby-face, just nowhere to look. If he pulled something else, maybe they'd get a better description.

Tuesday was quiet, with only a new unidentified corpse turning up, and a suicide.

And on Tuesday night Landers took Phil O'Neill out to dinner, at The Castaway high up in the hills above Burbank, the nice place with the quiet atmosphere and the magnificent view out over the whole metropolitan area.

They were late, because when he'd started out to pick her up he'd found he had a flat tire, and feeling disinclined for the job after a shower and a clean shirt, had called the garage, which was busy.

They didn't get there, to sit over preliminary drinks, until after eight-thirty.

Somehow they always had plenty to say to each other, and he thought she looked good enough to eat, little trim Phil with her short flaxen curls and freckled upturned nose, in a plain white dress with a bright red stole. They had a leisurely dinner, and lingered over more coffee. The waitress came tactfully with the bill and said, "We close at nine-forty-five, sir."

Landers was reluctant to move. "Well, I suppose—" said Phil. "Tomorrow a weekday after all." She slid out of the booth and put the stole round her shoulders. In the lobby the manager and cashier had the register open, and a stout canvas bag was on the counter. In the middle of the week, business was evidently slow; Landers and Phil were the last to leave, and when they went out, Landers' car the only one left in the customers' lot.

They got into the Corvair; it was a nice night, the air warm with just a promise of real coolness coming later.

"It really is a lovely, lovely view," said Phil.

"It really is," said Landers, looking at her profile tenderly. A car came up the hill behind and stopped up there by the restaurant. In the parking lot, by the low parapet at the top of the hill, they sat quiet in the car admiring the view.

"Dearest darling Phil," said Landers, "I do love you such a hell of a lot. I'm not good at saying things, Phil, but please will you marry me?"

"Well—" said Phil. He could tell she was smiling. "Yes, I guess I will, Tom."

"Darling love!" said Landers, and a wild salvo of gunfire shattered the night, a bullet slammed into the side of the Corvair and confused shouts sounded from the door of the restaurant. Landers shoved Phil down on the seat and leaped out of the car, clawing for his gun. More shots, and two men came running down from the building, with a man in pursuit firing at them. One of the first two went down with a yell.

My God, those damned heisters, thought Landers, and ran, and

[247]

tackled the second man with memories of high-school football, and brought him down flat.

The restaurant manager came running up, brandishing a .38 Police Positive. "It was a hold-up—they came in—I'd heard about them, I brought my gun in just in case—"

"For God's sake," said Landers. "Of all the—"

One man had taken a bullet in the leg. The other one was just swearing.

Phil came running up excitedly. "Have you got them? Honestly, Tom! Honestly! Well, we'll never forget the night we got engaged, will we? Maybe typical, for a couple of cops!"

Landers called the night watch. They'd get some names from the heisters tomorrow; a car came up to take them in. The night watch, amused, called the boss.

Mendoza was still laughing when he came back to the living room, where Alison sat reading with Bast and Sheba in her lap. Nefertite, insulted when Mendoza put her down to answer the phone, was sitting on El Señor on the sectional washing his ears. Cedric was asleep at Alison's feet. The lamp turned her hair to burnished copper.

"Once a cop always a cop," said Mendoza.

She looked up. "*¿Qué?*"

He told her about Landers and Phil O'Neill, and she laughed. "And I still wonder why I'm there, at the thankless job. Watching all the stupidity and cupidity happen."

The twins, hostages to fortune, were asleep down the hall. And you couldn't help worrying, as a parent—old or young.

"*Amado,*" said Alison, smiling, "all of you at the thankless job need reminding—always more of the good people than the other kind. *Se dice—*"

"It is to be hoped," said Mendoza. "And as you were about to say, *mañana será otro día,*—tomorrow is also a day."